PAGAN RAGE

Sam Taw

This is a work of fiction. Names, characters, organisations, places, events, and incidents are either products of the author's imagination or are used fictitiously.

Cover art supplied by Carantoc Publishing Ltd
First edition, 2020
ISBN 978-1-9163059-4-6
Carantoc Publishing Ltd.
www.carantocpublishing.com

Please note that this novel was created by a British author. Except for Cornish words, slang and dialogue, spelling and grammar are corrected to **British English**. There are also scenes which may offend more sensitive readers. It is not deemed suitable for children.

CHAPTER ONE

The long shadows cast by the rocks at the top of the escarpment favoured us. We stayed low, scurrying between the boulders and scree to gain a clearer view into the valley beyond. Blydh led the way, stumbling and staggering along the western slope of the ridge above the Durotriges' borderlands. He muttered constantly, even when there was no one to hear him.

Tallack crept as close to his brother's back as possible. He too feared for Blydh's health; he'd barely been out of his sickbed for more than a half moon, but no amount of reasoning would discourage him. Blydh was fixated on killing the new leader of our neighbouring tribe, Brea.

None of us thought it sensible to risk such close proximity to our enemy, but Blydh was insistent that we had to see what the devious kyjyan was up to across the River Sid. It was becoming a tedious chore, scampering up and down the border watching and waiting.

Tallack begged me to travel alongside them for the half day's ride out east, despite the fact that my presence seemed to rile Blydh's temper every time he looked at me. I kept my mouth shut and carried what few supplies I had left in my medicine kit on the off chance that he'd need my healing skills. It was too soon after his head injury to be scouting.

Kewri and Senara trailed after us a little further down the track with Renowden. I was glad of their company. Each and every one of them had proven themselves to be dear friends and trusted warriors in their own right, but volunteering to scout out our enemies put them in as much danger as our Chieftains ahead of us.

I watched Blydh fall to all fours as he neared the crest of the ridge, scrambling the last stretch on his knees next to Tallack. The chalky soil kicked up a plume of dust against the evening sky and I wondered if he had given away our position. Senara drew level with me and winced at Blydh's incompetence. She was the best scout our tribe had ever known.

Fleet on foot and horseback, skilled with bow and short sword, Senara was formidable. She had earned her place among the Dumnonii warriors by leading a number of our men on a successful night raid, showering our enemy's camp with fireballs of wicker and willow. If Blydh had been in his right mind, he would have sent her alone to spy on the Duros while we drew up plans of attack back in camp.

As it was, Blydh's senses were in short supply since the crushing blow to his skull. Only a golden sun disc and a taut strip of skin protected the soft flesh of his brain from further injury. I noticed that he muttered a great deal to himself, in between shooting looks of pure evil in my direction. Only his twin seemed able to get through his belligerence.

"This is a bad idea, Fur Benyn." Senara whispered to me as she passed me by and dropped to her hands and knees. All I could do was shrug. She crawled up the scree slope and peeped over the ridge top alongside our chieftains. I waved my hand at Kewri, signalling for him to wait for us at the lower level. His great hulking mass would be harder to hide if the Duros spotted us.

Despite my aching joints and growing thirst, I inched closer to my kin to view the scene below. The Duros were packing away their camp and loading shelters onto carts.

Others were felling trees further along the valley and rolling the trunks into the river upstream. It made me wonder if Brea hadn't taken the idea from our compound. Was she planning on creating fortifications similar to ours?

There were few women in the valley below us so she was not difficult to pick out. Large, heavily armed men stood in a circle all around her as she issued her orders from a tall boulder in the centre of their camp. Even from our distance, I could tell that her demands were not well received. She flung her arms about and bellowed at her men who gestured back with clenched fists and waving spears.

"She's not well liked." Senara muttered.

"Brea has that effect on people." Tallack replied ruefully.

One of the larger Duro warriors stepped up to the platform, spitting with fury and gesturing to the hills on the opposite side of the valley. A few of the man's companions clearly agreed with his assessment, shouting and jostling forwards in the crowd. We lay still and watched as Brea folded her arms across her chest and pouted in defiance.

She looked to be losing control of her tribesmen until two of her guards stepped forward, unsheathed their blades and stabbed them through the gut of the outspoken man. His belly ripped apart, spilling his steaming innards onto the boggy lower ground. As he buckled and slumped into the bloody pool of guts at his feet, the rest of Brea's guards unsheathed their swords and shuffled into an impenetrable wall around her. It was clear to all the price of disagreement; her punishment was swift and brutal.

Crows gathered on the escarpment, waiting for their chance to pick over the dead man's flesh; squabbling and bickering close by. We stayed pressed against the cooling gravel and sparse grass, trying to discern Brea's intentions. It was far too late in the day to be moving away from camp, yet the shelters were dismantled and loaded one by one onto the wagons. Distant sounds of chopping wood continued long into the twilight while the few womenfolk and children bundled belongings and began to walk on the riverbank in a long winding trail of human cargo. Where were they headed and for what purpose?

"Sssssss." Blydh hissed. "I should go down there and chop off its head."

Tallack twisted to look at his brother and then at me. His pinched frown conveyed his deep concern but he said nothing.

Blydh's behaviour had been most strange of late, but this was new. He wriggled about, his head swaying slowly from side to side. "A great serpent should not be left to slither like that. Sssss. Too dangerous." He lifted his torso from the ground and sat upright. "One slice from my axe is all it would take. Sssss."

"Shush, brother. We must not be found out."

"Nonsense. A snake is no match for a wolf."

We all looked into the valley at the meandering line of Durotriges walking with their bundles. Was Blydh hallucinating, thinking they were one massive snake?

He rocked back on his bent toes and stood tall. "This blade will skin it in no time." His axe grasped in his hand, Blydh lunged forwards to begin his descent. He was beyond the shadows and picked out by the setting sun. The polished metal of his bronze axe glinted in the evening light, attracting the attention from the Duros crowded on the valley floor.

Tallack threw himself forward, launching from a crouch until he could grapple his brother's legs. Hobbled, Blydh came tumbling down against the dirt and rocks, groaning as the force pushed the air from his chest. With

Blydh felled, Tallack rolled on top of him holding him close to the ground. I held my breath, peeping over the ridge top. Had the Duros spotted us? Would they send a pack of warriors to hunt us down and spill our guts?

Quick thinking Senara grabbed up a handful of small pebbles and hurled them at a flock of crows on the rocks nearby. They flapped and cawed making such a racket, that none of our enemy noticed Tallack yanking Blydh back to our hiding place by the ankles.

"Tallack, it's too risky to stay here much longer. We've seen all there is to see." I said, risking the ire of my nephews with my candour.

"Agreed, but with Brea on the move, we need to figure out what she's planning." Tallack said, still holding his brother face down in the dirt.

"I can stay." Senara offered. "They'll never spot me and I can report back as soon as I find out where they're headed."

I could have kissed the girl for her bravery. I thank Cernonnus daily for sending her to our camp. Handing over what was left of our provisions, I shamed my nephew into giving her some of his tin for bribes and watched as she slid back down the slope in search of her bay mare.

By the time Tallack released the pressure from his brother's back, I realised that Blydh's groans were not complaints about his treatment, but of genuine pain. We rolled him over to see his eyes screwed shut and his fists clenched to the sides of his head. The muscles in his jaw pulsed as he gnashed his teeth together. The jolt must have aggravated his skull again.

"Come on, brother. The longer we stay the greater the risk of discovery." Tallack reached down and grabbed Blydh's wrist to pull him up to his feet. The howl was mournful and loud. Renowden dipped low and peered over the ridge, panicked that the cries had been heard.

"Get off me. I need resin. Aunt Mel, I must have poppy resin."

It was at times like these when his hatred for me melted into fear. For just those few moments, I was no longer the evil kyjyan who botched his skull repair, but Aunt Mel, keeper of resin and succour. This constant swing from vulnerable nephew to scornful Chieftain exhausted me. I had only a tiny fraction of resin left and no way to procure more, but my soft heart could not bear to deny him.

Anxious that the Duros would come at any moment, I called out to Kewri and instructed him to help Blydh back to his horse while I mixed a small bead of resin in a cup of water. With a little help from Renowden and Tallack, we got Blydh in the saddle and dosed him with the resin just before the daylight failed us entirely.

I wasn't able to relax until we were well inside our own borders and trotting along familiar paths towards home. Tying the reins of Blydh's horse to mine, I was able to keep my eye on his changing moods and steer at the same time. I am getting too old for this kind of trek. Even with Kewri to help me, I find the journeys take me longer to recover from and my patience faltering.

It was almost dawn when we arrived at the northern gates and called out to the watchmen to lower the bridge. Blydh was already whining for more resin as we passed through the compound. I gave him some willow to chew on and directed him to his own house but that didn't seem to appease him.

Sliding down the flank of his horse he followed me into my hut and collapsed on my bunk. Tallack was a couple of paces behind. He grabbed a few logs stacked under my eaves to rekindle the low embers of my fire.

"Where's Kerensa?" Blydh murmured into my bedding furs. I stole a glance at Tallack. That was his mess to sort out. As far as I could tell, Tallack had tried several times to explain Kerensa's part in the attack on our people, only to have Blydh forget the fact that she was killed for her treachery.

"She's gone home to Bentewyn, Brother." Tallack lied, rolling his eyes at me to confirm the validity of his falsehood. I ignored the gesture. There were more important things to consider than the fate of a girl from the mining settlement.

It was almost as though Blydh's head injury was the cause of his confusion, which is strange since everyone knows that the heart is the most important organ in the body. Blydh's heart was strong and unharmed, so to have him behave in such an odd manner defied all the teachings from my ancestors.

Our compound was fully repaired after the Duro invasion, and Tallack ordered his men to begin work on the additional boardwalks across the muddy island to stop them from getting restless.

When our priestess walked into my hut through the door skins, I could see that she had not used them. Her feet were caked in soggy dirt and grass fragments which rattled loose from her wooden pattens and onto my fresh floor rushes. Between her and my nephews, it was almost impossible to keep the place clean.

"I saw your return, Fur Benyn." Endelyn said, scooting around Tallack and Kewri to the bedside. "Is there anything I can do to help?"

I don't know why the woman feels that she owes me. It was Tallack's decision to welcome her into the camp not mine. Nevertheless, I seldom refuse assistance when it's offered.

"You could warm a little goat's milk and a handful of grains, if you have the time. I'm famished, and I dare say the boys would appreciate a little porridge too." While I crushed and steeped more willow bark for Blydh's pain relief, Endelyn took a boiling pot out to my goat pen and set to work. From her furtive glances at both of my nephews, I couldn't make out which one she preferred. If I had to guess, I'd say that she was about their age, or maybe a couple of summers older but no more.

With Kerensa out of the picture, and Treeve keeping a low profile about camp, both our Chieftains looked to be free of suitable partners. Was Endelyn making a run for the position of Ruvane, like so many others before her? I vowed to speak with the priestess at the earliest opportunity. No good can come from chasing such a lofty position within our tribe.

Tallack sparked my fire back into life before heading off to the Long Hut. He said he needed to speak with his men, but I knew his real reasons for leaving. Ever since the great sacrifice of the Novantae Chieftain, Faolan at the Nine Maidens stone circle, Tallack had his work cut out for him taming his new slave. The old man's daughter, Sorcha was spared the indignity of death for her part in the plot to overthrow my nephews and take over our lands. In return for her life, Sorcha was to be Tallack's primary slave girl.

It was quite a fall from grace. She had left her homelands in Skotek with the aim of becoming our next Ruvane. Through ill-conceived plots and devious lies, her father and brothers had failed to bring us all to heel. Instead of ruling alongside Blydh and Tallack, she now emptied their piss pots and washed their clothes. With a strong will such as hers, Sorcha would not break easily. Tallack rarely left her to her own devices for more than half a day at a time, for fear that she might get hold of a weapon and begin slaughtering anyone in her path.

Endelyn milked my goats until the pot was half filled and set it among the embers to warm through with a handful of crushed barley. Blydh fidgeted in my bunk under my furs, but dozed off to sleep a short time later. By the time the porridge was ready, only the priestess and I were able to eat.

I watched her radiant face in the flickering light from my fire. She was slim and elegant, nothing like the sturdy, muscular women about camp. I supposed that was down to all the donations of food and metal she received in return for her priestly services. Endelyn was not built for hard work, nor hunting and gathering. She spent her days advising those in need of the gods' words.

It made me wonder how she would be received by our people. Our previous experience of those who followed the odd ways of the gods were not positive. While our Priest Sect were nomadic, we left them to their own devices, but when they settled within our camp, tensions rose and would not be quelled.

My nephews and I shared mixed feelings over the priests. As much as we'd like to see them all run from our lands, we know that there are times when their services are crucial in appeasing the gods. Perhaps I worried unduly. Endelyn was not of the priest family that caused so much discontent. There was every chance that she would bring fresh insight and stability after many moons of turmoil. We sat together, eating our porridge and listening to Blydh's murmurs and groans.

"Does he fret like this often, Fur Benyn?" Endelyn could hardly take her eyes off my nephew. He lolled about in my furs half naked and sweating. The battle scars on his upper body showed that his experience belied his young age.

"I can only go by the times he has slept here rather than his own bed, but since the injury he has, yes."

"And you say that his mood alters to the point of unpredictability?" She put her bowl down and folded her hands in her lap, contemplating my answers.

I nodded. "I dare say it's just anxiety that makes him angry towards me. Other times he is still the sweet little boy I always knew and loved."

"So, it's almost like there is another person trapped inside him, a character that is false and wild?"

"Um... well... I wouldn't put it like that..."

"Have you performed any rituals of late in camp, I mean other than the sacrifice I conducted at the Nine Maidens?"

"Um, I don't think so, only little Delen's naming ceremony."

Endelyn gasped, leaning away from me on her stool. "I mean no disrespect, Fur Benyn, but did you perform the ceremony as the oldest woman in the tribe?"

"I did. What of it?"

"And by any chance, did you ask Blydh to assure the protection of the sun?"

My head was spinning. What was she driving at? How could Blydh's condition be related to a simple ritual to welcome my new niece into the tribe?

"He did yes. It was all conducted carefully, with ivy to form a barrier and the sun disc to close the portal to spirits from the Underworld. She's perfectly safe. The ivy bindings were only open for a short time, just long enough for our ancestors to see her before her mother sealed the circle."

Endelyn closed her eyes for a moment and tucked her long hair behind her ears. Slowly, she rose from the stool and approached the bed. Looking down at my nephew, she sighed. "And you used the very same sun disc to bridge the gap in Blydh's skull?"

It didn't occur to me that it should present a problem. It was a clean, thin plate of gold and perfect for the job. I shrugged at the priestess. "I did. Why is that so bad?"

"My dear lady." She said, glancing around at my angst-ridden face. "You have brought this about. The sun disc was the only thing keeping the evil spirits out of camp after the ceremony. Now you have infected Blydh with a demon from the Underworld."

CHAPTER TWO

This news sent me reeling. What had I done? Rather than save my poor nephew from further harm, I had inadvertently embedded an evil spirit inside his skull. I went through my memory of Delen's naming ceremony, trying to figure out what could have possibly gone wrong. I did everything according to customs and traditions. The demon must have attached itself to the sun disc. How would the tribe ever forgive me?

Endelyn seemed to comprehend my upset. She returned to my side and patted my arm. "Let's not give up hope. There has to be a cure."

"He'd never survive a third procedure on his skull, and even if he did, I can't remove the golden disc or his brain would have no protection at all." My voice wobbled. I couldn't hold back the tears.

"That wouldn't do any good anyway. Once the spirit took up residence inside Blydh it was too late. No. We need to think of another way to drive out the evil."

I was glad that Endelyn was applying her wisdom to a solution. All I could think about was what Blydh's mother would say when she found out what I'd done. How would the elders and all the warriors react if they knew one of our Chieftains was under the influence of a demon? They would be unlikely to follow any of Blydh's orders from then on. I needed to break the news gently to Tallack.

Having learnt my lesson about hiding the truth from him, I knew that this was too big to keep to myself.

Leaving the priestess to watch over Blydh, I wandered out into the compound with the intention of looking for Tallack in the Long Hut. The moment I left my own shelter though, I found myself heading south along the boardwalks towards the horse pen. The white hart had grown used to me delivering a few handfuls of grain every day. Whether he truly was the vessel of Cernonnus or just a rare white deer, I'd grown immensely fond of him. Each time I visited, he seemed to wander a little closer to me until I could feed him straight from my cupped hands.

As soon as he saw me opening the gate to the enclosure, the stag appeared from the budding trees and rewarded me with soft grunts of welcome. With the wheat and oats mixed in my palms, I spoke quietly to my god. "I wish you'd taken my offer to free you the day of the attack. Your antlers are growing fast. As soon as they reach the same majestic proportions as when you were first captured, my nephew will sacrifice you and feed you to our people." The deer sniffed the air close to my hands before edging closer to lick the cereal into his mouth. "Did you stay to warn me about the sun disc? Well, I wish your message could've been clearer. I can't change the past. If this evil spirit really controls Blydh, our whole tribe is in danger."

The stag grunted louder and backed away by two steps. His ears flicked and he let out a steaming snort from flared nostrils. I turned my head to see Sorcha the new slave watching close by.

"It's alright, shush now. She won't harm you." I murmured, holding out the grain once again. Slowly, his fear subsided and he gobbled up the rest of my offering until my hands were empty and wet from his tongue. "I'll come back later, my god. Hopefully you will have some advice for me then." He didn't hang about once he knew I was out of food. The stag hurried back into the wooded section of the pen while I returned to the boardwalk.

Sorcha waited for me by the gate. "People say that you have the ear of the gods." She said it as a statement, but it felt more like a question. What did she want me to say, that I hoped the white hart was a messenger and that it showed that the gods favoured us? Did she think me special for enticing a wild and hungry creature with a handful of wheat?

"People have too much time on their hands." I grumbled, altering my course and aiming for the Long Hut.

"So, it's not true. You can't hear Cernonnus as you speak to the beast?"

I gave her a sly look and hoped that she would make up her own mind over the matter. "How are you settling in now?" I asked, keen to change the topic of conversation.

She pulled a face and then tugged at her dirty tunic. "He has me swilling out his clothes, cutting and laying new rushes and all in these filthy rags. I know what my family attempted to do was wrong, but they paid the ultimate price. I don't see why I should be punished daily too."

She couldn't see that Tallack needed her alive to discourage further attacks from her kinfolk, nor could she see that her treatment served as a deterrent for any other tribe who might plot against us. He couldn't afford to be kind or the word would spread that our Chief was soft. As much as I liked the girl, and wanted the best for her, I was not about to interfere. I had already pushed my luck in securing her life.

The former Ruvane, Cryda, was in the Long Hut with Tallack when we arrived. She sat by his side nursing the babe and wittering on about some jewels she wanted from a passing trader. I caught the tail end of their conversation as I approached.

"No mother, we can't afford to waste tin or copper on trinkets. We have to build a new fleet of boats and you have no idea how much it costs to trade for sail fabric, not to mention restocking the camp supplies. Make do with what you have."

I had to stifle a chuckle. At last Tallack was beginning to stand up to his mother and make sensible decisions. Of course, his snappy mood could also have been the result of no sleep.

"Aunt Mel." He broadcast in a loud voice, partly to silence his mother but mainly to compensate for his brother's animosity towards me. "Have you come to tell me that Blydh has recovered?"

"No, my Chief, I'm afraid I haven't. There is something I need to discuss with you in private, but I was also hoping that you might know if anyone about camp has any poppy resin I could trade for since I have just one dose left." I walked and talked at the same time until I stood just below his tall chair at the top table.

Tallack scratched at the new fluff growing on his chin for a moment and frowned. "No, I can't think of anyone. How about you, Mother? Would any of your friends have a bead or two stashed for emergencies?"

Cryda thinned her lips and narrowed her eyes at his insinuation. "Why would my ladies have need for such a thing. They're not addled priests or lazy sea warriors like your men." She scoffed, annoyed that she could no longer command the attention of our tribe. Her time of power had passed with the death of the twin's father, Aebba.

"Have you asked Ren? He might know where we can trade for some." Tallack stepped down from the top table and walked around the raised platform to my side. Sliding his arm about my shoulders, he turned me around and aimed our trajectory towards the back door of the hut. "Now what was it you needed to talk about?"

I dreaded telling him what the priestess had said, but he received the news with a calmness that surprised me. He took a deep inhalation when I had finished and exhaled with a noisy breath. "It would certainly explain his changeable moods."

"I'm so sorry that this has happened. If I'd known about the possibility of a demon escaping, I never would have…"

"Stop blaming yourself, Aunt Mel. You acted in Blydh's best interests, and whether he appreciates you or not, you saved his life. Did the priestess have any ideas about how to get the evil spirit out of him?"

I shook my head. "I left her pondering that very thing while I came to look for resin."

We were standing next to the roasting pits watching Sorcha struggle with a half-plucked bird between her knees. She was utterly out of her depth but none of the other slaves offered to lend her a hand. Perhaps she had offended them with her smart mouth and Skotek brashness.

Tallack lowered his voice and turned his back to the slaves. "Let's keep this to ourselves, Aunt Mel. There's no point in panicking the elders or their loose-lipped wives with this. You go and tell Endelyn to stay quiet and I'll ask about the resin among the men. If you have to, get Kewri to lash Blydh to the bed and we'll tell people that it's to protect his wounds."

I knew why he'd said that. If a demonic spirit had really taken hold of Blydh, we couldn't let him roam around the island causing chaos. The thought of restraining my nephew made me nauseous but I was glad to know that I had Tallack's support should the worst come to pass.

Endelyn was deep in thought when I returned to my hut. Kewri snored from his own bunk and Blydh was restless but asleep in my bed. With the patient's bunk moved out of my hut, there was no space for me to lay down except on the rushes by the fire.

Had the day been warmer, I would have rested in the shelter that Kewri built for me to treat the sick and injured but as it was, the cold breeze whipped through the open hurdle walls. Perhaps Kewri would finally get a chance to finish building it one of these days.

Endelyn was as I had left her, poking at the fire and supping my ale. I sat by her side and gave her our Chief's orders about keeping the news to ourselves. She seemed pleased to be a part of the secret, as though it bonded her to our family in some way.

"Tallack is going to ask the men about more resin, but I'm not holding my breath for a positive outcome. Most of the resin was used up after the attack on the compound. I doubt anyone has any from here to the other side of the moors." I refilled her cup with ale and poured myself a sizable measure too.

Endelyn nodded her agreement with my assessment and then looked up at me and frowned. "I don't suppose willow is strong enough, is it?"

"Sadly, no. I suspect he's used to the strong stuff. Now nothing else will do." We ruminated over this for a short time until Tallack pushed through the door skins.

"Any luck?" I asked, brightening at the sight of my handsome nephew in the entrance.

"The warriors only have hemp weed. Ren gave me all he had and shook down the rest of the men for their supplies too." He held out the pouches and pipes in his hands.

"It might dull the pain a bit, but not Blydh's temper." I thanked my nephew for his efforts. Endelyn poured him a cup of ale and patted the stool next to her. She shone with a hopefulness that frightened me. Everywhere my nephews go, women throw themselves into their paths. I'd say it was in Tallack's best interests to find a bride to bind with, but with his partiality for his crewman, Treeve, undiminished I feared that may never happen.

I had nothing against her, Endelyn was a fine young woman. It's just that the elders would insist on a match to further the tribal ties and trade routes for our tin. It was a pity that we were called away from the midsummer gathering at Stonehenge or he could have negotiated a bride with another tribal leader then. As it is, he will have to wait another two cycles before another such opportunity comes his way. From the glint in Endelyn's eyes, I knew that she would not wait for such an eventuality.

Sleep was all that I could think about, but just as I was about to shoo my visitors from my hut in favour of rest, Blydh began to murmur and thrash about in my bunk. From his half-conscious groaning, I could tell that he was in pain.

Tallack spoke quietly to us both. "You know, he really needs something to cover his head."

"Like the helmets the Phoenician Princes told us about?" I said.

He nodded, supping his ale at the same time.

"But wouldn't the metal rub against his skull and cause more problems?" I reached out and touched the furs laying across my bunk, finding the solution to my own question. "Unless the helm was lined with soft materials like sheepskin…"

"Would Blydh consent to wearing such a strange hat?" Endelyn said, looking puzzled at our suggestion. "No one else in the tribe covers their heads like that."

"No, but we have it on good authority that great warriors across the seas do. If we can convince him that it's a sign of a great leader to wear one, we might be able to persuade him." Tallack rose from his stool. "I'll go and speak to the smithy. See how much metal we have left."

"It won't stop his pain though, nephew." I called after him. "And we have nowhere to trade for more resin."

Tallack halted his retreat and sat back down to ponder the problem.

"Priests usually have some put by at the stone circles." Endelyn added helpfully.

"But the closest one is the Nine Maidens on the moor, and you and your companions abandoned the place more than a moon ago." I said. It was hard to think straight on so little sleep. My eyelids grew more difficult to lift and my chin sagged to my chest. These young ones made no allowance for my age. They might be fresh after a long night of riding, but my old bones lacked their strength.

"They're not the only circle of nine stones. There is always the Nine Petrified Children at Winterbourne." Endelyn lowered her voice as though it was dangerous to even utter the name. "I know the priest who leads the rituals there. He's bound to have resin to trade."

Tallack drew in a sharp breath. "Beside the fact that those stones are said to be cursed, the circle sits on Duro land. No one in their right mind would go there from our tribe. It's a suicide mission." He swept his hand in front of his chest in a defiant gesture. "It's out of the question. No."

We sat in silence for some time, listening to Blydh crying out in pain. Tallack's stern expression softened and then fell into deep anxiety for his brother. "They say that all who enter the circle get a fever within a quarter moon, then black boils appear under their armpits shortly after. Some cough up blood just before death takes them on swift wings into the Underworld." His voice tapered off into a whisper. I shuddered at his description.

They were just some of the reported symptoms of those who ventured into the sacred space. Some believed the legend of the nine fated children who strayed into the circle, close to the realm of death, and were punished for their trespass.

According to the tale passed down through the generations, they danced about the wooded dell mocking the gods and urinating on the altar. Cernonnus himself was said to have risen in anger and turned them all into stone for their misdemeanour. From then on, all who strayed into the circle felt the vengeance of the nine children, contracting various diseases and ailments with few recovering from their afflictions.

It was hard to think of the God of the Wild Forest and of Death as anything but benevolent, particularly since I felt I had his favour through the white hart in the pony pen. To me he was wise and comforting, but perhaps I had grown complacent to his darker side. Blydh awoke and cried out, grabbing at his head with both hands. The more he jolted the plate in his skull, the more pain he suffered.

Tallack looked to me for an answer to the problem. The way I saw it, there was only one solution. One of us had to make the journey across enemy territory, risking life and limb and the possibility of a gruesome feverish death to obtain the only comfort for our Chief.

"I shall make the trip." I said and the moment it left my lips, I immediately regretted my decision.

CHAPTER THREE

I'm not sure what I was expecting them to say. Perhaps I wanted them to talk me out of the foolish suggestion, or to insist that a group of strong warriors went in my stead. Neither happened. For an uncomfortable amount of time, Tallack and Endelyn simply stared at me.

"I shall need some sleep first, but I'll set off as soon as possible." I didn't sound very sure of myself. The more they stared at me the more my confidence waned. I stood up and rolled my knives in their leather wrapping and packed them into my healing kit. "I'm sure Kewri will come with me when he wakes." My voice had reduced to a thin rasp, barely audible to my visitors.

By the time I had gathered up a few of my things to pack, Tallack had risen from his stool and was standing behind me. He touched my shoulder, making me jump. "I can't let you do this, Aunt. It's much too dangerous." He said the words I was longing to hear, but they had no weight behind them. I could tell from his imploring look, that his concern for me was nothing compared to that of his brother. He had no intention of talking me out of going.

"Have you been there before, Fur Benyn? Do you know the way?" Endelyn said.

"No, but if I head east along the coastal path, I'm sure folk there will direct me." I didn't turn to look at her for fear my resolve would fail me.

"I should come with you. We can fly the black banners of the priests. That will allow us safe passage. I have the pennant in my shelter." She looked to Tallack and I thought I saw a flicker of a smile, urging him to come with us. Her wiles were lost on my nephew. Rather than rush to a damsel's aid, he offered his men instead.

"I'll go and find Ren." Tallack made a lunge for the door. "He and Kewri will keep you both safe. A small party can slip past the Duros under black banners far better than a great horde of us. Get some sleep, Aunt. I'll have it all arranged for when you awake." Before either of us could protest, he was gone.

Endelyn looked utterly crestfallen. Her noble offer failed to garner Tallack's interest. Instead, she'd saddled herself with a treacherous mission without either of the Chiefs accompanying us. With hunched shoulders and a faintly perceptible sigh, she left my hut and returned to her own quarters.

I shook Kewri awake and explained what we had planned. He rolled out of his bunk and set about the chores, giving me his warm bunk to rest in until it was time to leave.

It was past midday when I awoke to the smell of frying pork. Kewri cut the meat in half, wrapping the chunk in waxed fabric for our journey, and in half again to share with me. We ate some fresh traded bread, the meat and a little cheese, before loading up the ponies and walking them to the eastern gates of the island compound. Endelyn was sitting high on her steed waiting for us, next to Ren and one other.

"What's Sorcha doing here?" I shrieked. "We can't take a Skotek slave with us. The plan was to keep the numbers of our group small."

"Chief Tallack's idea, Fur Benyn." Ren announced. "Said she could be useful to us with building fires and cooking and stuff."

I pulled a face at him. From what I'd seen of Sorcha's skills, she would be more likely to hinder than help. The girl was used to having slaves of her own to order about. The reason had nothing to do with her usefulness. He didn't want her about camp reminding him of her father and brothers' slaughter. This was another attempt to palm her off onto me.

There was no use in arguing. Tallack was not there to hear my complaint. His absence did not go unnoticed by Endelyn, who was clearly hoping to twist his heartstrings in a ditch attempt to make him join us. Ignoring her scowl, I led the charge through the gate and into the narrow trail between the marshland on our eastern shores.

Ahead of us lay two and a half days of riding across enemy territory. Ren was our biggest asset. He knew the paths and tracks close to the coast better than anyone, but I secretly wished that Senara was among our group. She was the most skilled tracker our tribe had ever seen. As we rode out, Ren trotted alongside me, with Endelyn, Sorcha and Kewri at the back.

Every few moments, Sorcha complained. First her horse was too slow, then it was the heat of the afternoon making her sweat in her bulky slave clothes. By evening, she was moaning about how chilly she was. There really was no pleasing her.

As daylight faded behind us, Kewri lost his patience. "For the sake of Cernonnus, woman. Shut your kyjyan mouth!"

It was the first time I had ever heard him bark like that. It shook us all.

Sorcha was affronted. "It's alright for you. I'm the one forced to wait on the killers of my family or risk the same disgraceful death."

"Your father went back on his word. He betrayed us all. You should be grateful that they didn't slash your throat and be done with it." Kewri looked red in the face.

In all honesty, I was surprised. At the ritual of old Faolan's sacrifice, Kewri was the only one who showed Sorcha any compassion whatsoever. What had happened between them that sparked such a drastic change in attitude?

At dusk, Ren rode on ahead. We were close to the border of the Durotriges and we needed somewhere safe to spend the night. I also knew that he would keep his eye out for a bird or two for our supper. For a sea warrior, Renowden was a master hunter. It was almost as though he could sing the prey into his arms. I'd travelled with him on several journeys, and he was by far the most successful at keeping us all nourished.

This night was no different. When we caught up with him, he was sitting around a roaring fire with a couple of fat ducks roasting over the embers. I dismounted and let Kewri lead my pony to a freshwater stream at the foot of the valley. Ren had chosen a wooded dell in which to camp, but I was amazed that he'd risked lighting a fire.

"Won't we draw the attention of the Duros?" I asked him.

"Nope. I spoke to a man further up the valley. They said that all the warriors and able men have been called up to help build the new Ruvane's compound." He laughed. "Brea's obsession with power has done us a great favour. Even if there are other Duros about, they are in no mind for fighting. I got the distinct impression that they all hated her."

Endelyn clapped her hands together when she saw our supper sizzling and spitting meagre fat droplets into the flames. "I'm ravenous." She warmed herself by the fire and then picked at the meat, licking the juices off her fingers. "Hmm, not ready yet." It was an obvious statement. We could all see that the meat was practically raw.

Sorcha was tasked with helping Kewri with the horses. He rolled his eyes at me when I made the suggestion. What had got into them? She surely had enough gumption to get them to water and give them some grain? It wasn't as though I'd asked her to collect wood for the fire or build us a shelter. Did Tallack expect me to break her spirit and train her in the ways of subservience? If that was his plan, it was doomed to failure. This wilful girl had no intention of embracing her duties.

Endelyn was quiet after we'd eaten. She rolled out her bedding, swept away any ants and stones from her side of the fire and tucked herself into her furs. I took that to mean that she was still annoyed that Tallack had not fallen for her alluring ways. She was sulking. Kewri and Sorcha tired of sniping at each other and did the same shortly after, leaving Renowden and I to while away the time in peace.

"We crossed the River Sid back there." I said, tipping my head in the direction we had ridden. "This is Duro land."

"It is, but safe enough here. I did a quick circuit of the valley while I looked for food. There are no dwellings for miles, just a couple of old fishermen who had paddled down the Sid to the river mouth." He took out his pipe and packed the bowl with hemp weed. "Want some of this to calm your nerves?" He waited for the shake of my head before continuing. “You sure? I have another pipe you can use.”

“That’s good of you Ren, but I don’t much like the taste. I’ll stick to the ale.”

“You don’t know what you’re missing.” He chuckled, pulling a burning stick from the fire to light the dried weed.

I wrapped my bed furs around my shoulders against the cold of the evening while my front tingled with the heat from the flames. “Do you ever get sick of the sea, Ren?”

“No, not even on lengthy trips. I start to miss it if I’m on land for too long.” He puffed on his pipe and leaned against the trunk of an ash tree. “I sailed with Aebba and then with Tallack while he learned the ropes. I’m guessing that with Blydh out of action, it’ll be some time before we put to sea again.”

“If ever.” I said flatly. “If Blydh can’t lead the tribe, Tallack will have to stay on land to run things just as his father did before him.”

“I hadn’t thought of that. Do you reckon he’ll appoint another clan leader for the Sea Warriors?”

“Not sure he has much choice.” We exchanged glances, both of us landing on the same thought. “As long as he doesn’t pick Treeve to replace him.” I said. “There would be enough outcry to fuel a mutiny.”

“You’re not wrong there, Fur Benyn. He might be a favourite of Tallack’s, but his preferential treatment doesn’t sit well with the crew.” The corners of his mouth curled up into a sneer. “I did think at one point during the last couple of moons that Treeve was after the Ruvane’s position.”

“By the gods, so did I.”

“He’ll be borrowing Cryda’s furs and jewels next.” Renowden chortled, coughing into his pipe smoke.

The thought of the dainty crewman parading himself in front of our whole tribe as the highest lady wife of the Chieftain filled me with horror. “He’d ruin my nephew’s reputation in less than a quarter moon if that ever happens. Can you imagine the reaction our tribe would receive at the great midsummer gatherings at Stonehenge?”

That seemed to amuse Ren all the more. His laughter had him sliding down the tree trunk until he had to steady himself with an outstretched hand. When he stopped coughing long enough to speak, he said, “I’m sure Tallack knows what he’s doing. Our laws and customs are well known to all. I can’t see him breaking with tradition just to satisfy the ambitions of one sailor.”

“Hmm.” I said, unconvinced. “Let’s hope you’re right.”

Between us, we finished off the last of the meat and stacked more wood onto the fire. I must admit, the ale quickened my curiosity and loosened my tongue. “Did you ever wed, Ren?”

“Me? No, Fur Benyn. Who’d put up with an old sea dog like me? The ocean is my lady.”

“I find that hard to believe.”

“Never in one place long enough for women to catch hold of me.”

I sensed that he was steering me away from a troubled past. I should have stopped pushing, but the ale was in control of my mouth.

“Where are you from originally? I don’t remember you being born at the first compound on the River Exe.”

He could have simply refused to answer me, told me to mind my own business, but he didn’t. He looked me in the eye, all traces of humour erased. “I was born on a homestead on the north coast of Dumnonia.”

Now that he was talking, I stayed quiet in case I said something to interrupt the flow of information. He didn't break eye contact the whole time he spoke.

"My father was an evil man. I know, there are plenty of those in the land, but he was particularly vicious. He'd beat my mother until she'd pass out in agony." That memory pained him. He blinked a few times, clearing the excess moisture. "I tried to stop him but got a back hander for my troubles. I was too small at the time to overpower him and nothing would ease his temper." Renowden sat more upright against the tree and took a steadying breath. "One day I came in from feeding the goats and pigs and found my mother dead on the hut floor. She was covered in blood. I wasn't about to hang around for him to kill me too, so I took my few things and ran."

"You came south to the River Exe?"

He took a gulp of ale from his cup and nodded. "Ran over the moors. I had no brothers nor sisters so there was no reason to stay."

"And you joined Aebba's Sea Warrior Clan?"

"Not at first. I tried over and over again to join your brother, Cador's Head Hunters, but I was too young. I'd only seen nine, maybe ten summers. In the afternoons, I would sneak out onto the training grounds, but got my arse kicked out of there every time. Eventually, Cador fixed me up with the fishing crews, running about after the old men of the tribe. Spent my days fixing nets or gutting and salting fish. As much as I hated the drudge work, it introduced me to the sea. By the time Aebba was old enough to lead the Sea Warriors, I'd already learned navigation and sailed far and wide, mostly for trades with other tribes."

"And Aebba saw how skilled you were, especially in recognising tribal regions of the coastline and took you into his clan?"

Ren nodded. I could see his cheeks flushing in the firelight. He was embarrassed by his own admission. Humility was rare among our tribal members. "So, you see the longest time I've spent ashore was the odd winter when we were repairing the boats."

"I see, but I dare say some nice young woman would have been happy to bind to a man who was rarely in camp." I smirked, trying to lighten the mood.

It worked, he snorted at my jest. "Ah, maybe one or two tried to pin me down, but none were successful. How about you, Meliora?" He caught me off guard, using my proper name and turning the invasive question around.

"Eh? What about me?" I smiled. I liked him using my given name; *wise woman* is so impersonal.

"Did you not bind to another in your youth?"

I stammered my words, unable to form a meaningful response. "Oh, well, um, not really, although it was a close thing but not to be evidently." A rush of memories and emotions dashed into my mind, filling me with a confusion of feelings. I didn't want to be reminded of my past any more than he did, but unlike me, he seemed to be pressing the issue.

"Someone arranged for you by the Chief or someone you found for yourself?"

He'd been so open with me about his past that I felt I owed him something in return. The trouble was, every time I thought about the love of my life, my throat constricted and prevented me from forming a coherent sentence. How could I explain the most painful moments of my youth?

"It was a very long time ago. Hardly worth speaking about." I said, hoping that he'd lose interest.

"Someone as kind and smart as you must have had men lining up, surely?"

I narrowed my eyes at him, thinking he was making fun of me. His expression was neutral. He meant every word. I didn't know what to say to that. "There was a man I wanted to spend the rest of my days with, but my brother was not called Cador the Cruel for nothing. He set me up to wed a great Chief and was furious when he discovered that I loved another." It was my turn to stare into the flames, lost in my memories.

"And yet you did not go through with the ceremony your brother arranged?"

I took a long breath and let my lungs empty. "Let's just say that my knowledge of herbs and poisons made my brother think twice about controlling me."

"Were you able to take up with the man you loved?" He leaned forwards and rested his elbows on his knees, listening attentively.

I shook my head. "Cador made sure of that."

"I'm sorry." He murmured.

I shrugged. "Like I said. It was a long time ago." We sat in silence for a while, contemplating our shared stories. It made me feel closer to Renowden, knowing that he too suffered at the hands of another family member at an early age. Both of us had seen more summers than most of the tribe combined, yet found ourselves at the mercy of the young and inexperienced. He was respected among the Sea Warriors, they'd seen him in action, but he had to work hard to gain and keep the good opinions of Blydh's Head Hunter Clan. I enjoyed the rare privilege of being the Meterns' aunt. That alone gave me the opportunity to voice my opinions, even if Blydh was angry with me.

We began rolling out our bedding for the night. The moon was high and the wet buds and leaves over our heads were turning pale with the frost.

"Have you ever been to the Nine Children Stones at Winterbourne?" Ren asked me. His face was puckered into a deep frown.

"Never. Have you?"

"Just the once, with Aebba and a few of his young warriors."

"Well that should come in handy. At least you know the way." I covered my legs and pulled the furs high over my body.

"That's the least of our worries. What they say about the stones is true. I've seen it with my own eyes."

"What, that there is some kind of wicked magic at work for those who enter the circle without tribute or priest?"

"One of Aebba's warriors stepped into the circle before the ritual was complete on the night of a new moon. He died five days later from black pustules under his arms and rampant fever. I will never forget the look on his face. It was as though he'd been dragged into the Underworld by Cernonnus himself."

CHAPTER FOUR

Needless to say, I slept ill that night. Renowden's warning about the Nine Stones at Winterbourne swirled around my mind until the moon began to fall in the sky. Despite having a priestess among our party, I believed what Ren had witnessed all those years ago. He was neither a liar nor someone who exaggerates. If his friend died a horrific death just by stepping inside the circle, we had to be extra careful. As long as we could speak with the priest there without ever going near to the stones, we should be safe.

In the morning, Sorcha rode at the front of our group with Ren while I stayed at the rear with Endelyn and Kewri. With the bickering slave and my giant separated, we made good progress along the coastal path without the aggravation of their noise. Around mid-afternoon, we had a minor scare when Ren heard approaching horses along the cliffs.

Endelyn secured the black banners of the priests on a pole and held it aloft. It was a sensible thing to do, but we were not prepared to rely on it for protection. Rather than try and bluff our way through a conversation with people from our enemy tribe, we trotted further into the dunes and hid ourselves and horses behind the ridges.

Ren's best guess regarding the location of all the Duros seemed to be correct. Other than a few old people and those galloping warriors, the place was deserted. I started to relax, knowing that we had another night to catch up on sleep plus a further half-day's ride before reaching our destination.

We stopped to camp on the sheltered side of the cliffs beyond the high-water mark of the beach. While Ren wandered off to find our supper, Kewri and I built a fire and unpacked the cooking pots.

"Sorcha, walk along the wet sand and see if you can't dig up a few razor clams." I said, pointing down the beach.

"Can't see any. I'd be wasting my time." She snapped, sitting crossed legged on the bedding I was trying to unfurl.

"Get up girl." I chided, yanking at the furs from under her. "Of course, you can't see them. They're buried in the sand."

"Don't you know how to dig for shellfish? By the gods, you're stupid." Kewri sneered.

"I've never needed to find my own food. I was the daughter of a great northern Chieftain." She stuck her nose in the air and folded her arms across her chest.

My, they were tiresome. "Both of you shut up and go and dig for clams, cockles, whatever we can eat. Kewri, show her how." I looked up and shot him a glare. That shifted him. "Go on, daughter of a traitorous Chief. Make yourself useful, or Tallack won't have need to keep you alive. Just remember that, young lady." I tugged so hard on the bedding; she was thrown into the sand on her face. Endelyn laughed, almost making me lose my composure, but I was determined to stay stern and gruff with her. Sorcha picked herself up and followed Kewri, muttering and complaining under her breath all the way down the beach.

It gave me a chance to speak to Endelyn without being overheard. I repeated what Ren had told me the night before about the death of his friend at the Nine Children Stone Circle. Hoping that she might laugh at the notion of dark magic and a deadly infection, I grabbed her sleeve to make her turn and face me. She was not laughing. The skin above her nose wrinkled together and she sucked in her lips.

"I'm afraid that it's all true. A number of people have died from the same symptoms, but I trust my priest friend. He'll make sure that we're kept safe. We have plenty to give in offerings to the gods, thanks to Chief Tallack's generosity. As long as that Sorcha girl does nothing stupid, we can trade for the resin and set off for home before darkness falls tomorrow." She forced her mouth into a grin but it was not convincing. She was just as frightened about the possibilities as me.

Renowden returned with a couple of mackerel and a fat crab. They were almost cooked before Kewri and Sorcha returned with a few cockles resting in Kewri's upturned tunic.

"Is that all you found? You've been gone for ages?" I moaned, but neither of them answered me. They seemed distinctly sheepish, but I couldn't figure out why. "Did you rinse them well?" I squinted up at the huge man. He nodded, but they didn't look clean to me. "Hmm." Sorcha volunteered to take them to the shoreline and rinse them through again. Kewri went with her, smiling. For the love of Cernonnus, I hoped they had not taken a fancy to one another. It was bad enough when they were fighting, this simpering compliance was almost worse.

I let them be, choosing to ignore their changeable attitudes. There was enough to worry about without adding to our troubles. Ren maybe comfortable lighting big fires on Durotriges land, but I was not. We ate as soon as the fish and crab were ready, with a little boiled tender seaweed. The salty taste gave me a thirst, but I was not in the mood to stay up late drinking ale and sharing secrets two nights in a row.

Leaving the young ones to the chores, I dug out a dip in the soft sand closest to the warm rocks of the cliff face and rolled myself in my furs. The anxious thoughts had not left me, but I lay so still that eventually I dropped off to sleep.

Endelyn had to jog my shoulder to wake me in the morning. Our things were already packed onto our horses, except for a portion of thin porridge made with water and my bedding.

"Why didn't you wake me sooner?" I hurried to my feet and Sorcha grabbed my furs while they were still warm from my body. Kewri handed me my bowl and a spoon. What was happening? Had they suddenly paid heed of my warnings about Sorcha's place in camp or were they in as big a hurry to return home as Endelyn?

Rushed and disorientated, I let them all bustle around me until we were ready to set off on the last leg of the journey to the circle. The further inland we rode, the more homesteaders and campsites we had to dodge.

The horses picked up on our fear, nickering and trying to bolt every time a flock of birds soared into the air from the trees either side of the track. It was exhausting, keeping them moving along the trail while scanning for any potential hostile forces ahead.

By late afternoon, we passed through a shallow valley of grassland. On the southern side, the burial barrows at the top of the hill looked like cresting whales in a sea of black clouds. I shivered, although the day was not cold. You could feel the presence of the Durotriges' ancestors nearby. I wondered if their dead were trying to find a way to betray us to the living. We had nowhere to run or hide.

If the Duros chose to attack us now, there would be no chance of any of us surviving.

Our luck held out all the way through the valley until we reached a small stream.

Ren pulled up the reins of his horse and dismounted. "From what I remember, the stones are not far from here. We follow the meander in the stream and the circle is right next to the water. Make sure that you have removed anything that would give us away as Dumnonii. No jewels or metals on show for example. Sorcha, keep your trap shut or your accent will attract attention. Endelyn, you lead the way, since you know the priest." We all did as we were told, taking out hair rings and hiding metal in our underclothes and in my healing bag.

Before he mounted his pony, he looked back at us all. "Remember, don't step into the circle, for any reason whatsoever."

If his intention was to allay my fears, he did a terrible job. I could feel my porridge swimming about inside my stomach before it erupted into my gullet, but on we rode.

Our timing could not have been any better. It was too late in the day for morning rituals and too early for sunset ceremonies. Apart from a few old women and a tall man in long robes, the place was empty of Duros. My breathing steadied at our good fortune.

The circle itself was much smaller than I was expecting. The nine stones, said to have formed from the bodies of children when they were cursed by Cernonnus and turned into stone, were all completely different in shape and size. There appeared to be no equal spacing, nor anything to symbolise the usual beings represented at circles elsewhere. The stream ran so close to the boundary that I was worried about refilling my water bladder in case I strayed into the sacred ring. As I slithered down the side of my pony and crouched at the bank side, Endelyn stopped me with a hand on my shoulder.

"Not here, Fur Benyn. We'll refill on the way home upstream. Just to be safe."

I froze for a moment, not knowing which way to turn. The priestess tucked her hand under my elbow and gently pulled me in a sweeping arc around the edge of the circle and across a plank bridge over the water.

"I want you to meet my friend. He's almost as wise as you, Fur Benyn." Everything about her was calm, as though being close to the stones gave her comfort. Close proximity only served to give me the chills, especially after Ren's tale about his unfortunate friend. The same new moon sat below the horizon waiting to shine on the rock children at dusk.

She steered me towards the tall man in the long robes and introduced us. I admit I was not paying particular attention to what she was saying and completely missed his name.

As they greeted one another, my gaze was drawn to the stones behind me. One was large and stout, with a reddish hue. It was at least double the size of the tiny one at its side. I wondered how old the children were before Cernonnus cast his ire upon them, encasing them in rock for all time. Did they really deserve such wrath?

This place demanded deep respect and careful steps. Kewri and Sorcha rode their horses across the stream and dismounted a short distance from where I stood with Endelyn and the priest. Ren stayed well away, refusing to leave his horse.

The trees surrounding the dell were almost in full leaf, throwing us all into shadow. The stench of offal and charred herb bundles wafted into my nostrils from a pile of sacrificial offerings on the altar stone in the centre.

Thank Cernonnus that Endelyn had her wits about her. She began the negotiations to trade for whatever poppy resin the priest could spare. She offered him a handsome amount of copper to begin with, but he wouldn't accept the deal. He could see that we were desperate and that he was in a strong bargaining position. We had no gold to offer, but a sizable number of tin nuggets transformed his scowl into a smile.

With the small pot of resin sealed by wax drippings in my pocket, I heaved a sigh of relief. We could be away from this eerie site before the sun set. I turned around to begin the slippery crossing over the bridge, but stopped when I heard Endelyn speak softly to the man.

"While I am here, I should be grateful of your counsel." She whispered to the priest. I returned to her side, curious as to her question. Sorcha and Kewri were bickering again next to their horses. His clumsy dismount had over balanced his cart horse. To compensate for Kewri's heavy bulk, the creature stamped in the soft mud, jostling against Sorcha in the process. Their behaviour was no better than children. Perhaps that is part of the dark magic of this place, to regress those close by towards infancy.

Endelyn was encouraged by the old priest's expression and continued. "Our Chieftain suffers from the corruption of an evil spirit. It was the result of a careless naming ceremony and the misuse of the sun disc used to close the portal to the Underworld." She flicked her head around and saw my look of shame. "Not your fault, Fur Benyn. You are not to blame." She reached out and touched my hand, squeezing my fingers together tightly. "Wise priest, is there a way to banish this demon from a much-loved Chief?"

I watched him cover his mouth and then stroke his straggly beard, pondering on her request for aid. "Come and sit by the fire, Endelyn. This will require much thought." His offer seemed to include me, so I followed them to the bleak shelter between the trees where a woman ladled stew into a bowl.

We waited for the priest to arrange his robes around the low stool on which he sat. Once comfortable, he beckoned us closer and instructed the woman to serve us with what remained in the pot over the fire. Given the number of dead offerings in the circle, they were not short of food. Endelyn settled first, accepting the meal with her usual grace and gratitude. My bowl was less full than hers, but still warm and welcome in the chilly atmosphere surrounding us.

The priestess took her time in explaining Blydh's injury and the alteration to his behaviour since the naming ceremony for his little sister, Delen. All the while she spoke the old man nodded into his stew, only lifting his face to shove more bread into his mouth. From his dazed expression, I was beginning to think he hadn't heard a word of Endelyn's plea but at length, he put down his bowl and turned to us both.

"Dear ladies. It's clear to me that you care a great deal for this young man and his wellbeing. He is a lucky fellow indeed. As to his affliction, this is grave news and hopes for a cure are slim." It pained me to hear him say the words, although I was half expecting them.

Endelyn took in a sharp breath and leaned closer to him. "But not lost altogether. There must be something that can be done."

"Perhaps, but it's not a suggestion I make lightly."

Typical priest, loved to make every moment a drama centred around themselves. If it was not his supper time, I wouldn't have been surprised if he'd twirled around and doused us all with chicken blood.

"Tell us, wise one. What can we do to save our Chief from this wicked possession?" Endelyn was lapping up his performance, but then, she was as bad as him for craving attention.

"I have heard of a place where the water gushes up from a hole in the ground. They say it smells of the Underworld and is so potent that all demonic spirits are called back home from its power. You must take your Chief there and perform the Ritual of Eternal Solace, bless him with the stinking hot waters and intone the chant of Cernonnus. Make sure you give a generous offering to the gods or the ritual will have the reverse effect."

"You mean…?"

"Yes, rather than removing a dark spirit, you will summon more." The old man boomed his warning out across the dell for everyone to hear. Sorcha and Kewri stopped their jostling and bickering and stood slack jawed at the warning.

I grew tired of the show. "And where exactly is this hot spring of eternal damnation?"

He peered his rheumy eyes at me through narrowed lids, annoyed that I'd curtailed his performance. "Where the River Avon meets the Severn, and then two day's ride from the muddy eastern banks to the hot springs inland."

"That all sounds fairly straight forward." I said, rising from my stool. "Thank you for your hospitality…"

"But you must stop at the estuary first, at the mouth of the Avon." He interrupted, gesturing for me to sit back down. "The spring lies on Belgae land and they don't take kindly to strangers invading their sacred well."

I thought it sounded too good to be true. "What are they likely to want in return for granting us access to the spring, a first-born child sacrifice or my left arm severed at the shoulder?"

He was not pleased with my flippancy. He stood tall from his seat, stepped nearer, and glowered down at me. “Treat my advice with contempt if you must, but take that tone with the Chief of the Belgae and it’ll be the last joke you ever make.”

Suitably chastised, I gave him my sincerest apologies and bowed my head with respect. It was his circle, his shelter, and his food. He didn’t have to advise us. My quarrelsome ways will get me in hot water one of these days.

“Send a scout to request an audience with their Chief, and offer him a decent metal tribute. If he is satisfied with the level of respect shown, he will invite you into his camp to discuss your intentions.”

Endelyn chimed into the debate. “And if he doesn’t?”

The priest raised his brows and puckered his mouth. “You’d better hope he does.”

Neither of us needed clarification on the possible consequences of upsetting the powerful leader. It sounded like a dangerous mission with not much chance of success. “Can’t we just get Endelyn to perform those rituals and incantations at one of our own circles? Men an Tol has a good record of healing, or perhaps our Nine Maidens where she was the primary priestess.”

The old man gave me a searing glare from the corner of his eyes. “For something as ingrained as an evil spirit possession, no other sacred space will do.” He didn’t wait for us to argue the point. He took Endelyn by both hands and helped her to her feet. “It was nice to see you again, my child. Go now and prepare for the journey.” They touched foreheads together for a long moment, before parting. To me he said nothing. He simply turned his back and walked off towards the wooded region behind the stones.

Endelyn was tight lipped and cross with me. I hadn't made a very good impression on her friend. Their priestly ways had never sat well in my conscience and I found it difficult to take them seriously let alone revere them as others did. "I meant no offence." I said, but she wasn't content with my pathetic excuse for an apology.

The main thing was that we had secured enough resin to keep Blydh's headaches at bay. I stomped back over the bridge and glanced about me. Kewri was fiddling with the reins of his horse, Ren was exactly where I had left him and Endelyn followed on behind me. Sorcha's horse chewed the grass on the bank of the stream.

"Where's she got to now?" I blew out my cheeks in exasperation. "Kewri. Where's Sorcha?"

He had one foot on the stirrup straps, holding the horse's mane and the blanket covering the creature's back. "Said she needed a piss." He muttered into the soft hair of the cart horse.

I moved around Kewri's enormous pony and twisted in every direction. It didn't take long for me to spot her. She was squatting behind the largest stone inside the circle, emptying her bladder in their sacred space.

CHAPTER FIVE

Endelyn shrieked, Renowden gasped, I ran closer and beckoned Sorcha to hurry from the circle before she was seen by the priest.

"What? What's wrong? I had to pish." Her Skotek accent was broader than ever. "Even you have to do that, you know." Sorcha ambled towards me, pulling up her leggings and allowing her tunic to fall over her nether regions.

As soon as she was clear of the circle, I grabbed her by the wrist and dragged her to the ponies. "Didn't you listen to a word Ren said? The stones are cursed."

"Och, that's just a tale to scare the children." She was still tying the cord about her waist while I pushed and shoved her closer to her horse.

"Don't you see, you stupid girl?" Endelyn cried. "Those stones are Duro children and you have just desecrated their holy circle." The priestess covered her face with both hands, as though the ague that Sorcha was in peril of developing would jump across the air and infect her too.

Ren yanked his pony's reins to the left, kicking him gently in the side until he faced the way we came. "I did say this was a bad idea, not that anyone listens to me." Clicking his tongue, he urged the horse into a canter, setting the pace for us all to follow. I suspect he thought that by speeding away from the source of danger we might be protected. I knew differently. Curses seldom work that way.

It made me think of the Phoenician visitors to our shores, who needed a cure for a different type of curse. They pretended to be friends and allies all the way to the top of the world in search of their cure. Just when we thought we had found the solution to their problems; they stole away my Jago and slaughtered him as an offering to their gods. It didn't stop the curse from spreading and neither would galloping away from the Nine Children.

Youngsters like Sorcha always think that rules are made to stop them having fun, or to prove that we can control them. It's only when they've fallen foul of our advice that they begin to understand the purpose of customs, laws, and rituals. We rode the horses hard until we reached the beach where we'd camped the night before.

No one dared to speak, except for the generally quiet Kewri. Every so often, he would lean across to Sorcha sitting under the bedding furs next to the fire and ask her if she felt unwell. Her response was the same each time, a quick shake of the head and rapid blinking as she grew more anxious through the evening.

We ate a sparse meal of cooked oats with a few cockles and stayed close to the fire to sleep. Come morning, I awoke to see Kewri standing over Sorcha, watching her sleep. Normally, I would find that kind of behaviour creepy, but I wriggled out of my furs and stood next to him. I too was curious as to whether there was any sign of the ague upon her. When she stirred, we both scurried away, busying ourselves with bundling our bedding and cooking pots.

Endelyn was less subtle in her approach. "Let me see you, child." She demanded, pulling the covers off the girl and squinting in the early light at her face and neck. "Show me your arms."

Sorcha rolled up the sleeves of her tunic, exposing pale freckled limbs.

"Hmm. She looks fine." The priestess barked.

"I am fine. Takes more than a silly story to take down a Novantae Shield Maiden." She chuckled, jumping up from her bedding to eat the leftover oats. No one else found it a laughing matter.

Renowden's pace was gruelling. My backside was bruised and sore and the horses were foaming with sweat by the time we reached the second camping site. Being so close to our own border, the night was more relaxed than our first, until I saw Sorcha scratching her armpits. That was also when I first noticed that she had a new fur collar.

"Where did you get that from." I stomped over to her and prodded the animal hide fastened about her shoulders. "You were not wearing that before."

She wouldn't meet my eye. Sniffing and turning away from me, she said. "I traded for it. Not that it's your business how I clothe myself. I belong to Chief Tallack, not you."

How her attitude had changed from when I met her at the Novantae compound near to the top of the world. She was such a sweet and generous girl back then. I knew for a fact that she possessed nothing valuable to trade. The only explanation was that she'd stolen it from the priest and his woman back at the Nine Children Stones.

My face must have betrayed my incredulity.

"I found it in the circle. A bramble scratched my ankle and when I sat on the stones to examine the cut, I saw it folded on the ground. No one wanted it." She fondled the tatty pelt defiantly. Ren and Endelyn exchanged glances.

We all knew that she had taken one of the offerings to the gods, but it was futile to point out the error of her ways.

Later that evening, Sorcha scratched herself a great deal. A part of me wanted to help the girl, offer some of my famous plantain paste to cool the itch. A crueller part of me thought she deserved everything heading her way. What good would it do to waste my tinctures and salves on an incurable curse? The gods would either save and forgive her, or take her into the Underworld covered in black lesions and sores.

With no idea whether Sorcha was in pain or not, I slept with the poppy resin and my tin pouch under my furs. They were too precious to put in temptation's way. If Sorcha can steal a tribute to the gods, she would have little problem taking all I had and attempting to escape.

Ren stayed awake for half the night, keeping watch in case we were attacked by passing Duros. At least, that was the reason he gave. I rather think it was to keep an eye on Sorcha's movements while we slept. When the moon was high, I heard him wake Kewri to take the second watch.

At daylight, I expected to find Sorcha dead in a bundle of furs, but she was as sprightly and annoying as ever. As she stretched and yawned, I saw the raised bumps of a rash across her collar bone and neck. Her arms looked to be affected too, although she displayed no signs of being in pain. She kicked off her furs with bare legs, wearing just her long tunic to cover down to her thighs. Near to her ankle was a large square region of red, swollen skin with a black lesion in the very centre.

There was no doubt about it now. She had incurred the wrath of Cernonnus and the stone children. Ren saw the marks too. His mouth fell open but he said nothing.

When Kewri came back from the dunes, he took a rasping inhalation. "Sorcha, look!" He pointed to her ankle and stayed there like a dutiful hunting dog.

"Och, I know. I saw it earlier. Doesn't hurt. I expect a wee beastie bit me or something. Nothing like the midges we get in Skotek. Now they are a real pain in the arse." Her nonchalance seemed to allay Kewri's fears for her health. The rest of us kept our opinions to ourselves. Only time would tell if Cernonnus would take another life into his underground realm.

It was midday when the watchmen called out to open the eastern gates. The ingenious contraption Renowden designed lowered, allowing us to cross the deepest stretch of the River Exe to the island compound.

As we trotted towards the pony enclosure, I was relieved to see that my white hart still lived and appeared to be waiting for me. He must have missed me coming to feed him his grain these last few days. Passing the smelly end of the compound, where the hides were scraped and stretched, the weavers spun and dyed the wool and the meat butchered and salted, I saw Blydh standing on the new boardwalks with a hunk of roasted pork as big as my head in his fist.

I knew where he was headed. Ever since the attack on the compound, the twin's half-brother Paega was kept prisoner in an open-air enclosure strong enough to hold a raging auroch bull. The posts were thick and driven deep into the ground. Narrow spaces between them allowed our people to see through to him, but he was unable to get out. There was just one entrance that was secured with a thick bronze rod. Not even Kewri could have reached it from the inside.

Blydh made the decision to keep him alive after his treacherous betrayal, attacking us along with the

Durotriges. Some took pity on the pathetic creature, out in all weathers and having only the stream that supplied the ponies from which to drink. They threw food scraps through the gaps in the posts. Others took great delight in chucking their piss pots at him instead. Blydh preferred to sit and eat lavish foods and drink warmed ale in front of his disgraced kin, hurling insults and recollections of how he killed Paega's mother.

This day was no different. Blydh rolled a large log onto the boards and made himself comfortable. The warm meat juices trickled through his fingers and onto the planks. "Oh, mustn't waste those…hmm." Blydh licked the trail of grease from his hand and then sank his teeth into the tender pork. It was a constant barrage of torture. I sometimes think Paega would have been better off if Tallack had taken his life with the shiny grey sword that day.

He may have followed Brea and the priests into siding with our enemies, but he was still my nephew, my flesh and blood. I hated how low he'd sunk, but I had no right to meddle in his treatment. Perhaps, one day, the twins will decide that he'd suffered enough. Maybe then they'll allow him to make amends.

When we drew level with Blydh, I fancied that I might be able to distract him from his game of torment. "You are feeling better then, nephew?" I called out to him. At first, he didn't respond. I thought he hadn't heard me, so I bellowed louder. "Have your headaches gone, Chief Blydh?"

He turned and snarled at me. "I heard you the first time. Don't shout at me." His glare made me shiver, especially since one of his eyes seemed to be looking elsewhere. He hadn't regained the sight in that eye after the procedures

I'd carried out on his fractured skull. I don't think he will ever forgive me for that.

He was in one of his black moods, and from the level of swaying in his upper body, I'd say he'd replaced poppy resin for a serious quantity of ale in pain relief. This was not the right time to speak with him about the trip to the sacred hot springs. I said no more, expecting him to mellow later when he needed the resin I carried with me.

Lifting my furs and healing kit from my pony, I left Sorcha and Kewri to feed and water him and set him loose in the western enclosure of the compound. I headed north towards my hut, dragging my tired feet along the planks. The door skins of the Long Hut were pinned back, allowing the spring air to blow in and chase out the stink of addled warriors and burnt animal fat.

Tallack saw me passing by. He yelled for me to wait until he caught up. All I wanted was to collapse on my bunk and rest, but there was much to discuss.

"Look Aunt Mel." He held a shining bronze helm in both hands. The dome was of a thin sheet of metal, beaten and polished and secured with a ring at the bottom. The sheepskin lining was plush and carefully stitched inside, providing the perfect cushioning for Blydh's damaged head. "The smith did a fine job, wouldn't you say?"

"Indeed, nephew. The challenge will be convincing your brother to wear it. He's over there taunting Paega and in a foul temper." I edged forwards, hoping he would follow me into my hut. He did.

"Well, yes, it might prove tricky, but I'll think of something. How was your trip? Did you come across any Duros?"

I gave him a condensed version of our last few days, emphasising the importance of the advice from the priest and the trip to the hot springs, and playing down the foolish actions of his new slave.

"I knew she'd be trouble the minute you persuaded me to let Sorcha live." He sat on the end of my bunk and examined the helmet for scratches and unwanted dents. "You think she'll die?"

I shrugged. "Can't say one way or another. What I do know is that I haven't got an ointment or tincture to combat the effects of an ancient ague from the God of Death."

"Then I suppose we will have to get all the information about the Novantae Tribe before she drops. Might come in useful later." He laid the helm down on my bunk with some reverence and then helped himself to my ale jug.

"Did you hear what I said about the hot springs?"

"I'm not Blydh, Aunt Mel. I was listening. You think he has a trapped demon in his head and that we have to beg the Belgae Chief to let us take him to their sacred spring."

"I didn't say beg."

"But that's what he would make us do. By all accounts, he is a devious and disagreeable man with black teeth and stinks of death. Is Endelyn sure about the sun disc and the evil spirit? Can't we just shove him through the round stone at Men an Tol?"

I shook my head. "That's exactly what I said, but she seems to know better. The priest at the Duros circle agreed with her."

"So, we have no other option?"

"Blydh isn't getting any better. I don't think we have a choice."

He scooped up the helm and then loomed close to touch his forehead to mine. "Glad you're back. I've no doubt that Blydh will kick up a fuss. He never did like travelling unless it was to raid a Duro settlement." He stopped at my doorway and looked back at me. "Come and eat in the Long Hut this evening, you can help me to convince him."

He was gone before I could argue with him. I had all I could take of awkward young folk to last me a full moon or more, but he was the Chief and his word was my command. Taking the last of my kindling and dry sticks from beneath the eaves of the thatch, I lit my fire, refreshed the goat's water, and unpacked my bedding before taking a well-earned nap.

Kewri still hadn't returned from seeing to the horses when I awoke in the late afternoon. I figured that one of the twins had called him away to help them lift or carry something, but I couldn't see him about anywhere. With my pockets full of grain, I wandered down the boards to see my white stag. He hadn't forgotten me. The moment I stepped through the gate of the enclosure, he hurried out of the trees and nuzzled my hands for his feed.

"Dear Cernonnus, if you truly are the spirit of the God of Death, why would you inflict your anger on a silly girl who knew no better? If she makes you an offering, will you spare her life?" The deer snuffled and pushed against my cupped hands. Not once did he pause to give me a sign that he'd heard my plea. As soon as my pockets were empty, he sniffed me one last time, in case I was only pretending to have run out of oats, and then he wandered away.

There was nothing left for me to do but let events unfurl as they may. The roasting pits behind the Long Hut smelled delicious; juicy mutton and wading birds. That was when I remembered Tallack's summons to eat with him. I wasn't looking forward to an evening of abuse from Blydh, or the conversation that we needed to have with him, but I had no other choice.

With reluctance, I crossed the camp to the Long Hut and slipped in through the back door near the slaves cooking shelters. At least I could sneak in without Blydh making some snide comment in front of all the elders and the warriors. Ducking around the raised top table and Sorcha limping about carrying a serving tray, I slipped into my usual seat at the table next to the central fire.

Rather than hide among others as I had planned, I sat all alone against the table reserved for the twins' half-sister, Derwa and her Ordo husband, who'd been banished some half-moon or more ago. My solitary presence was more noticeable than ever. The moment I sat down, Blydh began his tirade.

"Oh, I wondered when you'd show your face. Come to take your fill and blind a few of my men?" His voice was loud enough to silence all those present. There was nothing I could say in my defence. My actions resulted in the loss of sight in his left eye, but then without my intervention, he'd be dead. I kept my head bowed and hoped that he would tire of his insults and jibes.

"Now, brother. Be reasonable. Look what I had made for you." Tallack produced the helm, gesturing for the elders and warriors to cheer and stamp their feet in praise of the item.

"I'm not wearing that." Blydh shot his brother a vicious glare.

"No? I think it shows status and bearing." Tallack lifted it onto his own head, striking a confident pose and flicking his fingers to encourage more cheering. "Great men across the seas wear things like this. They call them Kings."

Blydh snorted into his beer. "How would you know?"

"Maleek of Tyre told me. Great Phoenician Chieftains of vast settlements bigger than we could begin to imagine, wear bronze and golden head gear. This was made in the likeness of those worn by their best warrior lords."

"Then you keep it. You're just as much a Chieftain as me."

Tallack was stumped. He thought he could appeal to the competitive side of his brother. Instead he was bested by him. Confused, he looked at me to rescue the situation. I rolled my eyes; as if anything I said would make any difference.

I thought for a moment, and then stood and faced the top table. "You're right, Chief Blydh. Tallack should keep such a magnificent helm, it suits him well. Now all who set eyes upon him will realise his importance in our tribe."

I could see the veins pulsing in his temple. He stopped drinking and slammed his cup down on the table. "You think I am not worthy of such finery, Aunt? Is that what you think? You blind me and now I am incapable of being a Chief?" He stood up and wrenched the article from Tallack's head, shoving it down on his own. Wincing from the pressure on his scalp, he unsheathed his sword, held it aloft and roared. The men roared back, thumping their fists on the tables and stamping their feet. Tallack winked at me.

Blydh swayed, his left eyelid twitching rapidly. "Bring me more ale." He bellowed at Sorcha. She scampered to the platform and leaned across to pour from the large jug she carried. Just as the frothing liquid reached the rim of the horn cup, she teetered backwards, dropped the jug and fell to the floor.

CHAPTER SIX

"Get up girl. You'd better not have broken that jug." Blydh was unaware that Sorcha was unconscious on the rushes behind him.

Tallack just sat there and looked at her. "Is she dead, Aunt Mel?"

I hurried over to where she'd fallen. Her skin was wet with sweat and I could see that a blue line from the rash on her ankle snaked up her leg beneath her leggings. Some kind of poison was working its way through her body. "Can one of you strong men pick her up?"

Tallack glanced about him, taking his time in choosing a suitable warrior, but Renowden stepped forwards to lend a hand.

"Where shall I take her, Meliora?" He said. There it was again; he'd used my given name.

I was momentarily thrown by the familiarity and found myself blushing. "Um, right, yes. Can you carry her to my hut? I'll get Kewri to drag the extra bunk back in for her to rest on, if I can find him to ask."

Tallack's brows raised along with an amused smirk on his lips. I caught sight of him mouthing *Meliora*, to Treeve at his side. They'd interpreted the kind gesture as much more than friendship. I scowled at him, just enough to show him my displeasure, but not enough to stop me from leaving the Long Hut without stirring further rancour. In truth, I was glad of the excuse to get away.

Ren was such a help to me. He laid Sorcha down on my bunk while he sought out the patient's bed from the unfinished shelter outside. As soon as he'd dragged it through to my hut, he transferred the unconscious girl and set about banking up the fire. "Shall I stick around in case you need me?"

There were a few moments of confusion on my part. I wasn't sure whether he was simply being his usual kind self, or whether he wanted to share my company. Either way, I found myself nodding and growing hot in the cheeks. He smiled at me and grabbed two cups to fill with ale.

"I don't know that I can do anything to help her." I rubbed at my head, combing through my memories of treatments and cures that my mother had taught me all those years ago. None of them included how to reverse the ague from an insulted god. I fetched some cold water from the stream outside and pulled off her leggings. The blue line under her skin had forked at several points like the branches of a tree until her thigh was a mass of Sloe berry coloured veins.

The infection site was huge, a red raw patch of skin with a big black sore in the middle. All I could do was dab her with a wet cloth to try and cool her down.

"I should probably look out for Kewri." Renowden said, rising from his stool by the fire. "He and Sorcha got quite close over the last few days."

I must have looked aghast, since he laughed at me.

"You didn't notice them sneaking off together into the caves or hiding in the dunes?"

It took a little while to sink into my brain. "But they bickered and argued the whole time."

"Well obviously not all the time. You surprise me. I thought you'd noticed." Chuckling, he pushed through the door skins and disappeared into the night. Well that was a shock. There was far more to Kewri than met the eye. I shall have to pay more attention to his comings and goings from now on.

Sorcha did regain consciousness for a short time, thrashing about with fever and murmuring in her addled state. Something told me that this was more severe than the ague that Ren's friend had contracted. While he was out of the hut, I lifted her tunic and examined the areas she'd been scratching earlier in the day. Her armpits and beneath her chin were swollen. The rash was spreading and she was clammy with sweat all over. This could only end one way.

My cold compresses were doing nothing to help and she was too addled for me to ask her if she was in pain. I had a fresh supply of resin, but no way to get it into her body if she needed relief. Ren was not long in searching for Kewri. The pair of them stumbled into my hut, Ren trying to stifle a grin and Kewri red in the face and flustered.

It took a while for me to understand the comedy of such a grave situation; Senara was just behind them and fastening her clothes. From their guilty looks, it was obvious what they'd been doing. I peered at her and then at Kewri and finally at Ren, who burst into fits of laughter before apologising.

"I was just coming to see you with news." Senara averted her eyes.

"Is that so? You came straight here as soon as you reached camp?"

She squirmed all the more for my insinuation. I moved my gaze slowly to Kewri. There was no need to say what I was thinking. For all his gentle giant character traits, he was no better than any other hot-blooded warrior of the tribe. I wondered if Senara knew that he'd been rolling under Sorcha's furs as well as hers.

If I had to guess, I'd say she had no knowledge of the affair with the slave, or Senara might have skewered a sword through her guts before Cernonnus could infect her with the ague. Still, it's not my place to judge. I was young once and we've all been at the mercy of lust at some point I'm sure.

As soon as they all saw the sorry state of the Novantae slave, their attitude shifted to quiet concern. Kewri hovered near to the fire, Senara folded her arms behind her back and stayed close to the door out of respect.

Renowden was the only one who ventured to speak. "No better then?"

"Worse. She's burning up with fever and I can't get her to take water, let alone any of my tonics. Not that they would help."

"You've seen this before?"

I nodded. "The blue lines under the skin and fever, many times. Rarely does it end well. The black scab and rash are new to me, but from what you told me about your friend, her prospects are not good."

Ren comprehended my train of thought. "I should go and tell Tallack that he'll be one less slave before the day is out." He ducked back outside leaving the blushing couple standing around like spare parts.

Sorcha looked a pitiful thing, flailing her skinny little arms about and mumbling in her sleep. All I could think about was how she'd been spared the knife less than a moon ago and now she would meet up with her dead kin after all.

I stole a glance at Kewri, trying to decide whether he was pleased with this development or anguished. Sorcha's death would put paid to Senara ever discovering his duplicity, thus assuring their continued affair. From his expression, I detected a sadness, but little more. He is not easy to read at the best of times. I suspected that he would have been more vocal had Senara been absent from my house.

Rinsing my cloth in the cool water, I continued to dab Sorcha's brow and neck. "Have you spoken to the Chief about your scouting trip?" I asked Senara.

"Yes, I did that before..." She darted her eyes towards Kewri and then back at the floor rushes.

"And? What's Brea up to?"

Beginning to relax in my presence, she let her arms swing to her side and then to the tin pouch attached to her belt. "I managed to befriend a Duro scout, well... I say befriend; it took a few grains of the Chief's tin to get him on board." She unhooked the purse and held it out to me.

"How did that come about?" I grinned at her ingenuity, gesturing for her to hang onto the purse for another occasion.

"He was patrolling near to the campsite I'd built for myself. Blundering kyjyan made more noise than Blydh's Head Hunters coming back from a raid. I slipped around the perimeter, caught him in a headlock and threatened to slash his throat if he didn't tell me what I wanted to know." She shrugged. "One thing led to another and he's now my paid spy. Turns out, Duros are not the loyal creatures that we pegged them to be. They'd sell their children for a nugget or two."

I repressed a cackle. She really was something of a marvel.

"We were right about Brea." She continued. "They hate her. She's gathered a group of the best warriors together and pays them handsomely for protection and to enforce her orders within the tribe. Their elders are in uproar over her latest plan. She has commanded the tribe to build a compound like this one."

"Why are they against such a plan? It was our saving grace when they attacked us."

"Because the stupid kyjyan has learnt nothing after the fireball raid. She's insisting they build it in the Sid Valley."

I must have looked puzzled since she spelled out their problem in no uncertain terms.

"The site floods every spring." Her mouth fell open and her eyes screwed up tight chuckling with laughter and holding her middle. "Sorry." She stopped abruptly, remembering the deathbed patient at my side.

"How far into the build are they?"

"According to the scout, the warriors and able men are all dragging their heels. They've cleared some of the woodland, but hardly any of the defences are even started."

"I can't say I blame them." With our enemy's attention turned inward, we could assume that we'd be safe from further attack for the time being. That was something in our favour. It seemed to me that this would allow us to travel to the hot springs on Belgae lands to seek a cure for Blydh, without worrying about our people while we were away. I needed to speak with Tallack.

Looking at Kewri, I was hesitant to ask. "Can I leave her care with you for a little while? I have to go to the Long Hut." My features were set to stern and my jaw rigid. He could see that I needed him to be on his best behaviour. He nodded sheepishly.

"Good. Thanks." I grabbed my cloak, although it was quite clement for the time of year, and pointed at Senara. "You'd better come with me. I've a feeling I shall need your services again, my dear." She visibly brightened at my deliberate familiarity and strode behind me across the mud to the Chieftains' hut.

If only Tallack had extended the planking from the centre of the island to my house, I would not need to clean my pattens so often. The torches were lit, the guards were posted outside the front entrance, and the singing was bawdy and raucous. Senara's news must have gone down well with the warriors. They were all on the wrong side of many jugs of ale.

Pushing through those gathered in the doorway, we weaved between the elders' benches and Sea Warriors to get to the top table. The two Chieftain tall chairs were unoccupied. Treeve sat in solitary splendour in the Ruvane's chair between the two. The closer I moved to the top table, the angrier I became. I was about to spew forth a biting verbal reprimand for Treeve's arrogance, when Tallack grabbed me from behind around the waist.

"Aunt Mel!" He lifted me off my feet, squeezing the air from my lungs and crushing my ribs as he spun me around. "Come and have a drink with us."

"No time for that. Put me down you great oaf!"

His booming laughter was infectious, setting off his sailors and the elders, who shared in the amusement. "We have much to celebrate. Senara told you the news about the Duros I presume?" He let me down gently before pushing me towards the platform and his tall chair.

"She did." He sat next to his lover and patted the empty chair on the opposite side where his mother usually sat. I scanned the room. The elders and their wives filled one side of the hall, Tallack's crewmen on the opposite side. Where was Blydh and his Head Hunter Clan? "I can't see your brother." I meant it as a question for him to answer, but all I got in response was an ineffectual shrug.

Sitting by his side, I drew close to my nephew and explained what the priest had told us at the Nine Children Stones. I got the impression that he was only half listening, his hand strayed to Treeve's knee making him giggle. In hind sight, it was probably a stupid idea to reason with him while he was in his cups. I tried one last time to gain his support. Without that, I would never manage to coax Blydh into the trip.

"You know, Endelyn believes that he's likely to make a full recovery following the ritual at the hot springs; no more angry sniping or reckless behaviour. Blydh would be back to his old self." I thought that mentioning Endelyn might sway his decision, but it barely made a dent.

"If that's what she recommends, then you should do all you can to make it happen, Aunt Mel. I have faith in you."

I honestly believe that these youngsters only think about the night ahead of them and no further. That is no way to lead a tribe. All I'd achieved was to shift the entirety of the problem onto my own shoulders. How in the name of Cernonnus was I supposed to convince Blydh to travel into a dangerous tribal region to remove the demonic spirit he had no clue about? I tapped my foot on the platform, holding in my frustration.

Senara was yanked onto the warrior benches and was singing along with the rest of them until my head swam. This entire enterprise was futile. Tallack was in no mood to listen and I had to clear my head. Stomping from the top table, I left Senara to her revelry and slipped out of the back door by the roasting pits.

Not one of the slaves stopped me to ask about Dorcha. I know she'd only been in camp for a short time, but it seemed that she was not well liked among the warriors, elders nor slaves. At this rate, only Kewri and I would be sorry to see her leave this world. I took the long route back to my hut, skirting the southern end near to Paega's cage with the intention of walking up the eastern board walk to see if I could glimpse the white hart in the darkness.

Some of the elders' children were up late, taunting Paega through the gaps between the posts and hurling dead rats and midden waste at him. He was wretched. All skin and bone and covered in his own stinking mess. As soon as the slimy filth hit the ground, he rushed over and picked through it looking for scraps worthy of eating. I felt sick. Was there no one in this compound who showed any compassion at all? Did family honour and loyalty mean nothing to this generation?

Every time I closed my eyes, I could see him standing there, sorting through the piss-soaked eggshells, bones, and rodents looking for food. Not even a brief sighting of the white stag cheered my mood. Dragging my feet along the planks to shuck off the mud, I headed back towards home. Kewri and Renowden were standing in the doorway looking out for me.

"Has she…?" I asked, predicting their answer.

Ren nodded. "Just a short while ago. I'm sorry, Meliora. I know you were fond of her."

The moment he said it, guilt washed over me. I should have stayed with her to the end. She was forced to abandon her tribe, her mother's comfort and most of her kin to sail to our shores. Now she would never leave them. The men parted, allowing me to pass by into my shelter. The moisture had already dried on her pallid skin. Her face, once pink and dotted with freckles, was grey and haunting; that shock of wild red hair, lank and drenched in stale sweat.

"Shall I carry her into the unfinished shelter out there?" Ren offered. There was no point in leaving her on the bunk indoors. She had no one to mourn for her. There would be no songs of passing, nor ritual cleanse at the riverbank, nor pyre on which to send her into the arms of Cernonnus.

"Thanks, Ren. Can you make sure that the entrance is barred well? I don't want the camp dogs to get at her."

He gave me a thin-lipped smile and nudged Kewri to assist. Poor brute was stung into silence. He must have had some feelings for her, however fleeting.

I watched Ren take her by the arms while Kewri latched onto her ankles. She bowed in the middle like a skinned rabbit, her arse grazing the rushes on the floor. They saw me frowning and adjusted their grip. Following them out into the cool night air, I could hear the celebrations going strong in the Long Hut.

"I don't suppose either of you have seen Blydh have you?"

They both snapped their heads around to face me, stopping in their tracks.

Exchanging glances, they seemed to be conducting a silent argument over who should give me their news.

Ren lost. "He stopped by your hut while you were out. He took the whole pot of poppy resin and rode out of camp with his hunters."

CHAPTER SEVEN

I didn't think the day could get any worse. Blydh had sneaked out of camp with my entire supply of resin and without the hunters' usual whooping and hollering. With him controlling his own dosage, there was every chance he was crazed and leading his clan straight into the arms of the Duros. They would be outnumbered and butchered before dawn. How could Tallack have let him leave like that? Surely, he knew that his brother was not in his right mind?

There was nothing to be done but wait and hope for the best. Ren suggested that we make an offering to the Morrighan, to sacrifice a chicken or goat and ask her to spare our men in the raid, but I couldn't face anymore blood and death. If the gods had their sights fixed on taking my nephew, no amount of slaughtered livestock would alter his fate.

"No, Blydh has to live by his decisions." I turned to leave but stopped mid-thought. "Would one of you mind taking the left-overs to Paega's cage? He is in a bad way and he's still my kin when all is said and done."

Kewri said he would make sure Paega got food and water, which was a weight off my mind. I stayed in my hut and burned a fresh bundle of herbs on the fire, wafting the smoke around to help Sorcha's spirit on its way, and then turned in for the night. Kewri chose to sleep elsewhere, no doubt he and Senara had discovered somewhere private and sheltered for them to be together. My hut seemed enormous when they'd all gone. It was the first time I'd felt truly lonely in quite some time.

Under my furs, with the fire piled high with logs and the wooden panel barring entry to any who would disturb me, I wept a silent tear for Sorcha's passing. I was fond of her. The happy memories of my time staying in the Novantae camp with nothing but grief in my heart will stay with me forever. Her family showed me such kindness and in return we killed her father and brothers and enslaved her for one terrible mistake.

Come morning, I heard the muttering and coughing of people gathering outside my house. For a few moments, I pulled the furs over my head and tried to block out the noise, but curiosity got the better of me. Wrapped in my warm cloak, I yanked the door panel aside and peered out between the skins.

Slaves, elders and Sea Warriors were taking it in turns to peep around the door of the unfinished shelter. Initially, I thought they were there to pay their respects to Sorcha, but something about their postures and murmurs made me suspicious.

"What's the commotion?" I shrieked, sending the timid among them running. "If you're here to sing her passing, stay. If your purpose is to gawp at the body, move your kyjyan arses away from here! Go on, scat!" Many did indeed scurry away, leaving me to wonder why they had clustered there in the first place. I poked my head into the shelter. Sorcha's body was uncovered revealing the blue veins, the red rash, and the black sore on her leg.

Two of the slave girls from the roasting pits lingered behind. One stepped a pace closer. "Please, Fur Benyn?"

"Yes, what is it?" I snapped, looking around for something I could use to cover Sorcha's body.

"We worked closely with her." The girl stammered. Poor mite looked petrified. "People are saying that the black scab will kill us all, starting with those who shared her bedding."

So that was what all the rumpus was about. They cared nothing for a slave girl dying, particularly a foreign one from the top of the world, as long as they survived. "You can rest assured, girls that this was the result of dishonouring Cernonnus himself. I was there when it happened and only Sorcha was affected. Make sure that you spread the word across camp. No one else will die from this, you have my word."

They looked mightily relieved by my announcement, but I feared that it would take more than a promise to convince the elders. I stood and guarded the shelter until the last of the stragglers had melted away. Kewri was plodding up the boards past the pony pen. I beckoned him toward me and kept my eyes peeled for anyone else who might be trying to sneak a peek in the hut.

"How are you doing, Kewri?" I analysed his face. There were loose pouches under his eyes and mud smeared over his clothes. He puffed like he'd been running for half a day.

"I've been out to the forest at the northern side of the camp since dawn." He took a deep breath and released it slowly. "One of the weaver women made this for me too." From behind his back, he produced a ring of moss studded with early spring flowers.

"You picked them for Sorcha?" I was stunned. He obviously had deeper feelings for the Skotek slave than I thought.

"Not me, Fur Benyn. I traded with the weaver to make it for me." His face crumpled. "I know that normal slaves only get a hole next to the midden pile, but Sorcha was still a daughter of a Chieftain. I spent the morning digging her a proper grave next to the pond at the edge of the forest. I hope you will permit me to lay her to rest there."

It was hard not buckling alongside him. All I could do was nod my consent. He took one of the furs from his own bunk and wrapped her body within, stooping low to pick up the bundle into his arms. Together, we headed for the northern end of the island and waited for the watchman to open the gates.

By the time the bridge was lowered into position over the River Exe as it forked to surround our island, we had drawn quite a mass of spectators. Among them was Endelyn. She said nothing, but fell in line behind us as we walked to the grave site. For one moment, I thought that a few others might join us, but they stopped following as soon as we were clear of the river.

The breeze was fresh and easterly until we reached the edges of the forest. In the shelter of the trees, Kewri led us to the small trench he'd dug next to a pond. It was a beautiful spot. Catkins dangled from the weeping willows, sunlight streamed in between the new shoots and leaves, and birds sang all around us.

Kewri had laid a twisted trail of ivy around the grave to open the portal to the Underworld. Stepping into the narrow hole, Kewri lowered Sorcha's body down and removed the fur wrap. With great gentleness, he arranged her limbs into that of a sleeping babe, her knees tucked up to her chest, her hands close to her face.

From his pocket, he produced a tiny bone comb and a carved wooden horse. "Not much to help her on the other side." He muttered. "But it's better than nothing at all."

I wondered if he'd stayed up all night to carve the timber beast. My chest almost exploded with remorse. He was in more pain than I had imagined. It hurt him to think of her unable to pay her way into the afterlife. I might be a cantankerous old woman at times, but I'm not heartless. I dug into my metal pouch from around my neck and handed him a small nugget of tin. He gave me a teary smile and tucked it into her hand.

As he clambered out of the hole, he looked pointedly at Endelyn. It was an unsubtle hint for her to speak the funeral rites over the dead. There were a few moments of uncomfortable silence before the priestess caved in to his expectations.

She stood at the end of the trench and lifted her face to the sky, her palms raised to shoulder height. "Cernonnus hear me." She began. "Take this poor creature into your realm and forgive any offence she gave at the standing stones of the Nine Children. Sorcha was little more than a child herself and not aware of her actions. She has paid the price for her sin. Please allow her safe passage into the Underworld and a peaceful reunion with her kinfolk and ancestors, we beg of you."

Endelyn spoke at such a speed, with no pauses nor sentiment as if to reinforce her anger over the events from the past few days. Kewri and I intoned our own muttered farewells, barely audible to any but ourselves and stooped to push the circle of ivy into the grave around the corpse. Endelyn marched off immediately, leaving Kewri to back fill the soil and roots dislodged from the hole. I waited by his side for as long as I could bear, before turning towards home.

As it was, I spotted some fresh shoots of mallow growing on the way back and stopped to gather some. When I had finished my task, Kewri caught up with me, carrying the fur and a wooden shovel. We wandered the rest of the way without speaking, keeping our eyes on the track ahead and holding in the tears.

The gate and bridge were as we left them when we returned. The only difference from before was the noise of the crowds. It seemed that everyone was out of their huts to join in the bustle and clamour. Tallack stood tall in the centre of the gathering, his hands held up in an attempt to calm down an angry man in front of him. As we moved closer, I could hear what they were saying.

"You can't just throw some tin in my direction and expect me to be happy." The livid elder ranted. "It was my best horse and a good breeder. Tin cannot replace something as precious as that."

Another man stepped forward to voice his fury. "You're not the only one who had stuff stolen. He took my biggest knife, a good tunic and my best leggings from the washing."

"Please, men, I have heard your complaint and it will be resolved in time." Tallack said, but it opened the way for others to pitch in and claim losses whether they were genuine or not. The discussion descended into chaos within moments. Who could have rampaged through the compound stealing such strange items without anyone noticing?

I moved away from the commotion and surveyed the island. The horse pen was secured, the eastern, western and southern gates all closed and watched from the towers. It was when my old eyes fell on the small hatch that provided access to Paega's cage that everything made sense. My nephew had escaped and bolted through the northern gate as soon as it was opened.

My emotions went through several stages in rapid succession, first elation that he was liberated from such a pitiful existence, then fear that he would be killed for his crime, and then finally panic. I had sent Kewri to give him scraps of food before turning into bed. In his grief and confusion, had he left the hatch open by mistake? What would Tallack do to him if he knew? I turned and grabbed Kewri's sleeve, directing his attention to Paega's cage.

His eyes widened and he sniffed in a large breath. "I have to own up, Fur Benyn. It's all my fault." A huge hand flew upwards, slapping his forehead in self-punishment.

"Stop that, now then." I reached up to grab his upper arms, shaking some sense into him. "Tallack will understand given the circumstances."

He fretted, pushing me away and pacing about thinking. After only a short while, he stood still and calmed himself. "I can fix this. He won't have got far and he's well known about these parts." Kewri batted the elders and nagging wives aside until he was face to face with Tallack. "Chief, this is my fault. I'm sorry. I guess I forgot to latch the gate last night, but I can bring him back. Give me a chance to make things right."

Tallack looked at the giant. He must have seen the determination in his eyes. "Fine. Do what you must, Kewri, and hurry back. My brother will be wild if he returns and finds Paega missing." That was all it took to send my friend on his urgent mission, leaving Tallack to deal with the mass of shouting tribe's folk.

I hurried into my hut and gathered what food I could find for him in a waxed wrap and met him outside the pony enclosure. With a few extra grains of tin in his pocket, he mounted the enormous cart horse and set off towards the northern end of the compound. "May the gods be with you, my friend." I muttered, more to myself than anyone close by.

It took the better part of the afternoon for Tallack to appease all of those affected by Paega's rampage through the compound, but eventually things returned to normal.

Senara volunteered to help me with some of my chores, milking goats, feeding chickens, gathering bark and herbs for ointments and the like, but a growing sense of unease brewed inside my belly. I could feel that something was not right on the island but couldn't put my finger on precisely what.

It was nice having a quiet day for once. We chatted and ate together, bound the plants in bunches and suspended them upside down from the roof timbers to dry. Later, we traded for some fresh fish for our supper. As we went about our business, I noticed that the priestess had amassed quite a following. She'd taken to holding rituals and ceremonies outside her hut, encouraging people to bring offerings to sacrifice and bless on their behalf. I must say, it's an ingenious way to assure your meals.

By evening, I saw some burly Sea Warriors dragging in carved trunks of alder, ash and beech. Each bore different symbols and animal likenesses. One was painted in rich colours, with chalk dust and grease mixed with dyes from the weaver women. When they began digging post holes outside her shelter, I realised that she was creating a shrine to attract even more of our people to her door.

On the one hand, it made sense that we should have a central place to worship the gods and make offerings when it was impossible to make a trip to a stone circle, on the other I felt uncomfortable that Endelyn was deliberately trying to raise her status within the tribe. It reminded me of other ambitious womenfolk who thought they could push themselves forward in the past. No good came from their efforts and this would end just the same. I shook my head and made a conscious decision not to get involved in whatever she had planned.

At nightfall, Senara fidgeted on her stool by my fire. We'd eaten the fish with a little watercress and fresh bread and I was ready for sleep. She was not. She paced about my hut, offering to rinse our bowls in the stream, fetch wood, and all manner of other chores best done in daylight. It was when she ran to the doorway for the third time following an imagined sound, that I realised she was waiting for Kewri to return home safely. That endeared her to me even more.

"Would you like to sleep here in case he comes home in the middle of the night?" I said, tipping my head towards Kewri's bunk.

She grinned and gave me a slow blink. "Am I that obvious?"

I didn't answer. Stacking up the logs on the fire, I made sure the rushes were well away from the hot embers, tidied away the food bowls and leftovers, and got myself ready for bed. Just as I was getting comfy under my furs, her little voice called out to me.

"Kewri must have been extremely fond of that slave girl to go to all that trouble."

I froze. The question I'd dreaded was on the tip of her tongue and I didn't want to be the one to tell her.

"Were they lovers, Fur Benyn?"

I shut my eyes tight and held my breath. The creaking noises of the bunk she lay on told me that she was sitting up to get a clearer view of me in the firelight. I'm ashamed to say that I pretended to be asleep, faking mild snoring and tongue smacking noises in the gloom.

At dawn the whole camp was awoken by thunderous hooves, whooping warriors and squeals of delight. Blydh and his Head Hunter Clan had returned from their raid. Senara jumped out of Kewri's bunk and rushed to the door in a fit of panic. I stayed under my furs, but I too was beyond anxious. How long would it take my nephew to realise that Paega had escaped, and what would he do to the person who'd set him free?

CHAPTER EIGHT

When I say, whooping and hollering, most of the noise came from Blydh and a couple of the younger clan members. Those older, wiser warriors behind them, were subdued. At the rear of the group, three horses carried the bodies of fallen men. The sight of their blood-stained clothing and severed limbs silenced everyone in camp.

One I knew well. He may have been a sickly child, but he'd grown into a strong and courageous warrior. His life was cut short by my nephew's thoughtless and callous actions. At least he would be assured a seat in the Summerlands. I recognised the older man leading his horse too. It was the warrior's father. The further into the camp they rode, the more people gathered around them, watching, weeping and grieving.

Blydh cantered through the island to the central point outside the Long Hut and jumped down from his horse. The beast was burdened with the bloodied heads taken in battle. The hair of his victims was woven together in a chain of meaty skulls, their tongues blackened with dried humours and mud. Blydh didn't see me. The crowd was thick around him, obscuring his view.

A sick part of me was glad of the gruesome distraction. With such trophies on display, and the wailing from the kin of those departed, all thoughts of Paega's escape was forgotten. Tallack stood at the entrance to the Long Hut, drawn out by the noise. He looked in my direction as I waited by my shelter and then made a great fuss of his brother. I took this to mean that he would keep Blydh drinking and celebrating victory for as long as he could.

I had no desire to join in the revelry. We were neither under attack nor had need to defend our land or people. The motivation for Blydh's raid was spite and vengeance, and we paid the price with the lives of three of our best men. Our woodland was disappearing fast from the number of pyres built in recent times.

Senara pulled on the rest of her clothes and weapons and ran across the grass to hear Blydh regale his tale of bravery. I rekindled my fire and set about my chores. Before the morning was done, I'd tended to two shallow spear wounds to the belly, a broken nose and a severed finger. The unfinished shelter looked like the butcher's hut by the time I'd finished. Each of the men I had treated tried to give me tin or grain in payment, but I couldn't accept anything.

I felt responsible for their troubles. I had caused the loss of Blydh's common sense. It was my fault that his judgement was impaired. They would not have followed him into such a foolish raid, if I had not used the sun disc to cover my nephew's skull. As it was, I could barely look at them in the eye without tearing up.

As soon as the men were patched up, I watched them wander across the island to Endelyn's new shrine to make offerings to the gods. She welcomed them with open arms, covered in colourful daubs of paint and wearing necklaces of bones and beads. She was as determined to put on a good show as Paega's kin from the Priest Sect. I suppose they breed it into them while they're young.

By late afternoon, I went down to the stream to rinse out my best linens and saw the great mound of dead creatures stacked up against the central carved ash trunk outside Endelyn's hut. There were far more sacrifices there than a few warriors' offerings. People from right across the island and beyond were lining up to receive her blessing.

When I'd finished hanging out my washing to dry, I filled my pockets with a few handfuls of grain and wandered down the boardwalk towards the pony enclosure.

I was less than half-way down the path when Renowden caught up with me.

"Meliora!"

I turned and waited for him, taking note of his troubled frown. "What is it? Is someone hurt?" It was my usual response to expressions such as his. In my line of work, people usually needed patching up or a potion to quell the unwanted desires of their husbands.

"No, it's not that, it's…" He was tongue-tied. It was most unlike him and it worried me.

"What?" I looked in all directions, trying to see clues as to what was making him so anxious. That was when I saw them in the horse pen. A whole host of Tallack's men had my beautiful white hart cornered, with ropes tangled in the new growth where his antlers should be.

My gasp alerted Renowden to my intentions, but before I could scurry off to stop them, he threw his arms about me and squeezed tightly.

"Don't Mel." He said, with such gentleness and humility. "Blydh has made the order. He is to be sacrificed this night with Endelyn's blessing, to see the warriors into the Summerlands."

Ren held on while I writhed and sobbed. I pounded my fists against his sinewy chest but he didn't let go. We watched the warriors tighten the noose about the stag's neck and lead him, bucking and rearing up towards the open gate. The majestic animal's eyes were wild, his breath fast and steaming, his cries clawed at my heart. The vessel for Cernonnus was to have his throat slashed before being roasted for a Long Hut feast.

I didn't know what to do with myself. The more I saw him struggle, the more desolate were my tears, but I couldn't pull myself away. If only I had shooed him out of the pen during the Duros' attack on our camp, he would be free to live a long life.

"I don't understand." I cuffed the drippings from my nose and pushed Ren's arms away from me. "What has caused this sudden urge to make godly offerings?"

He lifted my chin and brushed away the drying tracks down my cheeks. "People are scared. Endelyn has told everyone that it's the only way to make sure they don't die from the black scab."

I scoffed. "Didn't you put them straight? We all know that you can't catch the Nine Children's curse. They'd have to be in the stone circle themselves." My voice rose to a shriek as the warriors forced the deer across the grassland in front of me.

"I tried. You know how the elders get when an unknown sickness takes hold. Besides…" He withdrew his arms and folded them across his chest. "No one listens to me. It'd take one of the Chiefs to convince them otherwise." The moment it left his lips, I could see he regretted voicing his opinions.

Bile and humours rose within me, sending my temper soaring. I rolled up the sleeves of my tunic and stomped off the boardwalk onto the grass.

"No, Meliora. That's not a good idea." Ren scampered after me, running alongside my determined strides.

I stuck out my jaw and swung my arms, marching as fast as my stumpy legs could carry me towards the Long Hut.

"Please, Mel. You can't just go in there and insist that they let your stag go free. Think this through, for the sake of Cernonnus, woman!"

It was no use. I couldn't hear his pleas. I'd seen enough pain and death to sicken the heart of the hardiest of elders. If my nephews chose to strike me down, then I was prepared for my end. The noise from the Long Hut was quieter than I had expected. Pushing through the crowd at the door, I could see Tallack and Blydh in their tall chairs, each with a cup of ale in their hands and the heads of the Duro victims oozing on the table where I normally sat. I should have guessed Blydh's mood towards me from that gesture alone.

The Head Hunter Clan sat on one side of the hall; Tallack's Sea Warrior Clan opposite. They talked in hushed tones, passing around the jugs of ale and sharing moments of bravery about the fallen. Blydh made the most din. He laughed and sloshed his beer about, yelled at slaves and beckoned the pretty young wives of the elders to sit on his lap.

"There she is." Blydh crowed, slamming his cup down on the table. "There's our not-so-wise woman." He'd spotted me. The room fell silent.

My courage failed me. I stood at the far end of the Long Hut struck with indecision. Everyone around me parted so that I was clearly visible to all who looked on. My breathing quickened, my fists clenched, I took a slow step forward, hoping that the menfolk would continue chatting and ignore my presence. They didn't.

Blydh stood up in front of his tall chair and sneered. “Here comes the blinder of Chiefs, the peddler of pain, the snake in our midst.”

Tallack rolled his eyes into the back of his head. “Come now, brother. You speak too harshly. Aunt Mel only did what I asked of her. If you have to blame anyone, blame me.”

Blydh screwed up his face, baring his teeth at me and hissing. “Snake!” His glare lasted a good long while, and I could see no way of broaching the subject of the white hart without losing my head too. By the time I had taken another three steps, Blydh was back in his seat and blinking rapidly. He swayed, steadying himself against the back of the chair. “How do we know that she’s not in league with Brea, eh?”

Tallack sighed as though he’d defended me of the same accusations for most of the afternoon. “You know that’s not true. Aunt Mel has done nothing to warrant such unfair treatment.” The bickering between the twins took on a low growling nature, each of them bowing their heads together and engaging in a lop-sided stare down.

Ren took the opportunity to grapple my arm. “Leave it be, Mel. You can only make matters worse if you speak with them now.” He was right, but of course, I knew better.

“Chief Tallack!” I bellowed at the top of my voice. It halted the brothers’ niggling snipes and silenced the men around me. “I am in need of private counsel if you can spare me your time?”

Ren shut his eyes and gently shook his head, as though the roof of the world would crash in on me for my impudence. Tallack froze, expecting his brother’s negative response. He was right to anticipate one.

Blydh toyed with the straggly hairs growing on his chin. "Is Tallack the only chief present, Snake? You demand counsel from one and not the other?" He gestured to his brother. "Didn't I tell you she's not to be trusted? She would have us separated so that we are easy to hunt. What will it be, poison, like my father?"

"You go too far..."

"Do I? Really? She could have been the one who supplied Brea with the berries for our father's stew..."

Tallack's patience wore thin. He tutted at Blydh and flicked his hand mid-air, dismissing his ranting as nonsense. Stepping down from the raised platform, Tallack hurried over to me and pushed Ren and I back out of the hut.

"Might be better if you keep your distance for a while, Aunt Mel. He's taken too much resin and doesn't know what he's saying." It was kind of him to blame the strong poppy water, but I knew that it was probably the evil spirit from the Underworld speaking through Blydh. It made me all the more determined to get him to the sacred spring on Belgae lands.

For a moment, I was lost in thought, distressed at the alterations in my nephew. It was when I heard the deep grunts and squeals of the white hart that I remembered the reason for my interruption.

"Tallack..." I reached up and cupped his cheeks between my hands. "My dear nephew. Is there any way that I can convince you to spare the stag from sacrificial rites?"

He leaned away from me puzzled. "Have you lost your mind too? You suggested him in place of a slave."

"I did, that's true, but these past moons I have taken a shine to him, and him to me. I firmly believe that he is the vessel of Cernonnus himself, and killing him might anger the gods." My thoughts blanked. I had no other argument to make.

Tallack narrowed his eyes at me. "So, the rumours are true, Aunt?"

"What rumours?"

"That you hear the gods speak when you feed the deer my best grain?"

I flushed with heat. I had no idea that he was aware that I fed much of my grain allocation to the creature. The shrieks and bellows from the poor man-handled beast grated on my temper. What harm could it do to play up to the stories?

"It's true. I hear him warn me about important matters and have his protection when I make him offerings."

"You'll need all the protection you can get if Blydh has his way." He rested his fists on his hips and released a noisy sigh. "I'm sorry, Aunt Mel. Blydh has made up his mind, and while his attention is on the stag and the feast, he might not notice the absence of Paega."

It was a valid point, but it didn't help me or the white hart. Overcome with emotion, I failed to make my argument stick. The warriors near to the rear of the Long Hut, over-powered the deer and tied its legs together with bindings that made me wince. The thought of the animal's pain filled me with horror. What if ill-treatment of this beast really did turn the gods against us? I was starting to believe my own story.

"When will you do it?" My voice was thin and tremulous.

"You know how this works, Aunt Mel. The sacrifice will be at high moon tonight, we'll have the rites and blessing thereafter and he'll be butchered for the pyre and feast tomorrow."

My guts sank inside me. Two of Tallack's men came out of the hut to take up their watch at the gates. As the door skins were thrown back, I could see Blydh smearing resin into his mouth straight from my little pot. He must have grown used to the dosage; it was enough to fell a bull. Tallack looked in the same direction and sensed my intentions.

"There's no use talking to him when he's like this. Let him wallow in his glory for a day or two, and then we'll have to see about getting that demon out of him."

Ren spoke up. "They were lucky to have only lost three men, considering the size of the Duro tribe."

Tallack pulled a face. "Luck, perhaps. From the tales I've heard from the men, I rather think that Blydh picked a hunting party on the outer limits of the borderlands to attack."

Ren and I looked at one another.

"Do you think the demon controlling Blydh is deliberately leading our men into danger?" Ren said.

Tallack shrugged. "Isn't that what evil spirits do?"

"All the more reason to keep the gods onside. Speak with Blydh on my behalf, nephew. Convince him not to kill the deer."

Before he could answer, Senara spotted us and came to the doorway, interrupting the Chief's answer. "Fur Benyn, have you heard anything about Kewri yet?" I knew her anxiety was for the giant's wellbeing, mine was for his speedy return with Paega.

I shook my head. "No child, there's no news on that front."

She pulled back her shoulders and planted her feet wide apart. "Shouldn't we have heard by now? I mean, there aren't many places or trails that Paega could have taken. Kewri should be back by now."

I thought for a moment, pondering the speed of the massive carthorse against the fleet and nimble pony bearing a skinny boy. We all glanced at Ren for guidance. He shook his head and held his palms aloft. “Don’t look at me. I have no answers for you.”

Senara would not be pacified. I tapped her arm with affection, softening my tone. “He’s a big lad, Senara. More than capable of looking out for himself.”

“Then why isn’t he back with Paega yet?” She almost screamed it at me. Her words carried into the Long Hut and along to Blydh who stood scowling at us from the hearth at the centre.

“What’s this?” He bellowed. “You let our treacherous half-brother escape his cage, or was he set loose?” I could tell from his one good eye that he was directing this accusation at me alone. His right eye twitched with anger, his nostrils flared, and his chest heaved with a seething fury.”

“I can explain, nephew…” It was virtually a whisper seeping from my mouth, as I watched him bearing down on me between the tables.

CHAPTER NINE

Blydh was almost at my throat when Tallack, Ren and Senara all blocked his path. I hid behind them quaking with fear.

Tallack stood toe to toe with his brother. "It was not Aunt Mel's doing. Paega the Wily lived up to the name our father gave him and took advantage of another in his bid for freedom."

Blydh growled, unconvinced. "Who? Tell me who and I'll slice him from gizzard to groin for his treason." Had he not heard Senara mention Kewri's quest to bring the prisoner back?

Tallack paused, his stare shifting towards the ground. For a moment, I thought he might give the blame to poor dead Sorcha, who could no longer feel the wrath of mortals, but he didn't. "It was Kewri, brother. An honest mistake. He's determined to make restitution and is out searching for him as we speak."

Blydh blew out his cheeks and then laughed, although it was infused with disbelief rather than mirth. "You seriously believe that? Can't you see the snake at work here?" He pointed to me over Tallack's shoulder. "She's the viper in this tribe. Kewri is her man, under her orders. She's in league with Brea." Blydh rammed his shoulder into Tallack, attempting to push past, but Ren and Senara closed the gaps between them. There was no use in trying to reason with him. Either the demon was in control, or he was seeing visions from too much resin.

Wild with fury, Blydh lashed out his fist. It connected with Tallack's jaw, making a cracking noise. Tallack was momentarily stunned, but he regained his composure and stood tall once again. This seemed to anger Blydh all the more. He rained blows down on Tallack, punching him in the gut and then to the face and finally lifting his elbow to swipe his brother with a devastating smack to the nose.

It poured with blood, but Tallack would not fight back. He raised his arms across his face for protection and let Blydh thump and kick until his spite was sated. Ren and Senara looked on powerless to intervene without Tallack's approval. At length, Blydh tired of his onslaught and stepped back. "You'll regret this brother. You mark my words." He spat on the ground and returned to the heart of the Long Hut to retrieve his ale.

The moment the door coverings fell and he was out of sight, Tallack bent over and pinched his nostrils, stemming the flow of humours. His eye was swelling fast and there was a rip at the bridge of his nose. I was overcome with remorse. My dear nephew took a beating on my behalf, from an evil spirit of the Underworld that was loose thanks to my poor decisions.

"I am so sorry that this has happened." I gushed, but Tallack just waved me away. I couldn't help but fuss about him. "Let me clean you up in my hut. It's the least I can do."

He didn't argue with me. The three of them wandered across the grass to my place behind me, all the while shushing my repetitive apologies and need for forgiveness. Senara lit some torches, Ren soaked a few lengths of dried cattle gut, and I bathed Tallack's wounds with water mixed with a little of my soured apple juice.

While I nudged the gristle of his nose back into position, I noticed Senara pacing around the fire. "Can't you sit still, girl? You're making it hard for me to concentrate."

She looked up at me and snorted, her brow furrowed with concern. "It's just… never mind."

"Out with it." I cried, dabbing at Tallack's jawbone with a cloth soaked in icy water from the spring.

"Something's wrong. I can feel it deep in my bones."

Ren lifted a flaming torch level with my hands to help me see better. "You mean other than one of our Chiefs being addled?" He said.

"You're right. There's enough trouble in camp without adding to it." Senara muttered, beginning her pacing once again. I knew to what she was referring. She'd done nothing but worry about Kewri since the moment he left camp, but I kept quiet.

It was Tallack who picked up on her thoughts. He had a peculiar respect for this young shield maiden that I'd never seen before; not an attraction as such, just admiration for her advanced skills as a scout and warrior. "Go on, Senara. Say what you have to say."

"I know he's big and strong and capable, but he doesn't have a lot of guile. Kewri's easily out witted and I fear that to chase down someone as cunning as Paega, he shouldn't have gone alone."

"You want to go after him?" Tallack looked up at her, keeping his head still while I sewed him back together.

"May I, Chief?" She looked animated, the first time in two days.

"I think it's a good idea. Aunt Mel, it'd be sensible if you stayed away from camp for a while too, just until Blydh simmers down."

I stopped stitching. For a moment, I thought he was banishing me for all my blunders in camp. He saw my look of consternation and took hold of my wrist. Peering up at me, he said, "We can do nothing with Blydh while he's in this mood. Come back when you've found Kewri and Paega, and I'll do my best to persuade him to travel to the sacred springs."

"As you command, Chief." I said despondently. What I really wanted to say, was that I would only slow Senara down and be a further burden, but the idea of upsetting my nephews further didn't bear thinking about.

Ren disrupted my preponderances. "I'll go too." He smiled at me, making my heart beat a little faster.

"No, Ren." Tallack said. "I'll need you here. I must have someone to keep a weather eye on Blydh's comings and goings about camp without drawing attention to our suspicions." He glared at Ren until he nodded his agreement. "Only Endelyn and we few know about Blydh's condition and I want to keep it that way for as long as possible."

We were under no illusions as to the huge tasks ahead of us all. Persuading Blydh to do anything was tricky enough before his skull was smashed. On reflection, leaving for a couple of days was my best option, but I was not looking forward to the trip.

Tallack asked me if I had enough tin nuggets and food to take with us, before he and Ren left us to our packing. We had initially intended to leave at daybreak, but the noises on the island sickened me. They were preparing to sacrifice my white hart when the moon reached its highest point in the sky.

We let my fire burn low and filled water bladders from the stream ready to load up on our ponies. When the drumming began at the pyre site near to the northern gate, my heart pounded in my chest like it was ready to jump from my body.

Senara noticed my agitated state. "You really care for that white deer, don't you?"

I couldn't stop the feelings from erupting into my eyelids. There was no need to answer her question. She understood me perfectly. "Come on, Fur Benyn. Let's go now. We can walk the horses along the trail until sun up and rest when we need to."

She didn't have to ask me twice. I grabbed my healing kit, food bundle, and my bedding, and followed her along the board walks to the horse enclosure.

There were tribe's folk wielding torches in just about every corner of the island. Some knelt in front of the new wooden idols outside Endelyn's hut making their offerings, others carried children from their shelters to watch the sacrifice. All those on their feet were moving in the opposite direction to us. The drumming grew louder when Blydh and Tallack appeared from the lit entrance of the Long Hut, leading their warriors towards the sacred circle that Endelyn had marked out on the ground. I picked up my pace, unlatching the enclosure gate and hurrying towards my old horse.

"You know, we can leave through the western gate so that you don't have to see it happen." Senara's kindness almost had me undone. I know I'm a silly old woman at times, and I should be a master at holding in my feelings by now, but the stag was more than a fine haunch of meat, he was my link to Cernonnus and the Summerlands. He soothed my temper and listened to my fears. Without his fully formed antlers, he was so vulnerable. It hardly seemed fair to attack such a defenceless animal this way.

Tying our bundles on to the ponies, we led them back out of the pen and headed towards the west gate.

"Ho there!" I yelled up at the watchtower, but no one was on guard. They must have left their post to watch the ceremony. Senara looked at me in the moonlight. Without discussion, we both altered direction and made for the southern gate. It was the same story there too. No one had stayed at their posts. We couldn't open the gates without the warrior's help.

The shield maiden waited for me to voice our only other option. "Looks like I can't avoid it no matter what we try." I said, the regret manifesting as a low grumble. With a loud sigh, I stood on the boardwalk and pushed myself up onto my horse. Senara followed suit, clicking her tongue to speed the ponies along our muddy route.

"If we hurry, we should be clear of the gates before it begins." Bless her. Senara is such a thoughtful person, for all her gruffness, but I knew that we'd never make it in time. The noise from the drummers was deafening, but not so loud enough to mask the sound of my stag's cries.

Endelyn was standing in a massive salt circle, the centre of which contained a flat altar stone raised on two rough-hewn lengths of wood. Despite the distraction of my stomach churning, I thought at the time that she would never get my stag to cooperate and stand on the stone, even with the help of many warriors. The white hart's legs were bound together with strong rope, his mournful cries relentless and agonising.

Great plumes of steam billowed from his mouth as he bellowed his threats at the men surrounding him. Poor beast wriggled and writhed on his side, exhausting what little energy he had left to him. I closed my eyes and let my horse follow Senara's towards the gate. A huge mass of people blocked our path, until Senara snatched up a flaming torch from a young lad and used it to illuminate our way.

The moment people saw that it was me, they moved aside to let us pass. We were just a few cart lengths away from the northern watchtowers, when the drumming halted. It was a natural reaction to turn and look over my shoulder, and one that I was powerless to stop. Sitting high above the crowd, I could clearly see the priestess waving her lithe arms about her head, holding a ceremonial knife and chanting her mystical words at the top of her voice.

Blydh and Tallack stood close by, waiting for her to complete the incantations. The bleating and groaning from the stag grew more pitiful the closer Endelyn drew to him with the knife. I knew precisely what she would do. For a so-called High Priestess, she had but a few different stages to her rituals, most ending in the collection and drinking of warm blood. It takes a brave woman to diverge from the things that please the crowds and try something new.

With every muscle in my body tensed, I yelled up at the watchtower, hoping that they would respond, open the gate and lower the bridge. I should have guessed that they were too busy watching the ceremony from their lofty position to take notice of me. Senara and I were stuck. We could neither move forward nor return through the crowds, who now had their backs to us.

All this swagger just prolonged the animal's suffering. Endelyn pranced and chanted, gestured up to the sky and then beckoned the Chiefs to move closer to the beast. For a moment, I thought that she would hand the knife to one of them, but she did not. Instead, Endelyn encouraged them to pick up the small bronze bowls from the altar stone and stand either side of her to catch the blood.

She addressed the tribe one last time, yelling her potent words over the heads of the closest elders and warriors, but I could not catch them. As much as I wanted to look away, I found myself transfixed. Endelyn crouched at the side of the struggling creature. Tallack did the same, clutching the small nubs of the growing antlers, while Blydh clamped the beast's head, keeping it still.

Even at my distance, I could see the panic in Cernonnus's eyes. His tongue protruded with one final deep squeal as Endelyn stabbed the blade into his neck and yanked it through his flesh. His beautiful white fur was thick with the red spray of humours; his cries silenced; his life poured into two small bowls.

I hung my head to my chest, gutted. Tears fell without shame. The whole tribe roared with delight as Tallack and Blydh raised their bowls and took a great gulp of steaming blood each. For that moment, I glanced up and saw the shared look in their eyes. I saw no demon in Blydh, but the fondness of twin brothers, forged over their many summers together.

Perhaps, just perhaps, this terrible loss was just what was needed to strengthen their bond and drive out any evil spirit from inside Blydh. Maybe there would be no need to take the trip to the sacred springs after all. I held that thought in my head, as the watchmen came to their senses and set about opening the gate and lowering the bridge over the Exe. As we trotted over the wooden structure, I said the same thing over and over quietly to myself, hoping that the gods would hear me. "Please take the offering my nephews made in good faith. Spare them from your wrath, Cernonnus, and release Blydh from the evil he possesses." I knew that my hope was a vain one, and unlikely to come about.

Senara held the torch for as long as she could, lighting our way through the woods to the north of the island, and tossed it into the undergrowth when it sputtered out. We got to the far end of the trail through the forest, before reducing our speed and walking the horses over the rough ground by moonlight alone.

For the majority of the time, Senara left me to my thoughts alone. She understood what losing the white hart meant to me, and concentrated on our route through frosty valleys and misty dells. She knew these lands like the back of her hand, and her senses were so finely attuned to oncoming danger, I had few worries that we'd come to any harm.

By dawn, we rested and watered the horses at a tributary to the west of the Exe and ate some of our packed food. Neither of us were in a talkative frame of mind. She stayed awake to watch over our things while I slept for a time. We were well inside our own borders, so there was little chance of attack. When I awoke, there was a crackling fire and warm porridge to gladden my aching heart.

I thanked her and ate my share, quietly mulling over the inevitability of loss when you reach such a ripe old age as I have done. The gods had taken Aebba the Wild, my niece Wenna, and my dearest slave, Jago in the span of the last cycle. Foolishly, I thought the gods would let me be after enduring so many losses in such a short space of time. I know that a deer is not the same as family, but it had provided me with such comfort.

When we had packed up ready to continue our journey, Senara wandered a little way from the fire on foot, stopping every now and then to touch the earth. "Kewri's tracks are easy to follow; a single carthorse with no wheel lines went this way a couple of days ago. They point towards the moors."

I watched her expression keenly. Instead of the animated features I'd witnessed the day before, she looked concerned. That was understandable. While Kewri stayed on the trails, near to homesteader's land and small communities, he could easily be found. If he strayed onto the wide expanses of the moors, we would struggle to follow his tracks.

The scant soils of the rocky ridges left few clues about past travellers, and the boggy areas filled with liquid mud and water in a space of a night. Mounting her horse, she urged me to follow her in a north-westerly direction, taking us close to the Nine Maiden's circle. It was when we crossed the River Taw that I remembered the reason for Kewri's journey. He was chasing after Paega; my nephew who was brought up among the Priest Sect of our tribe. I'm not sure why I hadn't thought of it sooner, but Paega was bound to run to the nearest stone circle in search of kin who could help him. The Nine Maiden's circle was the closest one to our compound.

I tapped my horse's flanks with my heel, forcing him to canter until I was alongside Senara. As soon as we were on firm ground, I began to explain my thoughts to her, but she held her hand aloft to silence me.

Stunned, I jerked my head around to see why she had stopped me from talking. Ahead of us, grazing on the heathland plants, was a large carthorse carrying all Kewri's belongings. He was nowhere to be seen.

CHAPTER TEN

"Let's not panic." I said, holding my hand up to quieten her rambling chatter. "He's bound to be around here somewhere. He's probably relieving himself in the shrubs and his horse wandered off." It didn't appear to settle her down. Senara galloped off towards the small clump of bushes in the distance, leaving me to shout after her. "Don't jump to conclusions!" She paid me no heed.

I trotted over to the huge horse and leaned over to catch hold of the reins. Pulling the huge beast closer, I checked Kewri's bags and bundles, with a passing thought that he might have crossed paths with looters or thieves, but his meagre tin pouch and blade were all intact. As far as I could tell, nothing was missing at all, other than Kewri himself.

The mist swirled in Senara's wake, but I could see that the closer she got to the bushes, the more her horse's hooves sank into the boggy ground. That's usually a sign that widespread flooding has transformed the peaty soil into a quagmire, just beneath the heather and mosses.

The pit of my stomach felt leaden. I guessed what might have happened. Wrapping the cart horse reins around my hand, I kicked my pony and steered him to a low slope just visible through the mists. If my suspicions were correct, I needed to approach the valley floor with great caution. This was not a time to go cantering off at full speed into more problems.

As I rounded the top end of the scrub, I could see Senara ahead, still mounted but at a complete standstill. The pony was above knee deep in a bog. It rocked from side to side, straining against the sucking motion dragging it down. Senara urged her pony to move on, digging her heels into the poor creature's sides.

"Hold fast, girl. Don't go any further!" I yelled, sliding down from my own horse and securing the reins of both mine and Kewri's ponies to a nearby branch. "The more it struggles, the less fight it'll have to pull itself free." Moving as fast as I could, I snapped a long stick off the bushes and stripped all shoots from the main stem until I had a rod with which to poke the ground. Jabbing it into the moss and squelching peat, I edged as close as I dared to and squinted into the low afternoon sun.

Without the weight of Senara on its back, I figured that the horse would be better able to pull itself out without too much trouble. I returned to my pony and unpacked my longest bed fur, grumbling under my breath about the filth I would have to deal with later.

After I'd explained my plan to her, I encouraged Senara to slide down off the saddle and lay flat against the mud to spread her weight. I tossed out the fur, clutching one corner until she was able to cling to its edge. Between her efforts and mine, she crawled out of the bog just as her horse tried to buck. In frustration, her pony squealed.

"Ho there!" The voice was feeble, but deep. It was also very familiar.

Senara cuffed the dirt from her face and looked at me. "Did you hear that, Fur Benyn?"

No amount of squinting could help me see through the diffuse light of the mists, but I knew he was out there. Kewri was alive and stuck in the centre of the mire. He called out a second time, causing Senara to lunge in his direction. I thrust my arm across her chest, stopping her from getting stuck a second time.

"Kewri, is that you? It's me, Senara, and Fur Benyn." She wailed, sniffing back tears.

The groan I heard was muffled, as though he was gargling. "Be quick, girl. I said" Gesturing towards the higher ground. "Go around with this and mind you don't get bogged down yourself." I gave her the stick and fashioned another for myself, before walking the horses along the higher path through the fog. I figured that if the cart horse had wriggled free, then Senara's pony would do the same in due course. Our priority was to reach Kewri before the mire sucked him beneath the surface into the Underworld.

When I finally got around to the other side of the mire with the ponies in tow, Senara was on her knees bawling her eyes out in desperation. Kewri was too far across the mire to reach. He fretted and gasped, spluttered and coughed as the murky liquid seeped into his nostrils.

"Keep as still as you can." I bellowed. "The more you struggle the quicker the dark spirits will pull you down." Grabbing Senara by the arm, I yanked her to her feet and issued instructions, hoping to Cernonnus that we had enough time to put my plan into action before Kewri choked to death.

The pair of us stripped off our tunics, leggings and capes, twisting them into make-shift ropes and tying them into one long length. Wearing only a thin shift to cover my modesty, I took the reins from my pony, attached one end of them to the clothing and fastened the other end around the cart horse.

"Kewri, listen carefully, we might only get one chance at this, do you hear?" I took his spluttered cough to mean that he understood. Backing the cart horse up as close as possible without it sinking into the mud, I looped the cloth into a bundle and threw it with all my might onto the surface of the mire. It was not close enough for him to reach. While he worked at getting his arms free, Senara and I slashed our bedding into strips and extended the rope.

My pulse throbbed inside my head, watching him thrash about, his actions slowed with the sheer exhaustion of survival. Senara took a turn at flinging the bundle of cloth. At last, her aim was true.

She stood and yelled at him, urging him to fight for his life. As his arms reached out, he dislodged an air pocket beneath him, creating bubbles that popped at the surface. Sinking much faster, the moss and peat smothered his face. Senara cried out. I held my breath. We could only see his hands and wrists flailing about trying to cling to hope.

"Get the rope closer!" I screamed, jolting her into action. With tremendous speed and agility, she pulled in our cloth bindings and tried again, hurling it right over his head.

Kewri felt the leather of the strapping with one hand and fed it into the palm of the other. When I saw that he'd bound it around his wrists, I smacked the carthorse around the rear. The rope went taut, straining at the loose connections until the knots bit tight. With gentle words of encouragement, I coaxed the horse onward until I could see the surface of the mire breaking. Gradually, Kewri's face reappeared, streaked in the blackest sludge. He took a massive gasp of air into his lungs.

"Don't let go!" Senara barked at him, but the giant was too exhausted and struggling for breath to reply. He was not going to let this chance to live pass by.

As soon as he was able, Kewri looped the leather strap around his back and under his arms, letting the horse take all the strain of pulling him free. How long had he been stuck in the bog? It was fortunate that we'd found him in time. Perhaps the gods had not punished us for sacrificing the white hart after all. Maybe they had greater plans in store for this gentle giant of the Dumnonii.

What a sight we must have looked; Kewri covered head to toe in stinking black filth and Senara and I stripped down to the bare essentials and soaked with tears. The poor man lay on the ground, panting and relieved. Senara threw herself on top of him, wiping his face clean of peaty water.

"I just knew you were in trouble." She gushed. "I felt it in the pit of my gut."

Kewri nodded and closed his eyes, planting his head down to rest. I felt awkward standing there watching their reunion, and busied myself in the reclamation of our clothes. Everything was thick with muck and filth, our bedding furs shredded and the fastenings of the reins stretched and useless. Even after a good wash in the river, the bedding was beyond repair. We'd have to return to camp without going on to look for my wayward nephew, Paega.

Senara collected some wood and stacked it up on her pony which had, as I predicted, worked itself free from the bog without our aid. While Kewri rested, we rinsed our clothes and found a suitable campsite on higher ground to build a fire. Using an old trick my mother taught me, I gathered up as many smooth stones as I could find and rested them in the embers until they were warmed through. It was a tiresome job, but with each hot stone poked out of the fire and wrapped in our fabric bundles, our clothes dried enough for us to wear.

Despite the damp and cold, Senara left us to hunt, while I gave what was left of our wrapped food to Kewri.

He looked at me with huge fretful eyes. "I am so sorry, Fur Benyn." His mouth flapped open as if he wanted to say more but couldn't think of the words.

"Never you mind about that. What's done is done. You're safe and that's all that matters. Now eat up and gather your strength." I knew that we were in for an uncomfortable night, huddled together for warmth without bedding or shelter. He paused for a moment, looking at the food and then at my wretched state, shivering in damp clothes.

"Go on, boy. Get it down you. Senara will bring us a couple of fat rabbits, you wait and see." I had every faith in the scout. She could survive in the most barren of places unseen by our enemy for many moons. Truth be known, I rather admired her. Where I preferred the warmth of a home fire and the security of compound walls, she was a wild thing, formidable and untamed.

When Kewri had eaten his fill and the colour had returned to his cheeks, I ventured a question. "So, what happened? How did you get stuck and not your horse?"

He rolled his eyes. "He bucked me off. Slammed into the start of the bog and thought better of it. Didn't give me the chance to object, just stopped all of a sudden and then threw me right over his head."

It wasn't a laughing matter, but I couldn't help myself. The snort, became a titter and when I saw his melancholy turn into a chuckle, I let rip with a cackle of my own. The carthorse had the sense to avoid the mire. Pity he didn't think to save his rider too.

When our mirth simmered down, Kewri explained that he'd followed Paega's tracks and, like us, assumed that he was heading for the closest stone circle to find members of his own clan. Despite asking local travellers and homesteaders, he lost Paega's trail over the stony tors and ridges. With such a lengthy head start, there was no way we would find him now. We both left the obvious point unsaid. How could we return to the island compound without Paega? The issue muted our conversation, but it hung between us like the fetid stench of offal.

I had a sudden urge to drink an unwise quantity of ale to numb all my senses to the cold and the futility of our situation, but we had none. Senara returned just as the mists started to thin out, revealing the star-filled sky. As beautiful as that was, it was not a welcome sight. The visible stars meant that we'd be in for another frosty night. Our camp site was on high ground and exposed to the elements.

Senara brought back a sizable trout, already scaled and gutted. Speared on a pole over the fire, it didn't take long to cook, but shared three ways it made fools of our mouths. My stomach groaned for more as we settled down in a small hollow next to the fire, with Kewri in the middle and Senara and I snuggling either side of him. We had just one small hemp blanket from beneath the carthorse saddle with which to cover us and our wood supply was running low.

Half way through the night, Senara and I swapped places and loaded the last of the fuel onto the fire. I tucked in as close as I could to share Kewri's warmth, but I was unable to sleep. My chattering teeth kept me alert and anxious until the mists formed once again to give the moor its ghostly dawn light.

With nothing left to eat and no wood with which to rekindle the fire, we drank a little cold water from our travelling bladders and saddled the horses. My innards felt like they were touching inside I was so hungry, but I said nothing. We had bigger problems to consider.

It was Kewri who broke the silence first, voicing what we'd all been thinking. "We can't go back. Not without Paega. We must push on, no matter how hopeless the search."

He was right, but we had to face the Chiefs at some point or we'd be banishing ourselves to live out our days on the bleak moors. Senara scraped a clod of mud from her boot on a sharp rock. "I've been thinking about that." She said, peering up at me from the corners of her eyes. "Fur Benyn, do you have any tin with you?"

I frowned, wondering where she was heading with this line of thought. "I do."

"And you could get more from the Chiefs if it was in the tribe's best interest?"

I pulled a face and sucked in my lips, puzzled. "What have you in mind?"

She laid out her plans to us both, explaining each stage of the process in detail so that I was left with a feeling that she had a mind to suggest it all along, perhaps since before we'd even left the compound. I came up with a few potential stumbling blocks, but she had answers for them all ready and waiting.

By the time we'd mounted up and turned our horses to the east, my head was spinning with possibilities. Not that I ignored the danger in what she had proposed. Kewri agreed to anything and everything Senara said. I think he was just grateful to be alive.

We followed the worn trail east, stopping at the first homestead on our route to trade for furs and food. They had little to spare, but gave us eggs and some cheese for our tin. The main thing was that we had the means with which to keep ourselves warm. Where we were headed, we couldn't afford to light nightly fires for fear of discovery.

Senara led the way and Kewri brought up the rear of our little procession, none of us feeling the need to chat. We stopped a few times during the day, mainly to gather what early spring shoots and leaves we could to supplement the geese Senara killed with her skill at archery. She was quite something to watch, bringing down hefty birds before they could launch themselves into the air, right from the back of her pony. Before we got close to the borderlands, she had traded most of her catch to settlers for flour and milk.

This was a woman well used to keeping her own counsel. More than a couple of times, she forgot that we were behind her. She'd gallop off the beaten path leaving us bewildered and all alone. When the sun was low on the horizon, Senara pulled back on the reins and waited for us to draw level with her horse.

"There's a hidden shelter not far from here with a good water supply and plenty of wood. No one knows it exists so it's perfectly safe. We can make camp there tonight and finally get some sleep." She caught me yawning as she said this, and grinned. "Nearly there, Fur Benyn, I promise."

I knew her notion of *nearly there*. The young always think great distances are *nearly there*. When you get to my ripe old age, everything takes more effort. Kewri seemed to perk up at this news. He trotted after the scout smiling, leaving my old horse and me to amble along at our own pace. I figured that the longer I was in the saddle, the greater the likelihood that a good fire would be burning by the time I'd caught up.

It was when they disappeared from view and into a forest ahead that I grew apprehensive. I knew the area, of course, but I had no clue as to where this hidden shelter might be. Tapping the flanks of my pony with my heels, I sped up to where they had vanished and crossed a stream. Was this a tributary of the River Sid? Had I just passed on to Durotriges' land?

The shade of the spring leaves cut what little sunlight was left to the day. I couldn't make out their tracks, nor could I see more than a couple of boat lengths ahead of me. The dense undergrowth snagged and ripped at my pony's legs, making him grumble and resistant to move ahead. We edged forward slowly, almost feeling our way through ash and oak.

"Psst!"

The sound came from my left. I craned my neck to see who was about. "Come out and show yourself." I said, thinking that Senara was playing me for a fool.

"Shush, Fur Benyn!" She whispered, stepping out from behind a clump of young beech saplings. She waved her hands at me, gesturing for me to dismount and follow her. I was puzzled as to why she was behaving so strangely.

"What's going on? Have we crossed the border? I thought you said it was a secret campsite?" Kewri flapped his arms at me, holding a finger against his lips and crouching low next to a shrub.

Leaving my horse tied up near the stream, I followed them deeper into the forest on foot. The pair of them were head and shoulders above my height, forcing them to bend low and slink towards our target.

When we reached the edge of a small clearing, I realised why they were creeping about. Someone had found Senara's secret hideout.

CHAPTER ELEVEN

Smoke twisted in a spiral up through the gap in the trees next to the little woven hurdle shelter. Several rabbits hung from posts in various stages of skinning and gutting. Whoever was in Senara's camp, meant to stay there for some time. An axe lay next to a pile of chopped wood and there were pots of food cooking over the embers. I looked all around the cleared space between the trees, searching for the interloper but saw no one.

Glancing over my shoulder, I opened my mouth to whisper to Senara, but she'd gone. I curled my lip at Kewri, but he just shrugged. This was how she managed to travel everywhere unseen. She had the stealth and cunning of a wolf that one. Neither I nor Kewri dared to move, in case a snapped twig or rustling branch gave away our positions. Just as cramp was making itself felt in my calf muscles, I heard a loud shriek coming from the opposite side of the clearing.

Within moments, a man shuffled out from the undergrowth, his leggings around his ankles and a blade at his throat. Senara had sneaked up and caught the man emptying his bowels.

"You can come out now, Fur Benyn, Kewri. He's alone." Senara shouted. To my surprise, she released him immediately, sheathing her knife and letting him pull up his britches. Kewri and I marched forwards, expecting him to make a run for it, but he didn't.

"You scared the kawgh out of me, Senara, literally!" He said, rubbing his neck where the blade had nicked his skin. I looked him up and down, taking note of the tattoo marking him as part of the Durotriges Tribe. This had to be the scout that Senara had bribed into spying for us.

"This is my place, you kyjyan thief!" She snarled, but there was a grin mixed in with her accusation. "How did you find it?"

"You are not that good at covering your tracks." He sniffed. "Easy really."

"I must be slipping." She grinned, holding out her arm for a more formal greeting. They clasped each other's forearms before introducing us. While she helped herself to his pot of stew and prepared one of his rabbits to roast, I glanced into the shelter. It was well built, but seemed far too small to accommodate us all. I sighed. After a night on the freezing moors, it was better than nothing.

As the night wore on, clouds gathered obscuring the moon and keeping the frost at bay. We were a merry little bunch, drinking what ale the Duro had and eating his stores of food. I'm not sure what I expected, but this rival of ours was nothing like I imagined him to be. My experiences of the Duros were limited, mostly taking the form of heart-breaking memories from my youth.

More recent time spent in their company, were through my niece, Wenna, who was forced into marrying their former Chief.

He was a great brainless brute, who possessed no redeeming features and bore grudges unto death. This scout was pleasant, hospitable and at times, fun. I liked him and could see how Senara had chosen to employ him in place of a swift death. Kewri sat on a log on the opposite side of the fire, watching Senara chatting and sharing food with our host. From his expression, I could see the jealousy bubbling up inside him.

I chose to distract them. "Perren," I said, interrupting the quick-witted banter between the two scouts. "What can you tell us about Brea?"

Perren swallowed his mouthful of rabbit and swilled it down with ale. "She's despised by everyone in the tribe. Most of us can't understand how she came to lead us at all, considering there were others in our Chief's family who could have taken the tall chair after he fell."

"So, she just declared herself Ruvane and Chief and no one tried to stop her?" I asked, impatient to get to the root of all.

"Of course they did, but she was too shrewd. She was paying our best warriors from the shared troves to keep her safe. Some of us think she put the idea in the Chief's head to attack you Dumnos in your new camp. Rumour has it that a few of the elders went against the decision and were executed for speaking out." Everything he said backed up Senara's observations, but then she took her information from Perren.

I sat and stewed for a while, contemplating whether he was someone who could be trusted. "Are there any elders left willing to stand up to her?" I knew that he could only guess an answer. This scout was too lowly in the tribe to know about the important camp politics.

"I'd say so, yes, especially those who had the right to make a challenge for their sons to become the next Chief." Perren looked at me with the kind of reverence I'd seen before. He was respectful of my position and age. If the rest of his folk were like him, perhaps there was hope for the Duros after all. Was it possible for Tallack and Blydh to forge a lasting alliance with the Durotriges after generations of conflict?

This was a possibility worth pursuing. It could help us to return to Tallack and Blydh's favour and win us a pardon for allowing Paega's escape.

Over the course of the evening, I grilled the Duro scout for details regarding their organisation and structure. From what I could tell, Brea had all but neutered the elders of their tribe through fear of death. She kept no counsel other than her own and through a combination of youth and hubris, had made some terrible decisions; the site for her new compound being but one.

It was tempting to put forward Senara's proposal to the scout there and then, but I figured that he could easily slip out of the shelter during the night to betray our whereabouts to his fellow tribesmen and have us all killed or worse. The matter could wait until morning.

Our night in the hut was beyond cramped, but it was warm and relatively comfortable. Kewri insisted on sleeping between Senara and Perren, leaving me squashed up against the hurdle wall at the end. At least she smelled less offensive than the men.

Come morning, we found Perren up and about before us. He cleared away the mess after our night of indulgence. Senara and I had quiet words together before leaving the shelter. It was a risk, but we decided to trust the scout to deliver our plan to the Duro elders.

Perren sat and ate flat bread and cold rabbit, listening to our proposal with a neutral expression. I couldn't make out his opinion at all, but we had little to lose by making the suggestion. When we had laid out the reasoning, time frame and locations involved, he finished chewing and swallowed.

"What you are suggesting has never been attempted before in my lifetime." He said, his friendly face turning quite stern.

"Nor mine, young man, although my brother attempted a union of marriage between our two tribes. The less said about that the better." I replied, reinforcing the gravity of the situation.

He cleared his throat, looking uncomfortable. "And in laying this at the elders' feet, I am admitting to them that I have cooperated with our sworn enemy."

So that was his issue. He was worried that his tribe would discover his friendship with our scout and realise that he was our spy. "You can tell them that we took you captive, but spared your life in return for delivering our message." That was an easy fix. I was surprised he hadn't thought of it himself.

Senara jogged his arm. "I can give you a black-eye if you think they'll need more convincing." She grinned at Perren, making Kewri glower all the more.

The scout smiled, rolling his eyes at her. "I think I can make it work.

Senara and Perren agreed on how and where they could leave signals for one another; a sun symbol scratched into a marker stone at the border crossing of the River Sid to indicate all was well, a crescent moon if discussions went sour, and a cross to bring the parties together by the spring solstice at the latest.

I butted into their conversation, adding further symbols if meetings were delayed or could be brought forward. In the end, both scouts agreed to make regular contact at the crossing to keep abreast of the changing situations in our camps. We'd need the rest of the spring to deal with Blydh's demon, that's if it hadn't already taken over the island while we were away.

With everything resting on Perren and his diplomacy with Duro elders, we packed our belongings, mounted our horses, and headed west towards the island compound.

We were a sombre party, riding in single file and letting the ponies dictate our pace. None of us were eager to return empty handed. We had no way of knowing how well our plan would be received, particularly by Blydh.

I spent the half-day's ride, pondering my approach. As ever, Tallack would be the most receptive to the plan, more so if I informed him that it was Senara's suggestion in the first place. She had earned his respect and admiration, and I'd be a fool not to trade on that fact. Kewri and Senara rode behind me, leaving enough distance between the horses so that I couldn't hear their mumbled discussion. There was no need to be coy, I knew exactly what they were arguing about.

Their lover's quarrel was of no interest to me at all. We had bigger problems to deal with than Kewri's jealousy. Considering the giant was laying with Tallack's slave right under Senara's nose, he had no right to behave in such a petulant manner.

When at last we reached the forest, marking the homestretch of our journey, Senara drew alongside me. "What are we going to say to them? Tallack's orders were clear. We were not to return without Paega."

She didn't need to tell me. It'd preyed on my mind since we'd left the borderlands. Why the young always think us elders have all the answers is beyond me. Most of the time, we wait and see what transpires. That was all we could do now. I tried not to think about the punishments that the Chiefs could impose upon us, banishment, imprisonment, flogging, or maybe worse. If Blydh had his own way, I would have already succumbed from one or more of those cruelties. I thank Cernonnus daily for Tallack's common sense and good reason.

The closer we got to the northern gates, the more I could feel my bowels churning inside me. Before we were close enough to call out to the watchmen, they saw us and blew a single note out on the horn. Were they signalling us as enemies? Could they not see who we were?

It took all my strength to press on and not turn back. Glancing over my shoulder, I saw Kewri and Senara slow their horses, leaving me a few lengths ahead. The bridge lowered over the River Exe in front of me. I pulled on the reins bringing my pony to a halt.

The imposing north gate rattled as the securing rods were drawn back. My breathing quickened; my pulse hammered in my ears. I imagined every conceivable weapon flying out towards us as the gap widened between the towers.

There stood Tallack and Renowden, both wearing grim frowns. Tallack made a show of tipping his head sideways, pretending to look for Paega. "You're about to tell me that my conniving kyjyan brother is dead and will never trouble us again, aren't you?" He glared directly at me but I could not hold his stare. I hung my head in shame.

"You lost him?" Tallack said, shaking his head and walking towards me across the bridge.

"I'm sorry, nephew. We tried, but Kewri and Senara both got trapped in a bog and then…"

"No, it's my own fault. I should have sent out warriors the moment Paega escaped. What was I thinking sending you and your little band of misfits?" He grabbed hold of my pony's bridle and led me into the compound. "We can talk about what to do later. Your services are needed again, Aunt. Blydh's in another mess."

It was a relief that circumstances had, yet again, saved us from the Chief's wrath. Our failure paled into insignificance compared to Blydh's continuous need for supervision. The rarity of my healing skills had saved us once more. My abilities made me a valuable resource. Tallack helped me down from the saddle and touched his forehead to mine. Relief washed over me until I felt giddy. There and then, I made a promise to myself, not to abuse this unusual privilege.

Renowden beamed at me and repeated the Chief's gesture. I was touched at how pleased he was to see me, using the greeting normally reserved for close family. Ren took care of my horse, while I spun about thinking where Blydh might be.

"I take it he's in his own house, or maybe the Long Hut?" I pointed towards the collection of Head Hunter shelters on the eastern side of the island, but Tallack shook his head.

"He's waiting for you at your place." He said, shepherding me towards my home.

"What? Why?" I spluttered, shocked that he would consider anything to do with me a comfort. "What happened?" I scurried through the mud and kawgh towards my house and pushed through the door drapes.

Tallack ran in behind me, snatching my healing kit from Renowden's hands on his way. "Nothing happened. He was drinking in the Long Hut last night, complaining that the new helmet made his head sore and this morning, there's a patch swollen up as big as a goose egg."

By the time we'd all squeezed inside, my hut was fit to burst. The twin's mother, Cryda was at the bedside, rocking backwards and forwards to soothe her babe and her own anxiety, Treeve stood guard at the door, although I've no idea why, and Endelyn was muttering invocations and wafting the strong scent from smouldering herbs about their heads.

I stood at the foot of my bunk looking down at my nephew. Blydh was whimpering, touching the swollen mass poking from the thin skin where I'd stitched his scalp back in place. The offending helmet balanced from an end post. He opened his eyes and saw me, and then held out his hand for me to grasp.

"Aunt Mel. Help me, it hurts so much."

At first, I thought it was a trick to get me closer so that his spite would have greater impact, but his anguish was genuine. He'd reverted to the frightened child I'd nursed many cycles ago. I detected not a trace of the demon as I moved in closer to examine the growth. Blydh took hold of my hand and wouldn't let go. It made me uneasy at first, but he needed the comfort.

"Can you do anything?" Tallack growled from the doorway.

"As far as I can tell…" I said, squinting at the milky fluid oozing from the scars. "The helmet has set the healing back. It sits too tightly against his skull. It needs less padding or for the smith to hammer the sides out to give him more room. I'll need to lance that swelling and let the bad humours out." Blydh squeezed my fingers hard. How could he be in this much pain? "Where's the poppy resin? Was he not completely addled on the stuff when I left?"

"He was, Aunt. That's the problem." Tallack grumbled. "He used it all up."

I couldn't stop my reaction. My sharp intake of breath was mirrored by Ren and Cryda. That small pot of resin would've normally seen me through a whole season. He was lucky to be alive. No wonder he felt the pain acutely now. He'd spent the last moon or more in a resin infused haze.

Endelyn broke my focus, leaning over Blydh to slip a necklace of carved bone symbols and feathers over his head. "For protection Chief." She whispered to him, lowering her chest so close to his face that she almost buried his nose in her cleavage.

"Kerensa?" Blydh murmured. "Is that you?" He let go of my hand and grappled Endelyn's wrist, pulling her down onto the bunk beside him. No one put him straight. Tallack and I exchanged worried glances. Blydh must be poorly indeed, if he could mistake the fair and willowy Endelyn for his raven-haired former lover, particularly since Kerensa was dead.

"I'll need everyone to clear out." I said. "I must have room to work." Most took the hint and left at once. Tallack handed me my bag and pushed Treeve and Ren outside.

Endelyn made no attempt to move. "I'll stay, Fur Benyn. He seems to be settled by my presence."

Cryda sighed. She knew when her children needed her, and this wasn't one of those times. She shot me a look on her way out, as if to say, *you brought this woman into our camp, you can deal with her.* How right she was. Endelyn was masterful in her manipulations. While I stabbed my finest needle point into the pustule, she stroked Blydh's cheek with her soft hands. As I drained the pus from the wound, she sang a distracting tune and nestled her face into his neck.

By the time I had smothered the loose flesh in plantain paste and wrapped his head in cloth, she had him smiling with closed eyes and calm breath. I washed my hands in a bowl of warm water and started to clear up the mess.

Endelyn sat up to face Blydh. "Chief, I know how we can clear your head once and for all."

He opened his eyes and frowned. "Clear it? There is nothing to clear. I was injured." His voice turned gruff and accusatory.

"I just mean that you can feel like your old self again. No one muddling your thoughts."

The Chief shifted on the bed, sitting fully upright. His mild manner evaporated in an instant. "You think that someone is telling me what to do? You think me weak?"

I knew his good temper would not last. His face flushed red, his lip curled and his fists tightened with rage.

CHAPTER TWELVE

I was sure that Blydh would vent his anger on Endelyn at any moment, pounding his fists into her fragile body. She must have seen the change in him too. Instead of backing away, as I would have done, she moved closer to him, laying her head on his chest.

"You are the most powerful man in the tribe, no one would question that, Chief. I meant that I know of a place that can rid you of pain, heal your troublesome wounds and make you more vital than ever. With a suitable offering, the gods would even return the sight in your left eye."

It was as though The Mother Goddess, Cerridwen, was speaking through Endelyn, choosing each word as a balm to his woes. She said nothing more, but resumed her lyrical singing. I watched from a safe distance as her soft voice lulled him into a stupor. The heaving in his chest lessened, his fists unclenched and his eyelids began to droop. She was better than resin for dulling his senses. I stayed until I was sure she wouldn't be in any danger, and then left in search of Tallack.

My nephew was in the Long Hut, holding more elders at bay. It seems that while we were away from camp, Blydh had eased his temper by destroying random structures about the island, the grain store, a chicken coop and the main posts supporting the smith's roof. Repairs were already underway, but the elders demanded compensation from the tribe's coffers.

I sneaked into the rear entrance, next to the roasting pits and surveyed the room. That salty young upstart, Treeve was sitting in the Ruvane chair next to Tallack, preening and posturing as though it was his for the taking. From the look on Tallack's face I could tell that he was not listening to the old men's gripes and moans, but it was his duty to hear them out.

Senara was sitting on the middle benches, directly between the Sea Warriors seats and those frequented by the Head Hunters. She was a shield maiden with no clan, an outcast, yet equal to most in all the necessary ways. I wondered if she'd discussed our plan with Tallack while I tended to Blydh, or whether she was biding her time. I'm ashamed to say that I hoped that she would put the idea before the Chiefs in my stead. I had a feeling that it would not be received well.

When I loomed into view, past the raised platform supporting the top table, Tallack used me as an excuse to be rid of the whining elders. "Aunt Mel. Come and sit with us." He'd often do this sort of thing, diverting attention onto others when he'd had enough. I did as I was bidden, safe in the knowledge that Tallack was ultimately on my side. He'd taken a beating from his brother for me, protected me on numerous occasions from Blydh's wrath, knowing that he was not in full possession of his own faculties.

He waited until I had climbed the platform to sit on his mother's chair at his side. Treeve narrowed his eyes at me from the central Ruvane position and I at him. This was not the time to open that old wound again.

"Good to see you, Nephew. It's been a tiring quarter moon, that's for sure."

"You've settled Blydh?" He asked, waving the elders away. They tutted their annoyance but did not press their luck.

"I've lanced, evacuated and stitched the pustule, but it was Endelyn who soothed him. She's with him now." My knees crunched as I lowered myself onto the chair. My spine felt like it was grinding against a bag of rocks.

"You heard him call her Kerensa?" Tallack said.

"I did." I studied the Chief's features. He'd aged in the last two seasons, the strain of leadership stripping his youth of vibrancy. The collective concern for Blydh was ever present in camp, but he felt it more than most. It mattered not how often they disagreed or fought, they shared a womb and that bond would remain steadfast unto death. "Maybe his sight was clouded." I offered up as an explanation for Blydh's vision. "You know he can only see through one eye, maybe the other had fogged over."

Tallack thinned his lips. "I appreciate the half-truths, Aunt Mel, but they won't wash with me. Blydh has to go to the sacred hot springs, or he will need night and day care like a new born babe for the rest of his life."

He had a point. I had dressed, treated, operated and re-stitched the Chief's scalp more times over the past two moons than I could count. The flesh on his head was so ragged, I struggled to find enough sound skin to stitch. I said nothing, staring towards the back of the Long Hut, searching for a solution. It was obvious what Tallack really meant. With the demon in charge of Blydh's body, we couldn't afford to let him out of our sight.

"You know that we can't keep news of Kerensa's death from reaching her father down at the mining settlement forever?" I ventured, knowing that it was likely to get a gruff response.

"One problem at a time, Aunt Mel. Her body is rotting in the marshlands. As far as anyone but you, me, Ren and Treeve knows, she died during the attack."

I took this as a snippy reminder to keep my nose out of his affairs. Whether it was Treeve or Tallack himself who dispatched the girl, the leader of the Alchemy Clan would most likely lead a revolt as a consequence. The more I thought about the outcome, the worse our position seemed. This was a kind and benevolent man, who managed the mining and smelting of all our tin in the western shores of our region. A man who'd sent his daughter to our compound with a view to her becoming Blydh's Ruvane. I knew enough about Kenver's character to understand his abiding love for Kerensa. He had the respect of all his clan and others besides. We couldn't afford to raise his ire.

The events from the last half moon hit me all at once, Sorcha's death, the sacrifice of my cherished white hart, and the continued troubles with my nephew. The pall of gloom hung heavy in my gut, leaving me crumpled on the chair. At the root of all this heartache, was my fateful decision to use the sun disc to protect Blydh's brain. If only I had asked the smith for a flattened sheet of silver or tin, none of this would have happened.

Tallack seemed to sense my despair. "We'll get Blydh to the sacred spring and all will be well again. Just you see." He gave me one of his famed cheeky grins. It failed to cheer me.

Taking a slow, deep breath, I bolstered my courage to tackle the subject of Senara's plan with the Duros. Tallack looked so much like his father, sitting next to me in the tall chair carved with a mighty bear head, my bravery left me. Senara glanced in my direction and then looked pointedly at the Chief, egging me on. My stare shifted uneasily and then returned to her wind-chapped face. Senara's response was to roll her eyes at me. She grabbed her cup of ale and stood up. Striding to the centre of the top table, she stood before Tallack.

"Chief. Your aunt and I have news from the borderlands which could prove extremely useful. I'd appreciate counsel in private, if it pleases you?" Her manner so forthright, her stance was confident and steady. Did this young woman have complete mastery over all her fears?

Tallack squinted at her, assessing her earnest demeanour. "Very well. Join me in my hut and bring some ale with you. I'm parched."

Senara slotted her fingers into a number of cups, clamped a jug of ale in the crook of her elbow, and followed me out of the Long Hut. When we reached the rear door, I stopped her with a gentle touch to her shoulder. "Thank you, my dear." I gushed, hoping that she would take it as a cue to lead the discussions ahead.

Together we stomped along the boardwalks for the short distance to Tallack's hut and let ourselves inside. In my jittery state, I hadn't noticed the whereabouts of Treeve. He scampered along in front of the Chief to claim his position next to Tallack on the end of his bunk. I thought I could keep a lid on my disgust, but it leaked out of me in the form of a high-pitched scoff. I received a scowl for my petulance from both men.

Senara had the sense to stay quiet on the matter. She launched into a full account of our journey to the borderlands and how she had secured the services of a Duro scout. Her careful choice of words and phrases made it sound as though it was a collaborative plan put to the elders of the Duros, even though it was solely hers.

She should have taken full credit for such an ingenious suggestion.

It was when I saw Tallack's reaction to her account that I realised why she had shared the glory. If the idea was ill received, she would not be the only one to incur the Chief's wrath.

Tallack's happy mood evaporated at once; the laughter lines pinching into a frown. "And you decided to do all this without my consent, without consulting either me or my brother?" His terse tone prickled the hairs on the back of my neck. He was on the verge of losing his temper.

"Chief," Senara continued, undaunted by the alteration in mood. "It was a fortunate encounter of which we took advantage. There was no time to ride back to speak with you or Chief Blydh. Nothing need come of this arrangement, if that's what you choose to do, but know that it could solve more than one significant problem if their elders agree to the terms."

"That's a big kyjyan '*if*' Senara." He roared.

"What have we got to lose? Brea and the Duros go on being our sworn enemies, Blydh carries on taking our men out to be slaughtered in idiotic raids along the borderlands and our homesteaders will be in as much danger as they've ever been. If we see how this plays out, we stand a real chance of forging a path towards peace; something your forefathers never achieved."

She was doing so well until that last point. I could see Tallack tipping towards her way of thinking until she made mention of our ancestors. His father, Aebba the Wild, had given his half-sister Wenna in marriage to the Durotriges' Chief in the hope of brokering peace. That didn't turn out so well for either of them.

Senara failed to notice the Chief's cool reception. She ploughed on with her reasoning as though it was a foregone conclusion that he'd agree. "We have it on good authority that the elders would jump at the chance to discuss terms."

"Good authority? You are relying on the word of a scout whose loyalty was bought for a few measly grains of tin. For all you know, he could've ridden straight back to Brea and told her everything. We'd be walking straight into a trap."

"No, Chief. I know this scout well; he can be trusted." She persisted.

"You are remarkably quiet on the subject, Aunt Mel. Normally, I can't shut you up. What's this fellow like?"

I swallowed, stalling for time. Both sides of the argument were equally valid. We had spent one night with the Duro scout, and in that time, he was a gracious host. There was no way of knowing whether Senara knew him more intimately, and I did not care to ask, but she placed a great deal of trust in him. I could also see my nephew's point. The Novantae were perfect hosts to us at the top of the world while we stayed at their settlement. It didn't stop them turning on us when the moment presented itself to them.

I scratched my head. "We have time to think everything through. There's no need to act on this immediately. If you do decide to meet and discuss terms with the Duros, you could send an emissary rather than go yourself."

Tallack did that irritating habit of his where he plays with the straggling whiskers growing on his chin. I swear he thinks it makes him look wiser than his young age. I have a better crop of whiskers than he does, foolish youth. When he'd finished his little display, he stood up from the end of his bunk next to Treeve. "And when did you propose this elder meeting would take place?"

"Senara agreed upon a system of signals for the scout at the River Sid crossing but, I doubt the Duros will be prepared to wait for long."

"Fine, I'll think about it, but right now we must make Blydh the priority. Not a word to anyone in the meantime." He flounced about his hut, flinging off his cloak and untying his leggings. Aunt Mel, come and eat in the Long Hut tonight, there's plenty of venison left from the sacrifice." As he pulled off his tunic and turned to face a grinning Treeve on his bunk, Senara and I made a hasty retreat.

On our walk back towards my hut, we passed the roasting pits. The stag's head rested on the end of the butcher's block, his tongue swollen and protruding, his eyes milky, his white fur caked in dried and blackened humours. Flies supped at the blood patches in his nostrils. I'm well accustomed to the stench of death, both animal and human, but this time I retched. I'd let my emotions loose from the cage of grief after my slave's death, and was rewarded with more heartache.

There are times when I curse the gods for allowing me to live for so long. Why must I persist while the young around me perish? Is there no respite in this wicked world?

Senara hurried off to find Kewri, leaving me standing next to the pony enclosure with no white hart to listen to my gripes. I sat on the edge of the boardwalk and poked the mud with a stick. I didn't want to return to my hut just to listen to Endelyn manipulate Blydh, or for him to turn on me again. There were more chores in need of attention than I could count, but none that were so urgent that they couldn't afford to wait.

I stayed there for some time, until the chill of the early spring evening seeped into my bones and stiffened the joints. No one paid me any attention. They went about their business as though finding me idle was an everyday occurrence. When the sun hid behind the trees at the western boundary, I heaved myself up and walked home.

Blydh was asleep on my bed, with Endelyn nestled against his neck. Both were fully clothed and above my furs. As much as I wanted to creep back out unseen, my fire was low and required more fuel. There was no way I was going to endure another freezing night without one.

The embers heated the sap inside the wood as I tossed on more logs, waking my guests with the crackles and spits. Sparks threatened the thatch for a time, but died before they could take hold.

Endelyn yawned and stretched, levering herself up onto an elbow. Blydh blinked a few times and then sat upright. I held my breath, wondering which version of my nephew would greet me, the demonic spirit from the Underworld, or my sweet nephew of old. His hand reached up to the dressing covering his scalp, touching the site of the pustule with great care. He winced and immediately moved his fingers away.

"It'll be tender for some time, I'm afraid." I said quietly, expecting a great barrage of complaint and anger.

"I expect so." Blydh peered up at me, rubbing his left eye with a bent knuckle. "Aunt Mel? Is there any more resin?"

I'd grown so used to the demon version of him that he took me by surprise. It was a while before I came to my senses. "Tallack said that you'd used up the whole pot. All I have is willow. Would you like me to…?" I reached over to my herbal stores and took out a little dried bark, hovering with it dangling from my clutches.

"Anything to dull the pain would be good. Thanks."

Keen to make the most of this brief period of calm, I heated my largest knife in the fire and plunged it into a cup of water. When it was bubbling furiously, I tipped the crushed stems into the liquid.

Endelyn sported a grin from ear to ear, content to sprawl across his legs with her own. Was she really alright with him believing that she was his dead lover? I couldn't make out what her intentions were. She couldn't keep the illusion going forever. As if Blydh was reading my mind, he scooted to the edge of the bunk and tried to stand. "The priestess tells me there's a chance I'll get my sight back. That's good news isn't it?"

I almost dropped the cup in the fire I was so shocked. This fleeting moment of lucidity was all it had taken for her to embed her claws. "Is that so, nephew? And what would that be?"

"She says that there's a sacred spring where the gods grant wishes. Endelyn and I are going there come dawn."

CHAPTER THIRTEEN

I stood frozen to the spot, waiting for my nephew's cordial mood to splinter into countless shards. In this solitary moment, he knew that the woman whispering into his ear was the priestess and not his former lover.

His reckless abandon was reined in to the point of civility towards me. Was her promise of healing at the sacred springs all it had taken to calm his noxious temper? More importantly, how would he react if he knew her real purpose for luring him to the springs was to drive out a demon from his head?

"Well, that *is* something to celebrate." I said, although it came out a little unnatural and forced. "Shall we all go over to the Long Hut and tell Chief Tallack?" I just wanted my hut back; in case the demon resurfaced and wrestled my sweet boy back into submission.

Endelyn shimmied to her feet and attached herself to his arm. "What a wonderful idea, Fur Benyn. Maybe we can all go and make a pilgrimage of the whole trip."

"Hmm, maybe." I grumbled, grabbing my cloak and following them across the grass. With the willow tonic in hand, I pondered on the time restraints involved in setting up a possible meeting with the Duro elders. We couldn't be in two places at once after all.

Tallack was overjoyed to see Blydh up and about. He ordered his men to fill their cups in a toast to Blydh's recovery. I loitered near the door, waiting to see what

Endelyn would do. She didn't disappoint. I could see her shallow designs on my nephews from a running distance. When she failed to interest Tallack, she had no other option but to cure Blydh, making him fit to rule with her at his side. He was a much harder quarry but the woman was determined, of that I had no doubt.

Leaning against the wall, I watched the twins embrace and sit next to one another in their impressive carved chairs at the top table. Treeve slithered from the Ruvane seat and sat on the opposite side of Tallack in Cryda's spot. Endelyn waited until all the cheering and noise had died down, before adopting a coy and bashful stance in front of both Chiefs. With one knee bent inward, she twirled a braid of fair hair around her finger. My, she's a shrewd one and observant too. That's precisely how their mother wheedles around them.

"Where should I sit, Chief?" She almost sang the words at the pair of them. Even Tallack was taken by the performance.

"Come and sit up here, priestess." Blydh announced, finding his old authoritative tone in front of his warriors. "Right here, next to me." He patted the bench at the side of his wolf head chair where visiting dignitaries usually sat.

The pipers began a jolly tune while the slaves brought in platters piled high with the cooked flesh of my white hart. My stomach turned at the sight. I pushed myself upright from the wall and handed the willow tonic to a passing slave.

"Give that to Chief Blydh if he asks for it, although I guess he'd prefer ale in its place." I turned to leave, but was stopped at the door by my friend, Renowden.

"You're not going already, are you? I thought we could eat together." He saw my distress at the enthusiasm with which the warriors consumed the venison. "I'm sorry, Meliora. It must be hard for you."

I shook off my emotions. "It was just a deer. People have to eat."

"He was more than that and you know it." His kindness almost had me undone. "People are giving Endelyn the credit for saving them from the black scab death."

"I thought as much. I can't believe she went along with it, knowing full well that only poor Sorcha was cursed at the Nine Children stone circle. None of us were in any danger at all."

"Kyjyan priests, eh?" He tittered, trying and failing to lighten my mood. "Come on, I've tucked some of Tallack's ale away and have a nice bit of cold pork in my hut."

It was the best offer I'd had in four full seasons, but as we made for the entrance, Tallack called out to us.

"Hey! Where are you two going? Come and help us plan the journey to the sacred springs. We shall need the pair of you to travel with us."

My heart sank. Couldn't they do anything without either Ren or I being at the centre of all the turmoil? This trip was bound to end in tragedy. It was based on too many lies. One careless word and it would send Blydh's demon into a frenzy of spite and bile none of us would survive. I'd scarcely spent a night in my own bed and they were ordering me to travel again. Was this punishment for Paega's escape?

Renowden saw my defeated expression and turned to face the Chiefs. "Wouldn't you prefer us to stay and watch over the camp in your absence?"

Tallack grinned. "My mother and Treeve can do that. We'll need your navigation skills and Aunt Mel's medicines."

I could see Tallack's urgency and his reasoning. The faster Blydh was back to normal, the easier we'd all sleep. There seemed to be no way out of this command. With great reluctance, Ren and I shuffled through the warrior benches to the small table next to the fire and sat down. Slaves brought us ale and pies, stew and fresh bread but my appetite had vanished.

It didn't take long for the conversation to descend into nonsense. Tallack wanted to take is fine Phoenician vessel along the coast past Duro lands to dock within the bays belonging to the Belgae. His intention was to show this huge and powerful tribe that we too were a force with which to be reckoned. I couldn't see how intimidation would persuade them to allow us passage through their region, but then I'm only an old woman. What do I know about such things?

Even Blydh could see that it was not only the longest route to take, but that the Belgae would skin us alive for our presumption. It was typical of Tallack to think that his charm and bluster would win out. He pouted and sulked in his tall chair, refusing to add anything further to the debate.

Blydh was in favour of riding our swiftest horses directly through the Durotriges territory and killing all the homesteaders and raiding parties in our path. Endelyn talked him out of that one, explaining her fragile state and lack of fighting experience, plus the overwhelming advantage our enemies would have in terms of numbers.

As usual, it was Ren's voice of reason that saved us from an entire evening of folly. "There are a few boats at our tin mine on the northern shore. We should send word to Clemo at the settlement, get him to sail up and meet us. We can ride along the borderlands and leave our horses with the alchemists, while we go on to the mouth of the River Avon."

"I thought the sacred springs lay further inland?" Tallack interrupted.

"It does, Chief, but Endelyn's priestly friend told us that we would need to send tributes to the Belgae Chief in the first instance. All being well, we can negotiate terms with him. I suggest that we fly our banners on the boats and hope that we are well received by their scouts on the banks of the Avon." Ren said. He had turned fully around on his seat facing the top table. He held such respect that both the Head Hunters and the Sea Warriors all sat in silence listening to his plan.

"And if we don't get a favourable welcome?" Tallack said, straightening his back to sit taller in his lofty seat.

"Then we'd better learn how to dodge their arrows. The Belgae are supposed to be the best archers in all the lands."

Blydh's brow pinched together and he briefly closed his eyes. He was clearly in pain. "We can take shields, for what good they will do us. Are we better to show our strength or take a small party and hope they don't slaughter us on the riverbank?" He touched the swelling on his head, dislodging the dressings.

"Can't say one way or another. We'd be stupid to go without any protection at all, but too many warriors would look like an attack." Ren's patience with my nephews was astounding. This was obviously why he was so well liked. He took time to steer their thoughts while maintaining the illusion that they were in charge. If only I could hold my temper in the same way.

"We could use my black pennants of the priests." Endelyn chipped in. "A voyage of pilgrimage would not draw fire."

"Begging your pardon, priestess, but we have no way of knowing whether that would provoke them more. They are a proud and worshipful tribe, but their faith is not ours. They have their own rituals and practices. It could make matters far worse." Ren held her gaze with a confidence that comforted me. He would not let her lead my nephews into unnecessary danger. She buckled and dropped her stare to the table before her.

"White then?" I ventured. "Banners of peace would be a show of intent. Even if they are suspicious, it should keep them from aiming their arrows at us until we have a chance to speak with them." Each of our leaders looked about them for signs of dissent. No one spoke for nor against my suggestion.

"Fine. White it is." Tallack said. "We'll take four of my men and four of Blydh's." He turned briefly to Massen, one of his warriors. "Send out our fastest riders to make arrangements with Clemo on the northern shore." And then to me he said, "Aunt Mel, come and help me sort out the tributes and offerings." He jumped down from the top table platform, took hold of my arm and, before I could protest, marched me out of the Long Hut.

Breathless and struggling, I tried to keep up with his long strides. "Hold your horses, boy. You'll yank my arm off." I complained, but it did little to slow his progress.

"You must send Senara to keep watch at the River Sid crossing. She can arrange a delay if the Duro elders request a meeting with us. Don't let on to anyone about what we discussed. With Blydh so changeable at present, we can't afford to let him be distracted by his quest for vengeance. First and foremost, we have to get that demon out of him."

I understood his fears and his logic, although I'd have thought an opportunity to forge an alliance with our old enemies would take precedence. We hurried into the Chiefs' storage hut, lit fresh torches and asked the guards for assistance with uncovering the trove pit containing the most recent tributes and tin deliveries.

Our wealth was vastly diminished following the raid on our old compound. Tallack's half-sister knew exactly when to strike us and where to find our entire hoard. We'd be stretched for offerings for some time to come. What we did have, was mainly salvaged from the estuary at low tide after we had burned the Novantae flag ship, killing many of their warriors in agonising flames.

One oak chest was all it took to house the treasures in the pit. Tallack lifted the lid and examined the contents. There was a small quantity of gold and a few bronze daggers, two charred breast plates and what jewels and metals our prisoners were wearing at the time of capture. What remained of our copper and tin supplies was pathetic and wouldn't amount to a reasonable tribute to anyone, let alone the Chief of a massive tribe.

"What are we to do, Aunt Mel? This won't appease the Belgae. If anything, they'd consider this an insult and kill us on the spot."

He was right. What little wealth we had was spent on supplies to build the new compound and grain stores. Tributes paid to us for passage across our lands had dwindled to nothing. The Duros had spread such vile rumours about us, that few tribes were still willing to keep our trade agreements. Those who were loyal did not have the means to travel, relying on our boats to make deliveries to their lands instead. Short of raiding new territories, we were stuck.

"What about your mystical sword? That would be more than enough on its own."

Tallack's eyes widened at the suggestion. It was as if I'd offered his life in exchange for the Belgae's favour. "They are not having that under any circumstances. Come to think of it, perhaps I should leave it behind. If we are to throw ourselves on their mercy, it would be too tempting to those religious kyjyans."

"And if we have to fight?"

"Then I will use my old sword. It stood me in good stead before."

I looked at Tallack in the dim lighting of the store hut. The guards withdrew to a respectable distance, allowing me to speak candidly with the anguished Chief. I could see that his burdens were more than his young years were able to carry. His brow was wrinkled and his eyes watery. All I could think to do, was to give him all that I possessed.

Taking out my tin pouch from beneath my tunic, I slid the strapping from around my neck and handed it to Tallack. "Here, take this. I can spare a bronze knife or two from my kit, but not my biggest nor smallest." As I started walking towards the door, he stopped me.

"I can't take your knives, Aunt Mel. You're our only healer. You of all people need to hang on to those, but I bet my mother has a fair few jewels and trinkets tucked away."

"So would the wives of the elders. Get Cryda on side and let her persuade the women of the tribe to contribute to Chief Blydh's recovery."

Buoyed with renewed vigour, he raced from the hut to elicit his mother's help in raising funds. My task was clear. I had to keep the hope of making a deal with the Duro elders alive via Senara. I stood outside the storage hut in the darkness and scanned the island. There was not much light from the moon and there were few fires outside of shelters and huts. From what I could see, the trainees were warming themselves and cooking their meagre rations near to their shared tents. It was the only place I could think to look for Senara.

Leaving the clean boardwalks, I trudged closer all the time wondering if Kewri was with her. As their rosy faces loomed into view, I slowed my pace. Would Kewri decide to accompany Senara to the borderlands, or come with us to the sacred spring? I wasn't sure whether I had the authority to give him orders.

They both smiled at me when I reached the fireside. Other trainees moved aside, allowing me to step closer to the warming flames. They had three ducks and two rabbits between more than twelve young warriors. A quick glance about, informed me that they had no grain or flour for bread, nor any leaves or roots. It was certainly more than the larger families had outside the compound, but I was instantly humbled at the extent of their meal. Sometimes I forget how spoiled I am, being of Chieftain blood.

Despite my shame, there was no time to dwell on the pitiful conditions our trainees endured. I called to my friends and beckoned them away from the others to explain the situation. Senara immediately began checking her weapons and securing her bow and quiver about her body.

"There's no need to speed off right now." I chuckled. "The morning will do just as well." I turned to Kewri and there was a long and uncomfortable pause between us. In my heart, I knew he wanted to ride out with Senara. I also knew that he would feel obliged to follow and protect me. With no specific orders about him accompanying us from Tallack, I let Kewri make the decision alone.

"It's entirely up to you, lad. You've put yourself in danger on my behalf for long enough. Go with Senara if you wish, but know that you'd be a welcome addition among our party too." The moment I saw his shoulders sag with indecision, I turned away and walked into the darkness heading north. I heard them whispering behind me but I didn't stop. There was much to prepare and little time in which to gather all that was needed for the trip.

It was late before I managed to get myself to bed. Everything I needed to take was bundled and stowed ready to strap to my horse, including what little spare metal I had hidden. Kewri didn't return to his bunk on the other side of the hut and neither did Blydh. I took this to mean that Blydh's pain was manageable and that Kewri was spending his last night with Senara before she left for the borderlands come dawn.

In the morning, I ate a little salted pork and stale bread and let the fire burn out. Dragging my bundle down the boardwalk towards the pony enclosure, I was surprised to see Tallack's men already mounted and prepared to leave. At first, I thought I'd been tardy, but I couldn't see any signs that my nephews were ready for the off, neither was Endelyn. When I drew level with the gate to the horse pen, Kewri was leading his massive carthorse and my faithful old pony in my direction.

Seeing the dear giant with his horse didn't necessarily mean that he'd chosen to accompany us. "Senara?" I inquired, avoiding the obvious question.

"She left at sun up."

I tried to assess his mood, but his quiet demeanour made it hard at the best of times. Did he make the choice or did Senara? Either way, a selfish part of me was pleased that he was coming along. Behind us, I could see Tallack and his mother in a heated exchange. Cryda let her body sag in an exaggerated sigh, before lifting her jewels from her neck and ears. Clearly, his mission to collect offerings of metals, amber and polished stones was more difficult than anticipated.

I left my bundle on the dry planks of the boardwalk and walked across the wet grass to join them. From inside Tallack's hut, I could hear Treeve moaning and muttering to himself. Cryda took no notice of my presence at all, continuing her nagging conversation with her son.

"You've already taken all that the ladies in camp can spare, surely you can leave your poor mother one necklace?"

"Sorry, Mother. We'll need all we can find if we are to make this ritual work."

"But you'll leave us with nothing. What will happen if we have need for more food?"

"Then you'll have to get off your arse and forage or hunt, like everyone else. Treeve will lend a hand. He's pretty handy with a bow."

Hearing his name being mentioned, Treeve stuck his head between the door flaps, dragging Tallack's packed bundle with him. "I can lend a hand with what?"

"You won't let my mother and baby sister starve in our absence, will you?"

A single brow rose high on his forehead. His sneer was unhidden and pronounced. "You could always take her with you, Chief. I know how you dote on your family." The jibe was not missed by any of us. This ambitious young sailor believed he had as much power as our Meterns themselves. I shot him with my most insidious glare but it failed to make a mark. It concerned me that he was left to govern the tribe along with Cryda, and she was too exhausted from nursing her babe to care about matters. What would we be returning to under his rule?

Tallack cupped his hands in front of his mother and accepted her jewels and the offerings from the women in camp. From the sound of metal clanging against metal, I realised that more copper and bronze sat in the leather bag slung across his shoulder. He'd obviously tapped up the men for their contributions as well.

It was when I saw young Treeve retreating, that I remembered something. He took the quill necklace from the body of Kerensa before sinking her in the marshes. It was filled with her family treasure; flakes of pure gold.

I was about to raise the issue of Treeve's offering, when Blydh appeared in the doorway to the Long Hut and bellowed at the top of his voice. "You are the traitorous scum who let Paega escape and went after him." I turned to see him staring at Kewri with the horses. "Well, man? Where is the kyjyan weasel?"

CHAPTER FOURTEEN

My hope of matters surrounding Paega's escape fading into the background were dashed. Blydh was no longer the frightened little boy we'd seen the night before. The demon was in full control again and he was spitting with rage. Even at distance, I could see his reddened cheeks and panting chest, his tightened fists and aggressive posture. Surely, he wouldn't be so dumb as to pick a fight with our resident giant?

Tallack saw the bile rising in his brother and ran to simmer the situation down. It took me longer, but I too moved in to soothe his bitter temper. Therein lay my mistake. As soon as the demon clapped eyes on me, the venomous monster altered course and spat in my direction.

"It's all your fault. You're in league with the Duros. You sent your man to set Paega free on purpose so that he could join forces with Brea and lead another attack." He stumbled forward and adjusted the helmet as it slipped down over his eyes. When he pushed the bronze helm higher, I saw him wince. It was enough of a distraction for me to wave Kewri away. The giant took my cue, placing himself between our two horses and leading them to the northern gates. If he found out that I'd sanctioned an approach to forge a lasting peace with the Duros, he'd drive a knife through my heart there and then.

I was left standing with Tallack and Blydh. There was nothing I could say to Blydh when the dark spirit was in control. To him, I was the enemy. Stepping backwards, I let Tallack lean in and hold his brother by the shoulders. He spoke softly and calmly until Blydh had simmered back down, but it was clear to me that we could not have Kewri trigger such outbursts while we were on the trails. Blydh was simply too volatile.

It grieved me to leave the giant behind. I'd grown accustomed to his steady pace, his quiet nature and his comforting protection. I knew that Ren and Tallack would not let me come to harm but their time was stretched enough without having to watch over an old woman as well.

Our numbers were reduced to just thirteen, counting me. Endelyn rode at the front of the line next to Blydh. Tallack was a short way behind them. Ren and I were closer to the warriors at the back, with an additional horse trailing behind us loaded with supplies.

Our peaceful white banners were tied about each of our arms, plus suspended from a pole on the spare pony, not that they were needed on our own lands but their presence might just save our lives on the banks of the River Avon.

I must say, we did not look like a peaceable group of travellers. Every warrior was heavily armed with spears and shields, long daggers and bows. If Tallack had left Blydh to his own devices, his horse would have been laden with the rotting heads from his last raid into Duro territories. As it was, none of the ponies could bear the extra weight. We had no time to lose and a long ride ahead.

Our route was a well-trodden one, scattered with ruined homesteads and abandoned moorland shelters. These were the borderland farms of those who'd been driven away by the constant Duro raids. As tragic as these remains were, they served to provide us with shelter along our journey. We even managed to barter with other travellers, providing us with some fresh fish for our first night out on the starry moors.

Blydh was unnervingly quiet in the evening. Endelyn entertained us all with stories from the rituals at the stone circles and the peculiar tales she'd heard from those journeying to engage her services. Tallack asked her if she knew anything about the Belgae and their religious practices, but she had not visited their region during her time with the Priest Sect. The odd snippet of information came from traders who claimed that the Belgae were a mean spirited and violent tribe and best avoided. That was not encouraging news for any of us.

It was after we'd eaten the trout and supped a little ale that Blydh began referring to Endelyn as Kerensa again. I couldn't tell if this was due to over consumption of beer, his poor sight, or a knock to his memory. Whatever the reason, it made Tallack and the warriors uneasy to see their Chief so confused. His manner was so gruff and obstinate, Endelyn chose to sleep next to me for safety. Despite all her bravado, she was just as frightened of his temper as me.

Come morning, the mist was thick. With dampened clothes and dripping hair, I set about the chores and began packing our things away. Endelyn still lay under her furs at the narrowest end of the shelter, warm and dry. Tallack loomed towards me fixing the belt around his tunic and leggings and securing his weapons ready for the ride.

Counting visible heads, I noticed we were short by two. I said nothing for a while, assuming that both would reappear when they had completed their ablutions but as time passed, neither Ren nor Blydh returned. Casting a glance about, I saw only one horse missing, the black stallion belonging to my nephew.

"Where has Blydh gone?" I barked at Tallack, suddenly fearful.

"He's ridden on ahead."

"And you didn't stop him?" It came out of me as a shriek of panic. Tallack just rolled his eyes at me in response. No one, not even his brother, could prevent Blydh from leaving us. The question remained, would he wait for us further along the track, or disappear altogether? More importantly, would he have one of his episodes and lay a trap for us thinking that we were the enemy?

I could tell that Tallack was pondering on a similar line of thought. Every muffled sound coming from the warriors, or from Endelyn as she stirred, startled him until eventually he rested his hand on the hilt of his blade in readiness. I scooped globs of porridge into bowls and handed them to the men. They were less perturbed by Blydh's actions, but then they had no reason to doubt him. Only Tallack, Ren, the priestess, and I knew about his true affliction.

After our meal, we kicked earth onto the fire and packed the last of our things onto the horses. The fog encircled us, unsettling the ponies and making it hard to fathom directions. Just as I was about to struggle onto my old pony, a dark shape blocked the white glow of the low sun ahead of us. Tallack drew his sword a short way out of its scabbard, expecting trouble.

I froze to the spot, squinting into the haze. As the figure of a man grew larger, I could just make out the limp bodies of dead rabbits swinging on either side.

Tallack blew out his cheeks in relief, pushing home his blade. "Can't you learn to whistle or something?"

Ren chuckled. "Why's that chief? Give you a fright, did I?" The men jostled together before exchanging light-hearted thumps to the upper arms. We were all together again, barring Blydh. Ren strapped the meat to the spare horse and saddled up next to me. I must say, he never fails to think ahead. We were aiming for the windswept coast on the northern shore to wait for the boats to arrive. We had no idea how long that would take, considering the alchemists' reluctance to comply with our Chiefs' orders in the past. Our stay could well be for days and a few rabbits would set us up for the night.

Throughout the day, we saw a surprising number of animals, many of which could have fed us for a whole moon, but we had no time to stay and hunt. Some of those creatures we passed were deer. With every head flick and ear twitch, I was reminded of my white hart and the sight of his bloodied lolling tongue. My nephews and the priestess may think that they were appeasing the gods by sacrificing him, I thought the opposite. The more I pondered on the subject, the more convinced I became that we had angered Cernonnus. If the stag truly was the vessel for the God of Death and the Wild Forest, then his life should have been preserved and respected. All we can do now is wait and hope that he will not exact his vengeance upon us.

Blydh was waiting at the end of the long ride to the northern shore. We saw the fire smoke from some distance and altered our course to intercept him. As we rode closer, I saw that he was forcing open shellfish with his blade and eating them raw. Tallack and I glanced at each other but said nothing.

Ren jumped down from his horse and set to work preparing the rabbits to roast. A couple of Blydh's warriors were kind enough to see to my pony, leaving me to help set up camp. Blydh had chosen a sheltered spot at the top of the beach and out of the biting wind. Even after Ren had staked the meat over the embers to cook, Blydh continued to chew on the salty raw cockles and mussels.

One look at his sinister glower was enough to know which personality was in charge of his body. I withdrew and took my blades in search of dry grasses for my bedding. When I got back to the fireside, Blydh was belching and complaining of a gut ache. It was hardly a surprise.

Before he could ask, I took what little dried mallow leaves I had from the edge of the forest back home and crushed them into a cup of water. A hot knife soon brought the water to the boil, turning the liquid green and murky. While the tea steeped, I stomped over to our ailing Chief and thrust it under his nose.

"What is it?" Blydh growled.

"It'll help or it won't. Your choice." I sighed, bending down to push the cup into the sand by his side.

"Are you and Brea trying to poison me, like she did my father?"

"If I was trying to kill you, nephew, I would have let you die when your head was caved in." I snapped. It had been a long day and my patience had worn thin. Every muscle in my back and shoulders ached from the ride and my arse was sore from the rough trails. We were all exhausted and had little effort for idle chatter. Tallack urged the men to curb their appetite for ale. Supplies were limited and there was no chance of trading for more.

Ren and the warriors built three shelters, one of which was reserved for Endelyn and myself, although I did wonder whether I'd end up sleeping alone. Blydh was sober and grumpy, but showed no inclination towards violence. He let my concoction get cold, muttering and farting, belching and rubbing his belly before giving in and drinking my mallow tea. I got under my furs and went to sleep, long before it had a chance to ease his suffering.

Come morning, the clouds cleared and the wind died down to a mild breeze. It was beginning to look like spring had finally arrived. The sun glinted from the rippling waves and gulls tucked in their wings and bombed the shoals of mackerel from a great height. I felt refreshed for once and keen to continue our journey. The only snag in that plan was that Clemo and the alchemists failed to show. We spent the day foraging and gathering, preparing food and collecting wood for the evening fire.

Endelyn was quite delightful company, cutting seaweed, harvesting cockles and collecting live crabs for the pot. Her chatter and lively stories were a welcome change from the one-word responses I'd grown used to with Kewri. It was almost like having my Jago back with me, although his conversations were usually tales about his homeland. How long would it be before my grief would leave me alone?

Our second night on the beach was filled with laughter and good cheer. Tallack sang a few of his bawdier tunes while one of his men played a pipe. Blydh seemed to be vastly improved. At one point during the course of the evening, I thought I saw him smile. This is what a decent night's sleep and a full day of rest can do for you. Endelyn must have decided the same thing as she sat close to the Chiefs and regaled them with a new selection of entertaining stories.

By the time the moon was high and the night air cold, I retreated to my furs. To my surprise, Endelyn joined me in our shelter, tucking my bedding around my back and shoulders as though I was her kin. I would have bet my whole tin pouch that she would spend the night with

Blydh. At the time, I thought I had misjudged the woman. Perhaps she genuinely cared for both my nephews. Maybe her sights were not on the Ruvane chair after all.

Come morning, I rose to find Renowden gazing into the horizon. Curious as to what he'd spotted, I wandered down the shoreline to meet him. "Can you see the boats?" I narrowed my eyes and strained my vision, but saw nothing except water and seagulls.

"Nope, but they'll be here by mid-afternoon." He smiled down at me.

"How can you tell?"

"Wind's changed direction. Should blow them here in no time at all."

I didn't argue with him. Ren had spent longer at sea than anyone in our tribe. He knew every stretch of coastline better than his own face and could read the weather a day before it arrived. "Gods willing." I muttered. It was more of a plea than a statement. We were at their mercy now, yet needed their protection more than ever.

Ren was spot on in his prediction. The Alchemists took their time sailing to shore, their inexperience with boats showing with every wave slap and near capsize. They'd brought two small boats, each with rough sails and oars but large enough to accommodate our party.

Clemo clutched the tiller in the lead boat, while a younger man steered the other. I recognised him at once. It was Kerensa's brother, Hellyer. Neither Tallack nor I could've predicted that two of Kerensa's kinfolk would deliver the vessels. I scurried back towards the fire to warn Tallack but his sight was far better than mine.

He already knew the potential for Blydh to create problems. "We can't tell them that she's dead. They will want the details and to make offerings. They could insist on going straight to Kenver and telling him the news." Tallack growled in a low voice. I knew what he had to say, but wondered if it was a sensible lie to tell.

Jumping to his feet, Tallack approached his brother. He leaned low and whispered into his ear.

"Remember our little talk about Kerensa. Should her uncle or brother ask, she is travelling back to the Bentewyn mines over land. Got it?"

Blydh just glared up at him. He made no sign that he understood the situation or whether he would go along with the ruse. My heart quickened as the boats were hauled up onto the beach and the men jumped out to greet everyone. Young Hellyer seemed particularly pleased to see me. After he'd formally grasped the forearms of both Tallack and Blydh, he approached me with a beaming smile.

"So good to see you again, Fur Benyn." He said, as though it had been a number of cycles since we last saw one another and not half a season. I guessed that his effusive greeting stemmed from the medicines I'd given to his family during the winter sickness at the Bentewyn mines. I also assumed that he was unaware of the fate of his sister or the manner of our meeting would have taken a turn for the worse.

"We set off as soon as we got news from the messenger about your trip." He turned back towards the boats where Tallack's men were unloading a wooden crate of tin ingots from the northern mine. "It was all that could be spared, but I imagine it's more metal than the Belgae have seen in a while."

Blydh and Tallack inspected the haul and extended their thanks to the Alchemists. The lull in conversation worried me. I felt compelled to steer the boy away from family matters for the sake of safety.

"Have you been at the northern mine for long?"

He smiled at me with pride. "Father sent me to learn from the men there shortly after you left us in the winter. He expects me to take over by mid-summer to prepare me for when I lead the clan." It seemed odd to me that someone so young and inexperienced should lead such a complex operation as the mining camps.

After all my time in this world, I still had not learnt how they managed to turn rock into tin. It was a guarded secret passed down from father to son and never outside their clan. It gave them a level of power that unsettled our Chieftains through the ages. Keeping them agreeable required patience and fortitude, more than either of our current Chiefs possessed.

"And I'm sure you'll do a fine job. You'll make your father proud."

Without prior warning or plan, Ren, Endelyn and Tallack occupied our guests with light-hearted chatter and good food until the daylight ducked behind the cliffs and threw us into darkness. That was when the ale flowed a little too generously. Clemo and the Alchemist warriors had brought their own beer to supplement ours and most had drunk to excess.

When we'd eaten our fill of day-old roasted rabbit and fresh caught fish, Hellyer relaxed and leaned back in the sand. "I think I would like to come with you on your journey to the sacred springs. It would give us all a chance to get to know one another better, before I become the leader of the Alchemists. What say you, Fur Benyn?"

CHAPTER FIFTEEN

Getting through one evening without speaking about Kerensa was challenging enough. The thought of extending the problem indefinitely, made me choke. Hellyer had caught me off guard. I was left sitting there with my mouth wide open and no answer for him.

Tallack jumped in to save me. "I'd feel easier knowing that you were back at the northern mine keeping your eye on things. After all the troubles we've had recently, I wouldn't put it past the mountain folk to paddle across from Kembra to invade and take control."

Clemo piped up. "Don't worry about that, Chief. My boy has it all under control until I get back there. The place is locked down tighter than a duck's arse. Taught him everything I know. It'll be fine while you're away."

Tallack forced a smile onto his face. We had no way of ditching this lad no matter what obstacles were laid down before him. Everything was settled before we had a chance to think of an escape. Come morning, the treasure trove and supplies were loaded back onto the boats, leaving Clemo and his men watching over the horses in camp.

Tallack took control over who and what was stowed in each boat, ensuring even distribution of weight and making sure that Blydh and Hellyer were separated for the journey. I'm ashamed to admit that I was relieved when Tallack insisted that I sailed with him, alongside his men and the young Alchemist. Blydh's constant swings in mood kept me on my mettle leaving no room for rest.

Ren took the tiller of Blydh's boat and led the way along the coast towards the mouth of the River Avon. Both vessels were low in the chilly water, making us vulnerable to the waves. I was tasked with bailing out as much as I could from the hull, but as soon as I scooped the brine over the side, more found its way on board. Endelyn was doing the same in the boat ahead of us, with the men all taking it in turns to row between the choppy waves.

When we were far enough away from the coast to defy the pull of the tide, Tallack hoisted the sail and kept his eye on the prevailing winds. Although it was unlikely that we'd be spotted by the Duros while we sailed along their stretch of the coastline, landing at the mouth of the Avon was fraught with danger. The river marked the boundary between the Duros and the Belgae. Ren had warned us before we set off, that the tidal surge and currents were strong.

If we were pushed off course and close to the Duros' shore, it was likely that we'd find ourselves showered in flaming arrows. Mind you, we couldn't rely on our white banners protecting us from the same treatment from the Belgae. All in all, we had too few allies and too many enemies surrounding our land. It made me even more determined to forge a lasting peace with our neighbours.

The men were in good spirits for the first part of our voyage, keen to take their turn at the oars to hasten the journey along. When they tired, they let the wind carry us in a north easterly direction towards the gaping estuary that funnelled into the vast River Severn. The further into the Severn Estuary we sailed, the clearer the southern coastline of Kembra became. We had no quarrel with the

Silures, and often traded with them, but their neighbouring mountain tribes were a slippery bunch.

By late afternoon, it was obvious to all that we would never make it to the Belgae lands beyond the mouth of the Avon before nightfall. Ren and Tallack steered our vessels until we were close enough to shout between boats.

The Chiefs had a decision to make. Would they insist on pulling in for the night, risking attack from our arch enemies or force us to push on through the darkness? I hoped that the gods would guide them into making the right choice. Blydh looked to be in pain once again. He squinted at his brother as Tallack explained our predicament.

Blydh rubbed at his eyes with a stiff knuckle. “We should land on the Duros’ side and enter the mouth of the River Avon in the morning.”

Tallack drew in breath and stole a glance at Ren. “The Duros may well have seen our sails. I don’t think that’s a good idea, Brother.” The swell of the waves parted us for a few moments, their boat soaring high while we plunged into a dip. My stomach went with it, making me swallow back bile. When we were almost level, the men held the oars out until they could grasp the shafts and pull the vessels together as one.

“If you’d already made your mind up, why bother asking me? I’m only the kyjyan Chief. What right do I have to give orders?” We could all see that Blydh was spoiling for a fight. It needed someone liked by all to break the deadlock. I shot a pleading look in Ren’s direction, hoping that he’d infer my meaning. It seemed to do the trick.

“Begging your pardons, Chiefs, but landing on either tribes’ land would be too high risk. If it were my decision to make, I'd weigh anchor in the Severn Estuary and set up a watch over night. All being well, we could row towards the Avon at sun up and hope for a favourable welcome."

The twins locked stares, neither of them big enough to admit that Ren's idea was the only solution. I was wind whipped, soaked through and frozen to my marrow, but better that than shot through with Duro bolts. The light was fading fast and the men grew tired of holding the boats together.

Only Tallack seemed to comprehend the gravity of the situation. "What say you, Brother? It makes sense to me."

Blydh glowered and looked away, hunkering back down in his furs. "Do what you want."

The moment Tallack nodded at the men, they released the oars and let Ren lead us further into the Severn Estuary. The currents were strong, eddying in great swirls and carrying us too far inland. The men dug in the oars and pulled hard, driving us against the tide sweeping us up the wrong river.

In the last of the daylight, the exhausted men repeated the procedure with the oars, until both vessels could be tethered together. Ren extended his rope length with ours, threaded one end through the hole in the flat stone and threw it overboard. The thick cable uncoiled rapidly, disappearing into the murky depths until there was no more to unwind. Snapping taut against the side of the boat, the rope stayed perfectly vertical. After a few moments, it was obvious that we were still moving towards land.

"Either the anchor isn't heavy enough or the rope is too short." Tallack said.

"That was my fear." Ren muttered, but it was loud enough for us all to hear. "I'd heard that these waters were deep, treacherous too."

His news was unsettling. Ren was our most experienced sailor. If he was concerned for our safety then we really had something to worry about. Even as he spoke, our boats were buffeted by the powerful surge of the spring tides.

Tallack thought for a moment, chewing a hang nail on his thumb. Without giving Blydh the chance to voice an objection, he said, "We should make for the mouth of the Avon and hope we remain unseen."

I couldn't understand what the problem was until we reeled in the anchor stone, unhitched the boats, and rowed towards the opening between two expanses of marshy grassland. Compared to the size of the Severn Estuary, the Avon was surprisingly narrow.

Now I understood Ren's reluctance to enter the river mouth. Tribes from both sides had cleared the shrubs and trees. If any scouts were about, we had no place to hide. Even if Ren and Tallack could keep both boats in the central current, we were close enough to either bank for the eagled eyed archers.

I trembled in the stern of the lead boat with my furs pulled up to my chest. Neither Chief needed to tell us to keep quiet. The men sculled in silence, letting the tide take the bulk of the strain. Shifting onto my right hip, I peered over the side of the boat at the western shore. In the gloom, the rotted stumps of trees were black against the pale clay silt. Each one took on the ghostly shape of a Duro archer, quickening my heart and fuelling my fears.

We cleared the first bend without any trouble. It gave us hope that we'd not been spotted on our way along the coast. The second meander was some way off and obscured. In this comparatively calm stretch of water, Tallack decided to drop the anchor testing the depth in search of a raised sand bank. This time, the stone hit the bottom, stretching the line out behind us and slowing our movement up the river. Ren navigated the other boat alongside, readying the ropes to tie off.

"Rest while you can, lads." Ren said in a hushed voice. "When the tide's fully in, the anchor will be useless."

I stared at him, my mouth gaping open. "But we'll drift…" I gasped.

He nodded. "You're right, we will. That's why they need to rest. We'll have to row against the currents to keep our position."

"What, all night?"

He gave me a look that said, *what else do you suggest?* But he said nothing. We had rowed directly between two enemy tribes and all for the man in the helm, snoring at the front of the other boat. His lack of regard for our safety was puzzling. I concluded that the evil spirit from the Underworld must still have control over my nephew since I couldn't bear the thought of his indifference. This was not the boy I'd spent many summers with, stitching his injuries and patching grazes as he learnt his clan's ways. He was always the quieter of the twins, but never unjust.

As much as I wanted to help, my strength was no match for the force of the currents and eddies in the river. Keeping us between the tribal territories would require all our men's efforts. Endelyn and I kept busy handing out salted pork and stale bread, water bladders and a few shelled hazelnuts we'd brought with us. Every sound seemed to magnify across the surface of the water, putting an end to any conversation.

When the tide was at its highest and shifted directions, the anchor rope sat fully upright in the water and we started to drift back out towards the Severn Estuary. When the rowing began in earnest, the clouds above us cleared to reveal the moon. Its wide glow picked us out as clearly as a pimple on a bride's face. We were completely exposed.

Endelyn muttered quiet oaths and incantations to her gods, promising extravagant sacrifices when we docked in payment for their protection. I had little faith that she'd secure their help. She had killed my white stag, my vessel of Cernonnus. Why would our gods favour us now?

When the moon was high and the men exhausted, a strong eddy carried us closer to the western shore. Another black shadow caught my eye, sending a flush of panic through my chest and neck. Inwardly, I scolded myself, remembering the rotted tree stumps from the cleared land. As I glanced back to confirm my thoughts, the shadow moved. Alerted to the possibility of discovery, I tapped Tallack's leg and pointed to the riverbank.

In the light of the moon, more shadows lurked, each of them taking the form of our enemies. "Brea's men?" I whispered to my nephew.

"Unlikely this far north. Probably borderland patrols." Tallack raised the alarm, urging all who could to grab the oars and scull us out of range. Their archers would need the muscles of a bear and the sight of an owl to hit us, if we could just paddle out of the main channel. Despite their aching arms and backs, our warriors heaved us from the force of the currents until we were closer to the eastern banks.

A few Duro arrows whistled through the air and plopped into the water, missing us by some distance. We were safe from attack and not far from dawn, when the sun would reveal our white banners.

All we needed was a little luck to see us through the rest of the night. With every one of our eyes trained on the western shore, none of us noticed the small flicker of orange light on the eastern bank. When that tiny flame grew to a blaze that hopped from torch to torch behind us, Endelyn let out a little gasp. One by one, we turned to see what she had spotted.

There were more warriors than we could count along the river holding their torches high overhead. Between them, Belgae archers took aim and waited for their Chief's order to loose.

How could we have been so naive? If the situation was reversed and they had taken a cruise past our lands, one or more of our scouts would have tracked their movements, while others sent word to our compound. This was a disputed territory, attracting a heavy guard in any season.

Our warriors' instincts were to reverse our direction and scull as fast as they could, but there was no way for us to escape their archers' range in time. Tallack stood up in the boat, rocking it from side to side. He steadied himself with a hand against my shoulder and held our white flag aloft for the Belgae to see. "We come under the banners of peace." He shouted towards the centre of the row of painted men.

From what I could see in the torchlight, their faces were daubed in red clay across their foreheads. Their beards were long and plaited. Most of their belts glinted with the sharp metal of blades and axes. This was a rich and battle-ready tribe, despite their reputation for their religious practices. We were left in no doubt as to their intentions towards us.

In the middle of the warrior line, was a wooden jetty protruding a short way into the water. One young man stood at the dock, holding an upright spear. It had long braids of coloured feathers and bones dangling from the tip that matched more suspended around his neck. At first, I thought him to be the Chieftain but I recalled Endelyn stories and this warrior was too young to fit the description.

When no response came from the river banks, Tallack tried again. "We are Dumnonii, travelled all this way to request an audience with the Chief of the Belgae. As you see, we are few in number and trust that you will honour the terms of peace under our flag."

"And you chose the cover of darkness to make your approach?" It was the feathered man who spoke. "That would hardly suggest a peaceful mission."

"We intended to wait until daylight to enter the river mouth, but the currents were too strong for us." Tallack wobbled in the boat, before planting his feet more firmly in the narrow hull. "We seek permission to perform a healing ritual at your sacred springs on behalf of one of our people."

I wrinkled my nose in confusion as to why he'd referred to his own brother as just, *one of our people*. It was a little while afterwards when I understood his canny words. If the Belgae knew that they could capture and kill two Dumnonii Chiefs this very night, our lands would be over run and our tribe taken as slaves before the moon was full. Our tin mines were the envy of the whole land and even more so with those across the ocean. Caution was the first lesson Tallack learned in negotiating trade deals, and half-truths formed part of his arsenal.

Before the young warrior could respond, he was pushed aside by an older, thinner man with hair as white as mine.

He wore no ritual garb nor weapons, but carried himself with all the dignity of a wily leader.

He strode out along the jetty and allowed his eyes to adjust to the darkness. "If you are who you say, you will have brought something from your land to favour us."

This was not a statement; it was a command. He wanted to see how much tin we had to give in tribute. Tallack looked at me and then at Ren. If the Belgae Chief saw the whole amount, he would give the order to slaughter us all and take the entire trove. Tallack crouched low and uncovered a single bar of tin, moulded to perfection as only our Alchemists could do.

"This is our finest grade of metal. You won't find anything like it anywhere else. We offer you this and four more just like it, in the hope that you will grant us passage through your lands and an opportunity to converse with the gods at your sacred springs. This was a colossal gift to bestow upon any tribe, far exceeding any we'd given before. The number of man hours needed to dig, process and refine a similar quantity again was incalculable.

We bobbed about in the fast flow of the river, with the men doing their best to maintain our position. We'd thrown ourselves on the Belgae's mercy, without a backup plan if things turned nasty.

The Chief walked closer to us along the jetty, the light of the torches behind him casting long shadows in his path. I could no longer see the man's expression. There was no way of guessing whether he liked what he saw or wanted a closer view of our impending doom.

CHAPTER SIXTEEN

The leader of the Belgae peered into our boats, leaning from side to side as though he was looking for something specific. At length, he gestured for his men to step forward onto the pontoon.

He grunted and turned away. "Throw your lines in and tie off. We'll speak on dry ground."

Tallack saw this as a good sign, sitting down with his tin bars and packing them back into the travel bags. I was not so sure. It all seemed a little too simple that he would consent to our request so easily, especially after all we'd heard about him.

Their men took charge of our vessels and the tin, which gave me an uneasy feeling. As they tied the ropes to the jetty and helped me ashore, I heard my nephew instructing the men to stay with the boats. There were so many Belgae that they would be useless in protecting us. We had to rely on the honour of their Chief to respect the white banners.

I pulled the pale cloth higher up my arm, making sure that it was clearly visible to all and then clung to Endelyn while we navigated the rough terrain of the riverbank. Tallack and Blydh led the way, with us ladies in the centre and Ren and Hellyer bringing up the rear. Their warriors held torches high, marching in single file either side of us. The closer we came to their settlement, the more I saw evidence of their deeply religious ways.

This was a tribe who not only had barrows and burials along a nearby tributary, but could boast about having the largest of all sacred sites, Stonehenge on its borders, in addition to the famed hot springs. Theirs was a massive region stretching in a dog-leg shape from the Severn estuary to the south coast.

They protected their boundaries as well, if not more fiercely than we did ours. Carved wooden icons of vicious creatures stood either side of their compound gates, with the skulls of their enemies suspended along a cross beam. Some still had fragments of flesh attached, as if their owners were clinging on to them.

My first impression of the tribe's folk was that they were suffering from an infestation of lice. Most of them had close cropped hair, shaved above the ears and up the back of their heads. It left them with just a tuft on top, even for their women. As we walked into the centre of the camp, I realise that this was their preferred style. Only the leader had long hair, woven into a thin white braid down his back.

Tallack and Blydh veered off towards the largest dwelling, expecting the old man to welcome them as his equal in status. When he continued walking, they had to scurry to catch up with him.

We stood outside a sturdy wooden structure with a solid door on thick rope hinges, where his men searched and stripped us of tin pouches, bags, and weapons. Tallack turned to speak, but before he could get out his words, the warriors pushed us inside.

Before the door was fully closed, Tallack cried out. "Please, Chief. My brother needs medicine. At least leave us the tonics."

The oak panel fit snugly into the doorway and I heard them wedge it closed with an angled post. There was no way out. Blydh slumped to the floor with Endelyn rushing to fuss over him. Ren and Hellyer checked every section of the shelter and thatch for weak points, but found nothing to help us. A pail of water sat on the rushes in the centre, alongside another empty one. This was the extent of the Belgae hospitality.

Wrapping my cloak about me for warmth, I sat with my back to the wooden walls and let my eyes grow used to the darkness. It was almost easier to distinguish our people from their smells rather than their shadowy shape. Tallack and Endelyn were both fragrant and clean, Blydh wore the two-day sweat from constant pain and fretting, while Ren and Hellyer smelled of the sea.

The men paced about the small space, complaining, plotting, making guesses as to what the Belgae might do with us, and filling the shelter with more bad odours. When light seeped between cracks in the door, we knew that dawn was well underway.

I could hear warriors outside as they changed shifts in guarding us. They were not taking any chances. No doubt our men left at the boats were also heavily watched too. I shuddered to think how well our tribe would fare in the instance that Treeve and the twin's mother were left to run things on a permanent basis. What if the Belgae reneged on the law of the land over our peaceable white banners?

Long after the cock crow, the door opened. The Chief stood there wearing a heavy scowl. Tallack rushed forward to speak with him but was dismissed with a flick of a hand. "Not you." He grumbled. "I've heard all about the reckless twins of the Dumnonii."

My heart fluttered in my chest. After all the care taken to choose vague words at our introduction, the wily old goat knew precisely with whom he was dealing. For a few moments, my hope failed me.

Before Tallack could protest, Endelyn rose to her feet and bowed her head to the Chief. "Fur Manow, thank you for receiving us. Long have I wished to witness your ceremonies and rituals. The rumours of their magnificence I'm sure are not exaggerated."

I held my breath, wondering if he'd be swayed by her gushing praise.

One brow flickered up, dragging the corners of his sour smile higher. "I'm pleased to see that at least one of your party has good manners. You may call me, Chief Rawley." He gestured for her to walk outside from the hut. "Just you. I don't care to hear what the others have to say."

Endelyn skipped after him, tucking her hand under his elbow. "Chief Rawley, please would you consider hearing our own Fur Benyn? She understands the high politics of tribal leaders in ways that a simple girl like me cannot." She gave him her best doe eyes until he agreed to her request. In no time at all, I too was ushered from the dark and damp of the shelter to follow the priestess and her new friend.

I was glad of the fresh air but keeping pace with them was hard going on my aching bones. We were followed by the outspoken warrior adorned with feathers from the riverbank. He strode alongside me, glaring the whole time. Their tribal compound was not so very different to ours, with tributaries snaking under the palisade walls, women bashing their laundry on rocks and the menfolk busy preserving and storing foods.

The only difference I could discern was the abundance of carvings and small offering posts to the gods. I recognised a few of the symbols but not many. This is a tribe who rely on priests for all their decisions; when to hunt, when to perform binding ceremonies, and when and where to inter their dead. As we walked out of the gates and along the River Trym, I could see the barrows in the distance. Their smooth slopes and flat tops were unmistakable.

I started to wonder why Chief Rawley led us along this path, until I saw the raised structures. Each of the wooden erections in the long row supported the rotting carcasses of their dead. The rooks and crows were not in the least bit disturbed by our presence as they scavenged and squabbled over the tenderest parts of meat. By the time we reached the end of the excarnation platforms, the bones were stripped clean.

At first, I thought that old Rawley was deliberately showing us how they dealt with intruders, but I saw the care with which the skeletons were handled by the women folk. Closer to the barrows, the bones were washed, dried, and carried in grass-filled baskets into the barrows beyond. Death was a laborious process indeed. This was not supposed to frighten us, but to illustrate the seriousness with which they took their religious practices.

Endelyn spoke quietly to Rawley ahead. I heard little of their discussion, but I supposed that she was buttering him up with regard to our mission. I decided to try and make friends with the young warrior. "That's a fine chest piece you're wearing." I pointed to the necklace of feathers and bones. "Does it symbolise something in particular?"

He turned his face towards me with a sneer. "What's it to you, crone? You Dumnonii care nothing for the gods. I saw your disgraceful behaviour at the last midsummer gathering at Stonehenge."

My mind whirled back to the time he mentioned. Our family had made a spectacle of themselves, it was true, but for good reason. I considered telling him about my niece and her treacherous plan to take over our lands, breaching all the rules of entering the sacred space. From his expression, I didn't think he'd be receptive to my excuses. "It was an unfortunate event, I agree, but I am genuinely interested in your beliefs and practices. Won't you tell me and make an old woman happy?"

He returned his gaze to the path ahead. When we'd walked in silence for some time and I'd just about given up on him, he said; "They are the finger bones of my ancestors. My father gave it to me when I became a warrior, and his finger bone will be added upon his death. We carry them with us into battle, we carry them with us to hunt and we carry them with us home. I am the keeper of their spirits."

I recalled something similar happening with the leader of our Priest Sect when the twin's father died. He was also keen to retain a bone from his thumb. Perhaps this practice was spreading across all the lands. I wondered whether it was some custom from across the sea, but I thought it prudent not to ask. "You do them great honour. I'm sure you are more than worthy of the task." I looked across at the sullen young man. He didn't smile, but I thought he'd started to look a little less severe. Perhaps I was making headway after all.

At the end of the path, we reached the entrance to the long barrow. I'd seen barrows before of course, but they were usually only open for special occasions, such as the interment of a Chieftain. Here, women came and went as though it was part of their daily routine. I watched Endelyn remove a copper clasp from her cloak and lay it down on a flat altar stone at the entrance. She bowed her head and muttered a few indistinct words.

I moved closer, trying to hear. If I was to repeat this ritual, I needed guidance. Offending these people was not an option. When Endelyn had completed her offering, they all looked at me. Plucking a tin clip from my hair, I laid it down next to the other offerings, and struggled to my knees. There were a couple of reasons for my decision to do this.

My knees crunched and clicked, my balance almost failed me and I exaggerated the pain it gave me, screwing up my face into a grimace. I could see from the corner of my eyes; this lavish display of respect was well received. Old Rawley looked dumbfounded. While I was nose to nose with flowers, bowls of grain, carved wooden animals and our metal, I intoned a complete load of made up kawgh under my breath. To anyone watching, I was as devout and humble as any of the Belgae.

Even when my knees felt as though they were crumbling beneath me, I waited there for far longer than was necessary. Endelyn came to my aid when I did finally look at her, hoisting me up to stand among them.

Rawley narrowed his eyes. "What name did the gods give you?"

I wanted to remind him that no god can bestow names on the living. That is the right of our parents alone, but I played along nicely. "I am Meliora, if it pleases you, Chief."

Endelyn chipped in; "She is known to us all as Fur Benyn, wisest of all the elders, best healer in the land and great aunt to the Chieftains of the Dumnonii."

When she boasts about me like that, I feel very small indeed. I never asked to be called a wise woman. Most of the time I am barely either. The young warrior had a better description of me - crone. If I'd been truly wise, Blydh would not be possessed by a wicked Underworld demon and we would not be begging this Chief for his favour.

"Is that so?" Rawley smirked. "Wisest of all the elders? Hmm." He flicked off his shoes at the entrance to the barrow and stepped inside. Endelyn and I looked at each other, waiting for further instruction. Rawley called out. "Paxton, bring them within."

We copied their leader and removed our footwear, stepping lightly on the rushes inside. The air was much cooler in this low cave-like structure; the atmosphere sombre and musty. From the wide entrance, we wandered around a stone plinth and into the main chamber. It was not set out as I'd expected.

At other sites such as this, bones of the ancestors were sorted into various piles, skulls in one chamber, long bones in another, backbone bits and pieces in a third section and so on. Here, their builders had constructed wooden shelves from the lowest level to the highest. I could tell from the size of the skulls, that the little mounds of bones were that of children.

What was even stranger, was that a number of women were cooking over the fire inside the chamber and ladling bowls of stew from a cooking pot. We watched them toiling away, chopping more roots and meats to add to the broth while others laid the steaming bowls in rows along the shelves for the dead children.

Did they really believe that this was a portal to the Underworld and their fallen kin could return to their bones to eat their mother's food? It took all my strength not to react to such wastage. Was this entire barrow devoted to throwing good food after the dead, and more importantly, had these children perished from the harshness of nature or were they taken before their time as an offering like my white hart?

A few seasons ago, I'd never entertain such thoughts, but my notion of common decency was drastically altered after my encounters with the Phoenician noblemen. Now I believed men capable of anything. I looked upon these women with heartfelt pity. If supplying their bones with nourishment gave them peace and comfort, who was I to judge?

Despite the new light this trip had thrown upon the Belgae, I was no closer to understanding why Rawley had brought us to this site. I glanced about the torch lit cavern, looking for signs of adult bones but saw none. In my fascination, I completely missed Paxton leaving the barrow and returning shortly afterward, clutching a rooster by the neck.

Endelyn forced a smile and touched her palms together. Clearly, she knew what they had in mind. Paxton grappled the bird until it lay flat against a large wooden bowl. When Rawley plucked a blade from the warrior's belt, their intention dawned on me. Our fate would be decided on the bloody entrails of a freshly killed chicken.

"Cernonnus, hear us. You have led these faithless men to our shores for a reason we cannot fathom. They intend to desecrate our sacred springs with their ungodly ways. Though you send emissaries to speak for them, I am not convinced of their sincerity." Rawley drew breath, the chicken tried to peck at him until Paxton thrust its head down with the heel of his hand. The two men exchanged glances. I didn't need a priest to tell me that it was not a good sign. The kyjyan cockerel was just as defiant as my nephews.

I closed my eyes and sent a silent plea up to the God of Death and the Wild Forest. *Please spare my nephews from the wrath of the Belgae. If they must sacrifice someone, let it be me instead.* When I looked up once again, Rawley dug the blade into the belly of the flapping creature, spilling out its guts and gizzard into the wide bowl. Paxton unhooked one of the finger bones from his necklace and dropped it into the stinking mess.

The Chief prodded the entrails with the blade, and then with his fingers. "I need more light, son." He muttered to Paxton, who obliged by retrieving a torch from near the wall. Under the flickering flames, the old man seemed to come alive, his face animated for the first time since we'd met him. Endelyn leaned in, examining the slippery guts and the shapes they made in the bowl.

She took in a sharp breath, suddenly afraid. What did it show? I squinted at the chicken guts but saw nothing but ingredients for supper. Endelyn hung her head and sighed.

"What?" I blurted before I could stop myself. "What did you see?"

Endelyn shook her head violently, biting her lips and refusing to answer.

I looked up at Rawley for an explanation. "It is decided." He said, straightening up and rinsing his hands with a jug of water. "Come."

CHAPTER SEVENTEEN

The walk back to the settlement was over in a flash. I scuttled along after Rawley and Paxton badgering them for an answer, but neither were prepared to say anything. Endelyn lagged a little way behind and was equally silent. I hold no faith in superstition and priestly nonsense, but Rawley did and that was all that mattered. Our fate was decided, for good or ill. Whatever was present in the reading of the entrails, Endelyn saw it too.

Filled with a sense of desperation, I stuck close to the old Chief and his son, hoping to steer a positive outcome. Belgae warriors stood guarding the wooden structure that housed our companions, each of them wearing belts laden with weapons. Our men were unarmed, exhausted and starving. I doubted whether they would have the strength to fight the Belgae off, if Rawley gave the order to kill.

The Chief gave a deep sigh and signalled his men to open the door. As soon as the wooden panel was removed, Tallack and Hellyer barged the warriors aside, yelling and flailing their arms in defence. The Belgae men stepped aside, allowing them to skitter past unharmed. When they came to their senses and saw Endelyn and I unmolested and unrestrained, they frowned. Ren helped Blyth into the sunlight, blinking and shielding his eyes.

Tallack approached the Chief. "What's the meaning of this? We come here under white banners and you treat us like livestock. We gave you our most precious commodity in tribute. A gift worthy of the gods."

"And the gods have made their wishes known to me." Rawley bellowed back. This was the first time he'd raised his voice to us since our arrival. Far from being a serene, retiring kind of ruler, he had a formidable presence. All those around him believed he had the ear and favour of Cernonnus, not in a benevolent way such as my white hart gave to me, but as the weapon of vengeance. In the eyes of the Belgae, our series of insults to the gods deserved punishment. Endelyn moved closer to me. I could feel her torso trembling against my arm.

"What did the entrails reveal?" I whispered to her, giving her my most impatient of looks.

Her fist shot up to cover her mouth, as though speaking the message from Cernonnus would damn her for all eternity. She uttered just one word to me, before closing her eyes and sobbing. "Death."

The humours trickling through my body ran cold. A shiver traced down my spine. There had to be a way to convince him that our motives for visiting their sacred springs were true. "Chief Rawley," I began, not knowing how to frame my gambit. "Forgive us this trespass on your time and lands. We heard that you were both honourable and fair or we would not have approached with this request. Please know that we respect your traditions and customs and would never do anything to jeopardise relations between us. Blydh is terribly ill. I beg you, Chief, allow us passage through your lands to the sacred springs."

Rawley switched his stare from me to the men in our party. Tallack and Hellyer looked to be preparing for a fight, Ren had both hands full keeping Blydh upright, and Endelyn was resolutely downcast.

Rawley analysed each of us and returned his attention to me. "I think you are not as wise as your name suggests. We Belgae have no ties with the Dumnonii, and as my son said, you have only ever shown disdain for our beliefs."

I bit my tongue. The old man had heard every word of my conversation with Paxton. Nothing I said would make the slightest difference to his decision. We all waited for our penance. If the entrails were to be believed, one or all of us would die.

Rawley cleared his throat. "I have no wish to cause undue animosity between our tribes and hope that in time, we can sit down and talk of trade. For now, I thank you for your gifts. Rest assured that the tin and jewels we found in your boats will be put to good use, as will your blades and axes. In return, and for the fine manners of your women folk, I give you the gift of your lives. Go now, paddle out to sea and never set foot on Belgae land ever again."

Tallack began to argue but the Chief had heard enough. He nodded to his son who in turn gave orders to the warriors. While our men complained and resisted the ardent shoves towards our boats, my relief was overwhelming.

Patting Endelyn's back as we walked towards the jetty, I noticed that she was not pleased with the outcome. "Why so glum? We can forge new blades, refine more tin. He will not kill us. Barring him actually granting permission, this is the best outcome we could have expected under the circumstances. Old Rawley defied the gods' message of death."

"You don't understand." She sniffed, welling up with tears. "He doesn't need to take our lives. Death is coming for us anyway." She stepped into the second boat alongside Ren and Blydh, before I could ask her for clarification. The Belgae warriors cut our moorings and kicked us away from the pontoon.

Tallack took hold of the tiller and steered us out towards the mouth of the river. I relaxed in my furs, thinking that we'd seen the end of our mission to the springs. Turns out, I had that wrong too. Paxton's men followed us for some distance along the riverbank on horseback, making sure that we did not land further along the estuary.

When we were at the confluence of the two rivers, Tallack called out to Ren. "Pull in close to us. We need to talk."

Tallack's puckered mouth and clenched jaw told me all I needed to know. I'd seen that look of determination before. Both he and Blydh would not allow anyone to tell them what they could or couldn't do. To them, having a fellow leader, a Metern of the Belgae, dictate their actions was the highest insult. It was akin to being sent to bed before a Long Hut feast.

The tide was out upstream in the Severn Estuary, allowing us to row hard through the strong currents to a sandbank and drop anchor away from the shore. We were out of the tribe's view by a considerable way, unless they had the sight of eagles. Here we ate a little of the salted meats the Belgae had left in our packs and drank the last of the stale water from the bladders. Having some food in his belly, Blydh perked up. He was revived enough to catch up with all that had occurred, adding his own brand of aggression to the talks.

"He has no right to deny us access to the sacred springs. If they are as godly as that kyjyan says, they belong to everyone in the land." Blydh helped himself to a gulp from our dwindling supply of water.

"The same could be said about our tin mines, brother. You can understand why he's so protective of the site. If a simple incantation can summon those from the Underworld, then you'd need to keep it under close guard." Tallack's reasoning was sound, but Blydh was not receptive to common sense.

"I say we go anyway. Ren, which stretch of this coastline is closest to the springs?" Blydh took another long swig from the jug, leaving us all short of drinkable liquids. Both the Avon and the Severn were too salted where we sat to be of use to us.

Ren stole a glance at Tallack. He was slow to respond, choosing his words carefully. "There are no safe places to land along this coast, Chief. Not unless we go home."

"That's not an option. My head will not be right until I have had the blessings performed at the sacred spring. Isn't that correct, Endelyn?" Blydh spun about to face her, but she was nursing her snotty nose and reddened eyes. She didn't answer him. Blydh grunted. "How far away are they by land?"

Again, Ren took his time. "We'd never make it across land on foot. Whichever way you approach, we'd be spotted by Duro or Belgae scouts and slaughtered before nightfall."

Bless Renowden for his mastery of the situation. He all but told them how stupid they were being, without them realising. Just as I was confident that he could change our Chiefs' minds, Tallack piped up.

"Didn't you say it was a short walk from the Avon River, further upstream?"

"I did, but…"

"Then that's how we'll get there. We'll stick to the original plan, permission or not." Tallack grinned, leaning across to the second boat to swipe the water bladder from his brother's grasp. "We'll wait until the tide goes back in and it's nice and dark and sail right past the lot of them. I sighed and glowered at Endelyn in the other vessel. It seemed that the gods were not finished with us yet after all. The chicken entrails were not a message, they were a warning.

Ren did his best to dissuade the twins, but they wouldn't listen. Hellyer sided with our Chiefs, even to the point of whipping up the rest of the men into a roar of cheering. Each of them took turns in swigging from the bladders and munching on the rations so that by the time the tide changed, we had nothing left to eat or drink.

Tallack deferred to Ren's experience, asking him to navigate the strong currents of the Severn Estuary shortly after nightfall. The Avon mouth was a flea bite compared to the vast width of the channel between Kembra and Belgae lands, but Ren's skill carried us along in the dim light until we were within spitting distance.

I kept my eyes trained on the Duros bank, while Endelyn and Blydh looked to the east. I was under no illusions. We would surely be spotted by scouts from both sides of the river. The whole plan was foolish from start to finish.

I'm ashamed to admit that I crouched low in the boat, keeping my head beneath the sides to avoid stray arrows. None of the men could afford the same luxury. They had to row like the Morrighan was on their tails, carrying us through the widest part of the river mouth and into the fast-moving current of the central channel once again. Ren knew its ways better this time, navigating by instinct rather than sight.

The clouds dulled the moonlight, shielding us from the sharpest eyes of the Duro and Belgae scouts. I held my breath, waiting for the torches to reappear on the bank side. We passed the first meander without any sign of us being seen. The next two, were sharper and deadlier.

I knew from my walk with Rawley and Paxton that the majority of their settlement huts lay along the Trym tributary, a short walk from the tightest bend in the Avon. Our men garnered their strength, collectively pulling the oars in unison without any need to beat a rhythm. Those of Tallack's crewmen kept the pace, leading Blydh's Head Hunters into a gruelling speed.

If only the tidal bore of the Severn reached this far into the Avon, we could have timed our approach to let it carry us up the river and out of harm's way. As it was, we had the gods with us, passing the Trym without detection. I was dizzy with fear, my trembling breath easing the further inland we rowed.

A dark mass of dense trees lay ahead on both sides of the river. It would either provide the perfect cover for attack, or shield us from our enemies' view. On we sped in silence, but for the swish of the oars through the muddied waters below.

Ren pulled on the tiller, taking his boat closer to the east bank. Tallack copied his actions, steering into a deep section of the flow. The additional shadows made it impossible to see the flock of geese, bobbing at the water's edge. Our oar splashes disturbed enough of them to cause panic, sending them honking and flapping into the air. If the scouts hadn't seen us before, they would now.

Instinctively, the men rowed harder, riding the tide deep into the wooded area. I closed my eyes, expecting a flurry of arrows at any moment. Other than the snap of twigs and branches, I heard nor saw anything to suggest that we were found out. On we travelled until the arms of our men tired. None would admit that their strength was spent, yet our pace slowed and their timing faltered.

When at last, we were close to the end of the tree cover, Tallack insisted that he took a turn with the oars. Tapping one of his crewmen on the shoulder, he stood up and balanced in the rocking hull, readying himself to swap places with his Chief. Just as Tallack sat down and picked up the oar, the first bolt flew past my ear and into the sailor's gut. He crumpled into my arms; spilling blood faster than it could be staunched. Tallack roared at the men to row harder. Ren glanced back to see us floundering. The more the men sculled, the closer we veered toward the Duros arrows.

I had two options. Press down on the warrior's gut to keep his humours inside, or take hold of the tiller and steer us to safety. It was not a difficult choice, leaving one man to bleed in order to save a boat full of our people. It had been a long time since I'd taken charge of a vessel, but I was quick to learn its ways. The hardest part was keeping my head down beneath the sides of the boat while maintaining our path behind Ren.

Arrows thudded into the wooden slats of our vessel, others fell short and plopped into the water behind us. I wasn't sure how long our men could hold out, rowing at full speed until we were beyond the Duros easy reach.

At the time, all I could think about was how much easier the whole trip would have been, if we'd waited until we'd heard from Senara about the possibility of meeting up with the Duro elders. A negotiated peace treaty would impact all areas of our lives, including the safe passage across their lands.

I could understand why Tallack and Blydh would be reluctant to deal with our neighbouring tribe. The grudges and hatred spanned generations. All our people were brought up thinking that Duros should never be trusted, making my plan harder to sell to my tribe.

When we were safely among the marshlands and reeds, the men slowed our speed and rested. There would be more opportunities to show their worth when the currents were against us once more. Tallack took over at the helm, while I tended the wounded warrior. I knew from the smell of him that the bronze tip had pierced his stomach. Vile humours and bile leaked out of him along with the blood, making it almost impossible to see the damaged flesh in the dark.

At any other time, I would have insisted that we docked, built a fire and taken my time to work my magic with a hot blade and a few lengths of soaked cattle gut. With a deep sigh, I resigned myself to the fact that this poor young man would probably bleed out before I could help him.

I packed his innards with dried moss, leaving the shaft from the arrow sticking out of him. I figured that more harm would result from pulling it out.

With a chunk of willow bark to chew on, I wished that Blydh hadn't polished off all my poppy resin. This fellow would enter the Summerlands a whimpering warrior and that would not impress the gods one bit. I cradled his head, bunched up together at the back of the boat, until he drifted off sometime in the middle of the night. His blood dried in sticky patches on my skin and clothes, but still I held on. How could we mark his death with dignity, stuck between enemy lands with no end in sight?

I lost track of the twists and turns in the river. When the force of the tide no longer carried us, Tallack ordered the oars back in the water. At a more sedate speed, we cruised through the night keeping a keen eye on the bank side for our foes.

When my dead patient lost all warmth, my nephew leaned into my ear. “He has to go overboard, Aunt Mel. We will make an offering to the gods on his behalf when we reach the springs.”

If we reached the springs, I wanted to say, but kept my mouth closed. Tallack chose a straight length of the river and ordered the closest warriors to help him lift the stricken man overboard.

“Rest easy, my friend. May you find the crossing to the Summerlands at sea.” Tallack said. I watched the solemn faces of our men, heads bowed in deep respect. We had nothing to offer to the Lady of Lakes and Seas for his passage; the Belgae had stripped us of all our valuables. That fact prayed on their minds; I could tell.

“The arrow was bronze tipped, perhaps the Lady will accept that on his behalf.” I spoke softly, hoping it would ease their troubles. As I said it, the clouds broke overhead, revealing the moon in all its luminous glory, along with a lone rider standing on the cliff top on the eastern side of the gorge. A Belgae scout was watching us.

CHAPTER EIGHTEEN

There was no point in hiding, the scout could see us clearly. Our white banners would be useless to us now that we'd defied their Chief's orders. The men and I looked at Tallack, waiting for his instructions.

"If I had a bow or throwing dagger, we'd stand a chance of bringing him down before he could ride off to their camp." He scratched at his stubble, in deep thought.

Hellyer looked agitated. "Put me ashore, Chief. I'll run the kyjyan down for you." The hubris of youth, bless him.

Tallack hid his grin. "Not on foot you can't. He'll be well away. No. The best we can do is out run them." He straightened his back and raised his voice. "Ren. How long would it take for him to get word to Chief Rawley?"

Ren thought for a few moments before he shouted his answer. "Not long at a gallop. Paxton and his men could take a shorter route across land than this winding river. We're about a half day's walk, quarter day's ride ahead. Maybe more if we pick up the pace."

Blydh knelt in the forward boat and peered back at us. "We'll make it easy. If not, we'll dispatch those kyjyans and take their heads and their metal in compensation."

No one agreed with him. We all recognised the voice of the brash spirit in charge of our Chief. Blydh would never have suggested anything so reckless. With little time to spare, the men finished their farewells to the fallen warrior and took to the oars. These men were tough, but

I could see the strain showing on their brows. They heaved and lurched in perfect time with one another, ignoring the weeping blisters bubbling on calloused hands. Nothing short of death would stop them from delivering their Chieftains to the sacred springs.

Throughout the night, the men alternately rowed and rested, until we passed into a huge valley with a wide, flat marshland at its base and steep grey stone hills either side. The sun peeped over the Belgae region, illuminating our path in between the reed beds and boggy lowlands. I knew that we were close, there was a faint smell in the air of rotten eggs. Ren steered the lead boat towards a jetty on the east shore. He bent low to alert Blydh and the men to the possibility that we could be greeted by irate tribesmen.

Two of Blydh's Head Hunters hopped out of the boat and searched along the ground for potential attackers. When they were satisfied that there were no threats to our safety, the rest of us came ashore. Tallack gave out his orders at speed. Ren and Hellyer went in search of food and living offerings to the gods, now that all our metal and jewels were confiscated. The Hunters found long poles of willow in place of weapons.

I looked in my kit for a blade to use in the ceremony, but Rawley's men had taken my knives. They were all I had left to remember the twin's father. Aebba made a gift of the set to aid me in healing others.

Tallack heard me cussing. "I promise that I'll have the smith make you some new knives when we get home. Even better than your original ones." He put his arm about my shoulders and gave me a squeeze. To his Sea Warriors, he said. "You'll be hard pressed to find flint, and even luckier if you can nap them into sharp edges for us." They took this statement as a challenge, but in the swampy rushes and thick mud, it was doubtful they'd succeed.

All the men were busy collecting, gathering or searching except for Blydh. He clung to Endelyn and whispered into her ear. She squirmed, pulling away from his clutches. I presumed that he'd forgotten who she was again. His former lover, Kerensa would have tolerated his lust-filled advances but we all knew that she was dead, including Blydh when he was in his right mind.

I walked in a large arc around the pair of them and followed my nose to the hot springs. Just as Ren had said, it was not far to walk and there was a well-worn track to a safe entry point. The Belgae had certainly left their mark. Carved tree trunks the size of boats stuck up at regular intervals, each one painted with smears of dried blood. Some bore strings of bones and feathers, like Paxton's spear and necklace. Others had notches scored in neat little rows, as though they were using it to keep count of something.

In front of the poles was a familiar altar stone propped up on two slabs of rock. It was obviously well used, since the central portion of the stone was worn into the shape of a bowl. At one end, they had cut a groove to let whatever fell inside the chance to drain away. Having witnessed a fair few of the priestess's ceremonies, it was my best guess that it was to catch the blood from their victims.

By the time our party caught up with me, I was already transfixed by the pool. I couldn't see where the spring gushed, as the old priest had described, but I guessed that the Belgae had dug out the surrounding mud and clay, allowing it to fill so that Rawley's people could bathe.

The wisps of steam rising from the hot water into the cool morning air gave it a magical feel. I had to pinch myself to remember that this was a dangerous place, not one of curious beauty. I recalled the words from the old priest friend of Endelyn, who warned us that if we failed to perform everything according to his exacting instructions, there was the possibility of letting more spirits out from the Underworld. It was bad enough dealing with one of the kyjyan things, let alone more.

I crouched down to the edge and bowed my head over the stinking water. There was not a breath of wind, nor ripples to disturb the spring. As the sun rose higher into the sky, I saw an image forming before me; a woman of some years, with clouded eyes and messy white hair. It was some moments before I realised that this was no threatening apparition sent by Cernonnus to capture me, but a likeness of myself. It was clearer even than when I saw myself in the polished copper disc belonging to the twin's mother, Cryda. She was the only one in camp vain enough to keep one. Aebba the Wild indulged her and had it made.

The warriors were more cautious in their approach, each of them jumping backwards as their image loomed into view. It took all my powers of persuasion to convince them that it was not a trick, nor a mean spirit taking on their form, but instead the magic of truly still water.

We couldn't afford to delay. There was no way of knowing when the Belgae would catch up with us and we still needed to perform two rituals; one to placate my nephew, the other to truly banish the wicked demon back to the Underworld. I hoped that our journey had given Endelyn time to think about how she would achieve both without alerting Blydh to our ruse.

Ren appeared with a single duck tucked under his arms. It pecked him a couple of times before he could grip its neck and shift its body into the dip of the altar stone.

Tallack's men were not successful in their search. They sidled in behind the carved poles, hoping that we wouldn't notice their failure. We had no blades with which to perform the ritual. Endelyn stepped in front of the wooden idols, faced us all and lifted a metal comb from her hair. It bore two long, sharp prongs on one side.

With a smile fixed on her freckled face, she said. "This will work. Chief Blydh, come and stand by me."

Poor dazed dolt did exactly as he was told, rocking gently backwards and forwards on the balls of his feet. I listened carefully, wondering whether Endelyn would combine the Ritual of Eternal Solace, meant to dispel the demon, with the blessing to Airmed asking her to heal Blydh.

While Endelyn prepared the altar and arranged things to her liking, I scooped up a little of the hot water in my cupped hands. My thirst was raging, but it smelled so rank, I was scared to drink. The heat was quite amazing. I let the water trickle through my fingers and scooped up a fresh batch, daring myself to stick my tongue into the murky liquid. "Well, here goes. If I keel over and die, you'll know that we've all been lied to." I gulped at the hot water and swallowed quickly. It was disgusting. My face contorted into a shudder, making everyone laugh.

Endelyn was not amused. She scowled at me for outshining her.

"Sorry. Please continue." I tried to sound contrite, but it was difficult with all the men smirking and hiding their smiles. I'd never tasted anything as peculiar as that in my life. To my mind, it was more likely to kill than cure, but Blydh was determined to go through with the ritual.

Her words blended into one incoherent sound for a few moments, babbling the way that priests do. Within moments, she took her hair pin and rammed the spikes into the throat of the duck. Its blood spurted a little, but the poor creature survived, squawking and flapping and making a rasping noise through the holes in its gizzard. Before Ren could offer his services, the priestess dropped the comb into the basin and took the neck of the bird in both hands, wringing the life out of the beast.

I looked at its green head, its pale beak and glassy eyes and started to worry. The old priest at the Seven Children's Stones had given us a clear warning; make sure that your offering is generous. One waterfowl was not a generous offering. It would barely account for an Airmed blessing, let alone convince the great Cernonnus to release my nephew from his torment.

Endelyn seemed to read my thoughts straight out of my head. She dabbed a little of the duck's blood onto Blydh's forehead, and then a little on his eyelids. Taking the comb in one hand, she grasped Blydh with the other and walked to the edge of the water. With a little dip in the knees, she lobbed the comb high into the air and watched it plop into the centre of the pool.

"Airmed, hear our plea. Bless this man with the gift of good health. Restore his sight and relieve his pain." The priestess flicked off her shoes and led my nephew into the steaming water. He followed her without a murmur, as compliant and accepting as a child. When they were waist high, Endelyn continued her speech. "Airmed, wash away all his troubles, all his strife and give him the strength of his forefathers, the kindness of his foremothers and the courage of his tribe."

The priestess reached up to the top of Blydh's head and pushed down gently on his helmet. He bent his knees, allowing her to submerge him beneath the surface of the warm water. I expected it to be just a quick dunk, but Endelyn held him under with both hands. While his ears were muffled to her voice, she began the incantation to Cernonnus.

"God of the Forest and of Death, release this great man from the wicked spirit sent to torment us all. He is a faithful servant to all the gods and an important leader of the Dumnonii." Those were the words I remembered, the rest came out of her as a long torrent of babble; her head thrown back, her eyes rolled and showing only the white. It was quite a performance.

The longer she intoned, the more suspicious Blydh became. His arms flailed about in the water as the air ran out in his lungs, but Endelyn redoubled her efforts to keep him submerged, forcing all her weight down on his head. It must have been painful, putting that much pressure on the tender wounds of his scalp.

I closed my eyes and sent my own little plea to the gods, begging them for their assistance in persuading Cernonnus to set my nephew free. When I opened them, Blydh sprang up with all his strength, coughing and snorting out the stinking water. As one last gesture of faith, I too removed the small metal rings from my hair and threw them into the pool, hoping that all our collective offerings would be sufficient.

"Are you trying to drown me?" Blydh choked. Endelyn moved closer to stare directly into his eyes, but Blydh pushed her away. She completed her ritual intonation alone in the middle of the pool. Tallack held out his arm to Blydh, pulling him out onto the bank. The twins sat together with their legs dangling into the steamy water. Blydh cupped a hand over his good eye, testing to see if his sight had returned in the other.

"Well, brother, has it worked?" Tallack whispered. Blydh turned to face him and gently shook his head. Both peered down at the sacred pool. "Perhaps it needs a day or two to fully take effect." Tallack was all kindness and forbearance, but I couldn't see Blydh taking this development lightly. If his sight did not return, I feared that his current mild manner would fade fast.

Ren wandered closer to me, noticing my pained expression. "You know, legend has it that Bladud, son of Lud Hudibras was cured here. He was blessed by Airmed for a raging disease and lived for some time after when all had given him up for dead."

"Some time?" I queried, puzzled by his statement.

"Oh, the illness didn't kill him. By all accounts, the stupid kyjyan thought he could fly."

I snorted and covered my mouth. It was not the right occasion for levity. There was far too much at stake.

He stood up and collected the mallard. "Pity we can't stay and cook this." He chucked the bird into the reeds for the foxes and turned to Tallack. "We shouldn't linger here, Chief."

My stomach grumbled, making Tallack smile.

"You're right, Ren. Time to go." Tallack approached his brother who still sat on the bank.

Blydh had stripped off his head gear and tunic and was wringing out his clothing. The inner fleece of his helm was as soaked as the rest of him. "Kyjyan waste of time. I don't feel any different."

Endelyn waded to the edge of the pool, swishing her hands about in graceful sweeps. "It won't happen immediately, Chief Blydh. The gods often wait until we sleep to bestow their gifts on us."

Blydh grunted, eased the helmet back on his head and turned his back to her. Tallack helped her out of the water instead. Whether Airmed had blessed him or not, it seemed that the evil demon was still in control of my nephew. Ren and I looked at each other, sharing our unspoken concern. There was no need to voice our suspicions. Cernonnus had not favoured us.

Before we could round everyone up and head back towards the boats, Tallack muttered in Endelyn's ear. "Is there anything that you might have forgotten, another ritual or a different incantation? Is there nothing else to be done?"

The priestess levered herself up from the muddy bank and dusted the bits from her hands. The tiny shake of her head made my heart sink in my chest. My botched treatment of his skull had condemned Blydh to misery and us along with him.

My belly wasn't the only one making itself heard. We were all ravenous and in need of a long drink of fresh cool water, or our strength would fail us.

"We can't go back the way we came." I said, glancing about for any roots or shoots that would curb my hunger.

"No indeed, unless we want the Belgae and Durotriges to pick us off one by one with their lethal arrows." Tallack said, looking to good old Ren for a solution to our problem.

"If I remember rightly, the Avon branches upstream. I'm fairly sure that if we take the right-hand fork, we'd paddle into the heart of the Duros region." Ren offered, although few of us could see the advantages of such a course of action.

"Why would we want to cruise right into enemy territory?" Blydh growled, his temper no better than before.

Tallack grinned. "Because all those in the north will expect us to return to sea, while the rest of their tribe are at their coastal camp with Brea in the south. It'll be deserted."

I scratched my head. "How wide is this tributary? Can we navigate through most of the Duro region?"

Ren shook his head and waited for the twins to catch up with what that meant. At some point, we would have to abandon our boats and walk for days along the trail back to the Exe across treacherous lands. Our choices were limited and stark. Only the Chiefs could decide our fate.

As we walked around the edge of the pool back towards the boats, we heard horses snorting and men urging them forwards. Ren hurried along the trail to where the new growth of reeds was shorter. "Belgae!" He yelled. They were closing in on us, their steeds struggling through the boggy ground.

CHAPTER NINETEEN

Thank the gods for that marshy ground. On anything drier, the Belgae would have ridden right through us while we were still at the sacred springs. Tallack, Blydh and the warriors all ran ahead, leaving Endelyn and I to dash as fast as my old bones would allow back to the boats.

Our men formed a line between the pontoon and the enemy to allow us safe passage, but none had better weapons than broken willow poles. The Belgae were a couple of boat lengths away from us, giving me the chance to climb into our vessel, untie the mooring rope and hang onto the pontoon until the men could jump aboard. Endelyn caught sight of my movements and copied me in the other boat.

One or two of their warriors hurled their spears, but they were easily deflected. It allowed two of our men to discard their wooden staffs in favour of bronze tipped weapons. There were so many of them. The smallest ponies carrying the lightest men made it through the swampy ground before our men could reach the boats. Our only hope was that the thick mud would slow down the heavy horses, giving our warriors an opportunity to fight a few at a time.

Paxton led the charge, roaring and cantering full speed into the marshy ground. You'd think that a young man growing up in these regions, he would have avoided the swamp and led his men around the edge.

Paxton's naivety worked to our advantage. Some of his men got fully stuck in the soft ground, their horses exhausting themselves just like Senara's had done on the moors. Before his warriors could dismount, two of Tallack's sailors clouted them about the head with their poles, knocking them from their steeds and stealing their axes and blades.

Paxton was in the drier reaches on slightly higher ground. Tallack caught hold of an axe from his crewman. He swung it about his head, taking enormous strides towards the heir of the Belgae tribe. Blydh's Head Hunters attempted a similar manoeuvre but met greater resistance. The Belgae left their horses in the swamp and slogged through the mud on foot, meeting our men armed to the teeth and in greater numbers than we could've imagined. Only five of our men had metal weapons. We didn't stand a chance.

Blydh's Head Hunters stayed close to protect him in his vulnerable state. Tallack, Ren and Hellyer stood firm, having the advantage of an axe, sword and spear between them. The first young Belgae lunged at Tallack with his lance, over-balancing to the point where Tallack could swipe at the shaft. The boy felt to Tallack's feet. One swift blow with the axe head and the young lad was no more.

Ren chucked the boy's spear to another of our men at his side. I held my breath, not expecting our luck to hold. They wouldn't all be as green and eager to die as that one. Paxton squared up to Tallack, picking him out and gesturing for his men to attack our warriors either side.

I had no idea who had the better weapon, Tallack's heavy and exhausting battle axe or Paxton's finely forged bronze short sword. My nephew was strong, but Paxton was agile and speedy. If I had to guess, I'd say that Tallack would be weakened after so little sleep and food for the last few days. All the Belgae had to do was tire him out.

Our men fought with whatever weapons they could snatch. There was no skill nor sophistication involved, such was the sheer bloody-mindedness of our warriors. They were desperate to survive. They kicked, punched and head butted those who came close enough. Others were run through with confiscated spears. By the time Paxton had made his first lunge, two of our warriors had already met Cernonnus in the Summerlands; one with a swift blade through the gut, the other with a spearhead embedded in his face.

I couldn't take my focus away from Tallack, even though the skirmish was fought on many fronts by our brave men. Endelyn screamed at our heroes to turn tail and run to the boats, which only distracted them further. The jetty was deceptively narrow. None dared to shuffle backwards for fear of losing their footing. At the same time, the onslaught of warriors would not allow our men to turn around and run.

Paxton's agile moves made me nervous. He danced about Tallack skipping closer to the swinging axe and dodging the blows just in time for what seemed like ages. He was clever, but he had to know that the reach of his sword was no match for Tallack's axe. One false move and Tallack could behead him with a single swipe.

"You sullied our sacred springs with your brutish and foul ways, prepare to make amends and die." Paxton goaded, although coming from someone so young and inexperienced, it failed to have any impact. My nephew laughed in his face. The Belgae heir was not done.

"Submit to us now and I might spare your men. My father will give you a dignified and honourable end as an offering to the gods."

"I'd rather take my chances with the Morrighan. She's favoured our tribe for years, picking off our enemies for her victims in battle." It was not so much the words as Tallack's sneer that fuelled the violence in Paxton's eyes. He lunged at my nephew's chest with his bronze blade. Tallack saw it and stepped aside, jabbing the butt end of the axe handle into Paxton's face until his nose streamed with blood.

Ren had a small pile of young men heaped up to his right, but there were more making it through the mud every moment. They had to clear a path back to the jetty or they'd be completely surrounded. Another of our Sea Warriors lost his life, protecting Blydh from two large Belgae.

Our ailing Chief stepped up admirably, disarming one and dispatching the other enemy in rapid succession. He may not be at his best, but Blydh was a Head Hunter through and through. He swung at a third and missed, falling to the ground before his weapon made contact with his attacker. He looked to me as though his sight was failing him. The Belgae fighter drew closer, determined to finish the job.

Just when I thought Blydh's days as Chief were finally over, Ren launched himself across the mud and blocked the spear aimed at his heart. It was as though the whole world stopped for a moment to consider the scene. Tallack gasped, distracted by his brother's brush with death. Paxton saw his chance.

He twirled about on the spot, using all his might to swing his blade about for a fatal blow to Tallack's throat. At the very last moment, Tallack returned his gaze to see the blade coming for him. Twisting to the side, the sword failed to slice his neck, but landed at an angle to my nephew's upper arm, knocking the axe from his grasp.

The keen edge scored a thick trail right through Tallack's muscle and sinew. His face contorted as he struggled to steady his stance. Paxton had knocked him off guard. Before my nephew could find a better footing, Paxton lunged for a kill shot. With a little guile and no grace, my nephew rolled onto the ground scooping up the fallen axe before righting himself further away.

A quick glance told him that Ren and Hellyer had cleared a space to the wooden dock, and that Blydh was spent. More Belgae were wading through the swamp and mud to replenish the horde of attackers.

"Ren! Get Blydh and the men onto the boats." Tallack meant to hold the line at all costs. He was just one injured man against an army. Hellyer hovered at his side until Tallack shouted at him again. The young Alchemist would not budge. He had his Chieftain's back, fending off any who would approach from the opposite direction.

Paxton grew angrier as more of our people staggered down the jetty. With a deafening roar, the Belgae warrior ran at Tallack, his sword held in both hands, ready to strike.

Tallack stood firm. As his enemy charged, he raised the axe and swung it with all his might. The two blades connected with a deafening ring, followed by a discordant clunk, as Paxton's sword splintered into pieces. Tallack's axe carried right on through Paxton's ribs and cleaved his heart in two.

My nephew let the warrior drop to the soggy earth, before treading on his chest to tug the axe free. "Go!" He pushed Hellyer towards the pontoon. "Go now!" The two men ran at top speed along the jetty. Tallack launched himself over my head, while I clung onto the mooring post until Hellyer was aboard.

He was within five strides of our boat, when his chest erupted with a spearhead, his face froze in panic and he crashed to the wooden planks below. I let go of the post and the men sculled for our lives. The Alchemist was no more. His lifeless stare will haunt me for ever more.

Rowing at full capacity, the men took us out towards the west bank of the River Avon, ducking from stray spears and daggers. We'd lost five brave young souls in total, and all to fix a Chieftain that was beyond our help.

I took the tiller in our boat, while Endelyn steered the other. With so few of us left, Ren sculled with two oars while Blydh came to his senses. Tallack tried to keep up with the men in our vessel, but his arm was torn to shreds. We struggled between us, but we managed to move far enough upstream to be safe from further attack. Thank the gods that there were no archers among them or we'd all be fuel for pyres come nightfall.

There was no opportunity to tie the tiller and tend to the wounds. The Avon was as winding as a snake and twice as tricky. I did my best to keep on the same course as the lead boat, but with Endelyn steering according to Ren's instructions, the currents carried us apart several times. Tallack rummaged in my healing kit and cleaned the gash as best he could, but he was losing blood at an alarming rate.

At least the river was fresh this far inland. We had plenty to drink but no food. I could see my nephew getting sleepier the more humours oozed from his arm. As soon as I saw the fork in the river, I knew that we'd be deep in the heart of Durotriges' territory within a short while.

"Tallack, we should pull in to get the men stitched and bound." He didn't argue. I called ahead to Ren who nodded his agreement. I suspect he was contemplating the same thing himself.

We continued up the tributary into Durotriges land, hoping that their scouts would still be at the northern reaches. The men were tiring fast, especially since we had lost five able men. Tallack was slumped at my feet, with little more than a strip of cloth tied about his arm to hold the wound together.

Ren found us a stretch of the river bank where it was easy to land, making sure that visibility around us was good. While the men took it in turns to keep watch, I did what I could for the injured; stitching, binding, and covering with plantain paste.

Endelyn soothed Blydh with quiet words, but he seemed particularly agitated to me. I watched them for a while. Every time she said something that he disagreed with, rather than speaking directly to her, he would turn his head to his blind side and whisper over his shoulder. It was as though he thought someone was sitting there listening to his murmurs.

Packing away my kit, I moved closer to Ren. He too had noticed Blydh's strange behaviour. Keeping his voice low, he muttered; "Doesn't look as though it worked."

I shook my head. What was there to add? Blydh was worse than ever. His moods went from placid and contrite to spiteful and venomous in moments. I admired Endelyn's patience with him. No matter what he said or did, she remained calm and comforting at his side.

There was still plenty of daylight left and Tallack was keen to make a move. Before we returned to the boats, I needed to know just how we intended to get home.

"How far up this river can we go before it's impassable?"

Ren smoothed his whiskers and sniffed. "Not much farther. See how the banks narrow and the current speeds up? We'll bottom out before long."

"And then what? Just how far are we from the Exe?"

He shrugged. "We'll have to abandon the boats and go on foot, few days, maybe a quarter moon if we don't hit trouble."

I scoffed, my hand resting on the top of my head. How could we walk right through enemy territory with weak and injured warriors for a quarter of a moon? We'd barely escaped with our lives, had no food and no metal to trade other than the stolen weapons. Ren's forehead pinched with anxiety. The more youthful members of our party might be filled with enough pride and hubris to quell their fears, but we elders knew better.

Tallack urged us all back into the vessels and tried to take his turn at sculling, but his stitches ripped with each stroke. It must have been painful, but he bore it with a smile. Every now and then, he would tell us a story about his travels at sea to cheer us all, but they fell on deaf ears.

We'd lost dear friends, young warriors and old, and felt their absence keenly. I wondered how the leader of the Alchemist Clan would react when he heard the news. Both his children were dead, one by fair means and one by foul. They were a powerful clan, with secret knowledge of smelting and processing that no one else in our tribe possessed. If Hellyer's father chose to rebel, we would lose access to the most valuable commodity in our land.

As I pondered on what the future might hold, Ren did his best to skewer fish during the rest periods between rowing furiously upstream. A cold supper of raw fish was all we had ahead of us. At dusk, we spotted grey smoke trailing up to the orange glow of the sky. Mooring in among the new growth of reeds, Tallack sent one of the men to scout ahead on foot. All was silent, but for the addled murmuring of my poorly nephew. Endelyn did her best to keep him quiet, but he was insistent that he went ashore. Nothing would stop him.

It was fortunate that the scout returned when he did, or Blydh would have stomped off towards the smoke looking for more trouble.

"Well?" Tallack hissed. "How many Duros did you see?"

The scout panted, holding his side as if it was cramping. "It's a homestead. As far as I could tell, it's just a couple of families, mostly young 'uns." He took a few breaths. "Best of all, they have horses. Most look wild, but there's a few that are broken - still wearing reins."

Blydh stumbled to the bank with his Duro axe in hand. "Then we'll slice off their heads and take the lot."

I didn't expect anything else from Blydh. That demon was most definitely still in charge of his body. I stole a glance at Tallack, hoping that he would see reason without me having to spell things out. If the Duro elders discovered the indiscriminate slaughter of two defenceless families, they would never forge a peace treaty with us.

No one dared to argue with Blydh. Tallack looked indecisive.

I had to do something to lessen the bloodshed. "Can we not trade with them? We have spears, a couple of swords and that axe."

Blydh snorted. "And leave us defenceless. Not a chance."

Tallack Stepped onto the bank. “They’d recognise the weapons anyway. We don’t exactly look like Duros, none of us have the distinctive neck tattoo. We don’t want them to ride out to warn the scouts of our whereabouts.”

“Alright then, if trading is out, we can steal the horses and maybe a little food, but we don’t have to kill them.” I tried to sound forceful, but it came out as pleading. Blydh scowled at me, tossing his axe from one hand to the other.

Ren stepped up to defend me. “She’s right. They are not warriors; they don’t deserve to die.”

“Then we shall take them as slaves and burn down their roundhouses.” Blydh growled. I closed my eyes and took a slow breath. He was becoming more tedious to deal with every day. Every discussion was a battle, every sound idea met with objections. I soon realised that there was nothing I could say that he would accept.

We all had to rely on Ren to be the voice of reason. He turned to the scout. “Was the horse enclosure close to the roundhouses?”

The scout pulled a face. “Not right next to them, but fairly close.”

“And the doorways shuttered against the cold?”

The scout frowned thinking for a moment and then nodded.

With a beaming smile spreading across his salt-worn face, Ren said; “There you have it. They’d be slowed down just removing the door panels. We can take their horses before they realise we’re there. As long as we let all of them bolt, it’d take days for them to raise any kind of alarm.” The fact that this was Ren’s suggestion and not mine, made it more than palatable to the twins. It was hardly different from what I would have suggested myself.

Blydh did argue a little, trying to convince his brother that it would be better to capture and torture their young, forcing them to divulge the best routes across country, but Ren reminded him that there was no need. All we had to do was to head south-east until we hit familiar trails towards our own borders.

We waited until it was fully dark and then left the boats tied to stakes pushed into the soft mud. I hoped that they would go some way to making up for the theft of the homesteaders' livestock. Tallack mentioned to his brother that they would need to compensate Clemo and his kin too. We had intended to return both his nephew and his boats safe and sound. Hellyer was a brave young warrior who, like the others, missed out on a tribal farewell and ritual pyre. There was nothing of equal value to the heir of their clan that could be given.

We sent the scout ahead of us. He knew the way and could warn us about any wild animals or birds that might take fright and alert the Duros to our whereabouts. I hid with Endelyn in the long grass at the edge of the homestead boundary. Tallack and Ren sneaked closer, sending the scout and another lithe warrior to fetch two of the tame horses at a time from the pen.

Taking their time, the scout whispered to the ponies, gaining their trust and keeping their whickers to a minimum. On their third trip to lead another two over to Tallack and Ren, Blydh grew restless.

"Come on, what's taking so long. Just open the kyjyan gates and have done with it." He yelled at the top of his voice. The door panels to the houses squeaked and groaned as they were removed. Light poured out of the huts from the fires.

CHAPTER TWENTY

Barking dogs spilled out of the roundhouses, closely followed by their owners. Tallack and Ren mounted the horses and held out their arms for the scout and warrior to vault up behind them. Before the scout could grasp Tallack's forearm, an arrow whistled through the air and caught him in the neck. The tip poked out of his throat. Great spurts of frothing blood spilled down his front as he fell choking. He was dead before his head hit the ground.

Ducking low against the manes of their ponies, they rode towards us with the dogs snapping at their heels. We scrambled onto the horses at the boundary to their property and fled. Blydh took delight in swinging his axe into the dogs' paths, cleaving the head of one in two. It gave a single horrifying yelp as it died and tumbled along the rocky path.

We galloped for some distance before we dared to slow down. The horses tired quickly, most carrying the weight of more than one of us at a time. Endelyn shared a pony with Blydh, although others offered to share with her. She was determined to stay by his side, foolish girl.

Ren's horse struggled with both he and another heavy man on its back. The only sensible solution was for the warrior to take my pony. As Ren said at the time, I was nought but skin and bone anyway. His steed seemed to prefer the lighter load, trotting along easily with the both of us.

Even with the stolen horses, we were still two full days ride from our borders and another half day on top of that to make it back to the compound on the Exe. We'd lost too many young men on a failed quest. None of us were looking forward to the explanations we'd have to give to the families of those slain and left on the wayside.

We were a sombre crew for the whole night of riding. At dawn, we rested and watered the horses and foraged for what little food we could find. It was risky, but we did make a small fire to cook a little broth from two fat wood pigeons and some bulrush roots. It was warm and welcome, considering the scant meals we'd had since leaving the northern shores of our land. As soon as we'd eaten a small portion each, Tallack kicked dirt over the flames and ordered us back onto the ponies.

The second night, we stopped in a sheltered dell and roasted a whole mallard. The men told stories about those who'd fallen, singing their lament to the gods. Endelyn performed a brief ritual in their honour, asking the Morrighan to carry them to the Summerlands from battle, and to forgive their inability to pay the gods for their passage. Tallack repeated his promise to make a generous offering as soon as we got home.

After we'd all bedded down next to the smothered embers, I looked up at the stars and tried to count the number of lives given since that fateful night when the Duros smashed Blydh's skull. Any other man would have died right there on the spot. Since then, our tribe's misfortunes have doubled. Surely the gods would tire of testing us and move on to torment another tribe in our stead?

When the moon had begun its descent in the sky, I heard faint mumbling near to where the horses were tethered. Fearful that we were being watched by Duros, I wrapped my cloak about me and went to investigate. The shadowy figure of my nephew was unmistakable; Blydh was standing between the ponies. I crept closer, listening to him speak. He didn't see me.

"I know, you're right." Blydh said, nodding slowly. "Can't trust her for a moment."

He faced the bay mare he'd ridden for a couple of days, still nodding. "That's what I said, but you know my brother. He just won't believe me. It's obvious when you think about it, she makes the perfect spy in camp."

Was he talking to the horse? My foot dislodged a pebble, sending it skittering across the dry earth. He snapped his head around.

"Who's there?" He growled.

I hurried back to the fireside and covered myself over before he could return to accuse me. This was a bad sign indeed. My nephew was addled in the head. More than that, he truly believed that the horse was his friend.

In the morning, Endelyn once again insisted on sharing Blydh's pony. She clung onto him around his middle, as though she had captured her prize. I don't think she fully understood what she was taking on. The ritual was a spectacular failure. Blydh was unlikely to ever recover. If she thought that he would suddenly return to his old self and make her the Ruvane of our tribe, she was sadly mistaken.

We pushed on at some speed, keeping to the valleys covered with woodland and avoiding the flat expanses where we thought Duro scouts might lurk. By late afternoon, we crossed the River Sid at a narrow point and stepped onto our own land. We'd been extraordinarily lucky to pass through the Duro region without encountering further problems.

Ren suggested that we make camp and rest up, with a view to continue on to the compound at sun up, but Tallack overruled him. Either he was still in pain from his injuries, or he sensed that Blydh was getting worse. After a short break, we walked the horses on through dusk. The trails were so familiar to us, we were hardly slowed by the darkness.

I have to admit, I craved my warm bunk and furs. I'd barely made use of my hut all spring. As we reached the final stretches of the forest to the north of the island, I began to wonder what had occurred in camp since we left. Would Kewri still be at the agreed meeting point with Senara, awaiting news from the Duro scout? Had Cryda and Treeve managed tribal affairs in our absence without coming to blows?

I was soon to find out. Tallack called up to the guards in the watchtower, who in turn signalled for others to lower the bridge and open the gates. Ren took the horses to the enclosure, while Tallack and I sneaked into the rear entrance of the Long Hut.

All was quiet and orderly, much to my surprise. There were no fights, nor evidence of rebellion; just a few warriors drinking next to the central fire and eating the Chief's supplies with Treeve sitting in the Bear's head chair.

There was no sign of Cryda at all, but then it was late. She'd probably retired for the night with the baby Delen. Blydh dismounted and swaggered to the front entrance of the Long Hut with Endelyn close behind. She slipped her hand under his elbow just as they walked in together. All those inside cheered to see them, stamping their feet and thumping the tables welcoming them home.

Endelyn puffed out her chest and lapped up the attention. She had assumed the Ruvane role without any need for a formal binding ceremony. I watched Treeve's reaction. He seethed from the top table, pouting and glaring at the priestess, making no attempt to move from the lauded spot. It was only when he saw Tallack that his temper eased. He shot out of the carved chair, treating our Chief to a disarming smile.

"You're home. It's so good to see you." The young crewman gushed.

Blydh rolled his eyes, leading Endelyn to the Ruvane's seat between the two tall chairs. "Kerensa, you sit there."

Tallack and I shared a look of dismay. Blydh's senses were lost again. I made a hasty exit, leaving the Chiefs to bicker over which of their favoured folk deserved the seat most.

My back clicked and crunched as I walked across the damp grass to my hut. Every part from my tail bone to my neck was sore from the ride. More than anything, I wanted a warm meal and my bunk, but I knew my fire would be stone cold.

In the dark, I almost missed the shelter just beyond my house where I had laid Sorcha's body overnight. It had proper walls and a door panel, a full thatch and shuttered windows. Someone had completed its construction. Puzzled, I continued the few paces to my house and lifted the door from the entrance.

Much to my surprise, I found Kewri tucked up in his bed next to a roaring fire. My noise awoke him. He squinted at me, adjusting his sight to the low light.

"Fur Benyn." He almost jumped out of his bunk. "I wasn't expecting you back so soon."

"Nor I you. How come you didn't go with Senara to the meeting point in the borderlands?" I chuckled at his state; his black hair sticking up in all directions, the sleep still gluing his eyelids together.

"I did ride out there. Stayed a couple of days but she got annoyed with me and um…"

"She sent you back?"

He nodded; his eyes cast down to the rushes. I guessed that her familiarity with the Duro scout, Perren had put a strain on their relationship. Poor fellow had managed to lose both his lovers in one season.

Kewri milked one of my goats by torchlight, so that I could have some tasty warmed grains while I sat by the fire. The strain of the last few weeks had exhausted me beyond anything I could describe. I silently thanked the gods for delivering us home and vowed that I would do all I could to ease the suffering of those bereaved families left behind.

The tribal tribute chests and secret stashes of tin were empty. My knives and the men's weapons were all seized by the Belgae. It would take more than a full cycle to replenish the tin and jewels we gave as an offering. If the homesteader harvests failed come autumn, we'd have nothing with which to trade for grain.

Our people would need to scavenge to feed their young, like in our ancestors' times. My fears for our people were justified. A lasting peace with our neighbours was more important than ever.

Kewri sat with me while I ate, telling me all the news from the compound; which of the women had squabbled, others who had recovered from illness and more who had not. I thanked him for finishing the shelter for my patients and healing herbs. He smiled with embarrassment.

The soft-hearted giant was not used to praise. It wasn't until then that I realised how much I'd missed him. He was not chatty, like my Jago, but his quiet manner and wit put me at ease. I'm fortunate indeed that the gods saw fit to send him to our camp.

When my eyelids began to droop, I retired to my bunk. Kewri fixed the door so that there were fewer draughts and climbed in to his own bed. We could hear the warriors in the Long Hut celebrating the safe return of our Chiefs and the passing of our fallen into the Summerlands. I was glad that such things were not expected of me. I mourned their loss in my own way; in silence with the shedding of a few tears.

Death of ones so young always provoked contemplation. Why had the gods spared me and taken the youth and vibrancy of others? As the oldest tribal member, every day I awoke was a surprise. I'd outlived wives, mothers, Chieftains, warriors, and lovers. I'd seen so many pyres, so many ritual burials, I didn't think I could cope with any more.

I recalled my beautiful white hart, and the solace it gave me whenever I spoke with him. It tickled me that the tribe thought I had the ear of the gods. When they discover that my blundering attempts to treat their Chief's skull allowed a dark spirit from the Underworld to take him over, they would think it was done on purpose.

Despite my extreme exhaustion, I lay awake listening to the crackles and spits of the wood sap on the fire, pondering my existence. It seemed to me that the rowdy warriors were getting louder. I waited for a while, expecting it to die back down.

"Fur Benyn?" Kewri spoke softly. "Can you hear that racket?"

It was enough for me to drag my weary bones back out of bed and stand behind Kewri as he dislodged the door panel again. Wrapped in my bedding, I slipped my wooden pattens on and stepped outside to find a whole host of our men and elders gathered near to the Long Hut.

At first, they were all shouting and jostling, those at the back straining to see over the shoulders of men in front. Within moments they all went quiet. Kewri and I moved closer. He stayed at the outer limits of the circle, I bobbed under elbows until I had a clear view. Endelyn lay on the ground in the mud, her hands raised in submission. Blydh stood over her, his helm askew, his mouth dribbling.

"Tell me what you've done with her and I might spare your life." He snarled.

Endelyn scrambled to her knees, keeping her gaze low and meek. "Who, Chief Blydh? I don't understand…"

"Kerensa, daughter of the Alchemists, and fine warrior maiden in her own right." He prowled around her as though she was his prey. "I know you priests and your wicked ways. Where is she?"

It was obvious that he was having another episode, but Endelyn was unable to coax him back to reality. I glanced about the circle, looking for Tallack. He was the only one who could talk some sense into his brother. The Head Hunters and the Sea Warriors all hung their heads. Blydh's behaviour was shameful.

I tugged on the cuff of a man standing at my side. "Where's Tallack?" I whispered.

"He went off with Treeve, Fur Benyn."

I rolled my eyes, tutted, and shook my head. "Then go fetch him." And when he hesitated, I raised my voice. "Now man!"

"All I can say, priestess, is that you'd better not have used her for some vile sacrifice or you'll answer to me." Blydh thumped his chest. His eyes were wild, although it didn't help that his blind eye was directed at odds to the other one. He was deteriorating fast.

"Please, Chief Blydh. I have never known a Kerensa in my life. I'm truly sorry that she is missing, but it was not my doing."

"You lie!" Blydh reached forward and grabbed her fair hair, yanking her backwards. "You know what I do with liars?" His face was close enough to her that she blinked from the flying spittle. Endelyn clasped her hand to his, trying to ease the pull on her bunched locks. I could see that she was shaking from head to toe.

Tallack forced his way through the crowd, still fastening his clothes. He took in the scene and assessed his brother's condition. "What's all this, Blydh? Come and have a drink with me, brother."

"I don't want ale. I want Kerensa. This kyjyan holy woman has taken her from me." He raised his fist and was about to land a punch when Tallack stepped in and blocked him.

"Kerensa went home, Blydh. Don't you remember me telling you? We gave her a horse and she rode back to the Bentewyn mines." It was better to lie than tell the truth, especially in front of so many of the tribe. Blydh scowled at Tallack. His expression slackened just a fraction and for one glorious moment, I thought that Blydh was persuaded. I was wrong.

"You are too trusting brother. Can't you see that we're surrounded by spies?" He let go of Endelyn's hair and leaned closer to Tallack. "She's in league with the Duros. You can't let them win. It's precisely what Brea wants."

Tallack slid his arm about his shoulders, trying to turn him away from the priestess, but Blydh would not be distracted. Pushing the helmet square on his head, he shoved Tallack away and returned to his quarry. Grabbing her by the wrist, he yanked her along the grass, her knees and feet gouging tracks in the mud. Her cries for help grew more insistent as he made his way across the compound to his hut.

His warriors stepped aside, leaving his path open. None of them dared to challenge him. Tallack ran to catch up, pleading with his brother to see reason. It fell on deaf ears. Blydh's mind was set. If he couldn't punish Brea, he would take out his fury on the innocent Endelyn instead.

I scuttled along after them, not sure what help I could provide. We could all see what Blydh was planning to do to the priestess; a punishment that only a man would think to inflict. This had to be the work of the dark spirit in his head. Blydh would never sink to such depths, surely?

When they reached his hut, she spun about on her behind. Despite Endelyn's sorry state, she managed to fight back. She lashed out at his arms, clawing his skin and kicking against his shins. For someone who was normally so serene and composed, she turned into a wildcat of fury.

Sadly, her willowy frame was no match for the leader of the Head Hunters. With a single back handed swipe, Blydh stunned her, before dragging her by the ankle into the roundhouse.

"Do something, Tallack!" I called out, but he was already ahead of me. He pushed his way through the door skins of his brother's hut, only to be confronted by Blydh's fist. With one single knockout blow, Tallack was thrown backwards onto the ground. A quick peek told me that he'd lost consciousness.

As I reached the entrance, Blydh thrust the door panel in place and wedged it from the inside with a stake. No amount of me hammering with my fists would convince him to let her go. I slid down to the floor next to Tallack, with tears streaming down my face. Endelyn's screams echoed throughout the whole camp, and there was nothing I could do to help her.

CHAPTER TWENTY-ONE

Kewri caught up with me at Blydh's door and without asking, lifted Tallack up from the ground and carried him to his hut. I stayed for a short time longer, pleading through the wooden panel on Endelyn's behalf, but to no avail. None of the elders or warriors in camp were prepared to gainsay a Chieftain as volatile as Blydh, especially one who swore revenge unto death. When her tortured moans became too hard to bear, I paced the boardwalk back to my hut and waited. Kewri stayed with me. Whether it was my nervous state or that he sensed a need to be watchful for my protection, I wasn't sure, but I was glad of his company.

Endelyn had become a camp favourite among our people. Her treatment sent shock waves through the community. Initially, the buzz was in transmitting the news from weaver women to elders' wives and finally to the new recruits. Within moments, everyone knew what our Chief had done. Endelyn's cries prevented any fitful rest for most of the night. No one stirred until it was over.

Before dawn, there was complete stillness in the compound. Even the livestock and wild birds were silent. I was beyond tired, but too fretful to sleep. At first light when the cock finally crowed, I heard a little voice at my door.

"Fur Benyn. May I come in?"

I was sure that Blydh would kill her after he'd done all he could to make her suffer. Rushing to greet the pitiful creature, I didn't know whether to laugh or cry. Endelyn was alive, but only just.

"I have nowhere else to go for help." She shuffled in, wincing with every step. It'd taken every morsel of strength to get to my door. As soon as she was across the threshold, she collapsed in my arms. Her eyes were swollen and purple, great welts garnished her once pretty freckled face, and her clothes were shredded and barely covering her beaten body. Kewri offered to lift her, but she flinched every time he drew close.

"He won't hurt you, child. Isn't that so, Kewri?"

He shook his head with some violence. "Never." He looked as though he was about to sob.

"Go and fetch me some fresh water from the stream and then stand guard, if you will, please." I thought it best to get him away for both their sakes. She needed herbs and healing without fearing the men about camp. I struggled to get her to my bunk, lifting her legs up gently and covering her over. Dabbing at her face with a cloth soaked in cold water, I stroked her hair back out of her eyes.

She reached up and took hold of my hand. "Please don't say I told you so." Tears streaked down her temples and wet the bedding furs.

"Shush, now. Try to stay calm."

She didn't let go of my hand. I dragged a stool closer and sat by her side, assessing her injuries as best as I could without being too invasive. How could I make her feel safe with that demon loose about camp? I had no way of knowing what Blydh would do if Kewri refused him entry. Having seen his behaviour at first hand, he wouldn't think twice about running him through with a sword or spear.

As the day wore on and my exhaustion took hold, I drifted off to sleep leaning on the edge of my bunk holding her hand. It wasn't for long, and certainly not enough to fully restore my faculties, but my anger returned with a vengeance. Kewri was such a good lad. For one so big, he came and went with the stealth of a fox, balancing split logs on the fire, fetching more water and standing watch at the door. It was only when I heard Tallack's voice that I roused myself and poked my head through the door flaps, ready to start my day proper.

"Aunt Mel. Is she… did he…?" he fidgeted and stared down at his feet. He felt the shame on behalf of his twin.

"She lives and yes, he did, the vicious brute."

"Can I…?"

"No, you most certainly cannot. No men are to enter this house until further notice, is that clear?"

Tallack nodded apologetically. "Is there anything I can do?"

"Get me some poppy resin. I don't care if you have to swim to Iwerdon to get it, just get some, and don't let it anywhere near your kyjyan brother."

He nodded again and hurried away.

Kewri kicked the tufts of grass near to my goat pen. Why is it men would rather scale mountains or fight bears than be near to those who are ailing? He opened his mouth to speak and changed his mind.

"What? Spit it out, man. I haven't got all day."

"I thought that I could give an offering to Airmed outside the priestess's hut."

It was a lovely thought and I could see why he would want to make a sacrifice to the goddess of healing, but I needed his protection. "Later. I need you here with me, right now. Can you do that? Make sure no man enters, no matter who it is." He gave me a half smile and a nod. We both knew what was required of him. He was prepared to lay down his life to keep Blydh at bay.

One or two of the elders' wives stopped by to offer their support and a few provisions they had spare. Both had needed my services in the past and knew that a meal would be welcome at times like these. I took the salted pork and bread to Endelyn but could not persuade her to eat. All I could get down her was a small cup of willow bark tea for the pain. While she lay still, I stitched a cut above her eye and warmed water for washing. I laid out one of my clean tunics and turned to leave.

"No, don't go. Please." She whimpered, the panic returning.

"I was just going to stand at the door…" She grabbed my wrist until I agreed to stay. I babbled about her well-wishers and how concerned Chief Tallack was when he called earlier, mainly to distract myself from the wretched state of her broken body. She wasn't listening to a word I said, but my voice seemed to soothe her. It took all my concentration to stop myself from breaking down. She needed me to be strong. When she'd cleaned herself and dressed, I convinced her to get back under the furs. Sleep would do more to heal her than I could.

Kewri coughed loudly outside. "Fur Benyn. There's someone here to…"

"No visitors, Kewri."

"It's Senara."

I looked at Endelyn to see how she felt about the possibility of a shield maiden entering. She nodded and closed her eyes.

"Fine, tell her to come in."

Senara pushed through the drapes and stacked her bow and quiver against the wall by the door. "Kewri told me what happened. Do you want me to slice him from balls to gizzard? Just say the word, Fur Benyn. I'm your warrior, not that kyjyan monster's."

Her vitriol almost had me undone. I sucked in my lips to suppress a smile. I believe she'd do it too, despite Blydh being my nephew. I have to say, it was a tempting offer, but he was family after all. We were in no position to hold a Chieftain to account. Only the gods had that power.

"It's good to see you. Senara. What news have you?"

She was still seething about Endelyn's unjust treatment and only half listening. I had to tip my head into her line of sight before she snapped to attention. "Sorry, yes. Perren met with me when the moon was high last night. Tensions are boiling over in Brea's camp. She's doubled her guard and tripled their pay to ensure protection."

"So, the elders won't turn against her?" I was crestfallen. It was the only hope I had left after a full cycle of troubles.

"On the contrary. All the elders and their families want rid of her, and they think that can be achieved with as little bloodshed as possible."

"I'm guessing that means they have no need of our peace agreement."

"Well, Perren said that the families who are set to succeed Brea's rule are sick and tired of this ongoing feud between the Dumnos and Duros. He explained that they were amenable to a truce, but only if we agree to their terms."

It sounded like they were on the brink of a leadership revolution whether we were involved or not. She gave me a list of demands and then fell silent as I assimilated what it would mean if we agreed. I blew out my cheeks, wide eyed. It was quite a list. One of their terms would not be accepted by my tribe under any circumstances. Senara stood watching my reactions, awaiting a response. I had no answers to give.

"Where is Perren now?"

"He's at the meeting place until I return with your response."

I nodded. That made sense. At least while the lines of communication lay wide open; there was a chance to bring about peace, but at what cost? "Can you stay with Endelyn while she sleeps?" I thought that if anyone could provide the priestess with a sense of security it would be her.

Senara unsheathed her dagger and adopted a fearsome stance next to the bunk. "No one will get past me, Fur Benyn. You can count on that."

Bless that girl. I believed her too. She was tougher than any of the men about camp and possessed a sharpness of wit unlike any other. The morning was chilly and damp. I wrapped my cloak about me and headed towards the back door of the Long Hut. Kewri hopped from one foot to the other, unsure of what he should do.

"You're off the hook, lad." I yelled to him. "For now, at least. Senara's keeping guard." I thought he would hang around to attempt a reconciliation. If not that, then I expected him to use the time to find something to eat. He did neither. Lumbering after me like the old times, he seemed content to be my protector.

Sneaking in the rear entrance, I crept towards the platform supporting the top table and peered about the room. The fire was low and smoke had pooled in the roof space. It stank of piss and stale ale. Blydh's men were sleeping on the rushes, but there was no sign of either Chieftain.

I backed out and walked across the wet grass to Tallack's hut but only Treeve lay within. My nephew was elsewhere looking for the resin I'd demanded. In desperation, I trudged across the compound towards Renowden's shelter with Kewri following close behind. When I got to Ren's door, I held up my hand to my trusted guard. "I think I'm pretty safe in here."

Ren heard my voice before I stepped inside. He was standing with a bowl of steaming milk and grains. "Meliora. Would you like me to spoon out a bowl for you?"

"Kind of you but no, thank you. I need your counsel."

We sat around his fire while I explained all that had happened. When he heard the demands from the Duro elders, his eyes widened and his mouth fell open. "They can't ask that, it's impossible."

I nodded. "You're right, but according to their scout, they won't budge."

"How long does Tallack have to decide?"

I peered at the floor. "I haven't even told him yet. He's off to find poppy resin for Endelyn."

Ren picked at his nails. He couldn't look me in the eye. "That was a bad business all round." He swallowed hard, as if by being a man, he was partly responsible for the actions of Blydh. I patted his arm. It was not my nephew's actions after all but that of an evil spirit from the Underworld. Perhaps the creature was seeking revenge for our attempts to send him back into the arms of Cernonnus at the sacred springs.

We sat in silence for a time, each of us pondering the dark turn in tribal affairs. I drank a little of his ale and yawned.

"You look exhausted." He said rising to his bunk and shaking out the bedding. "Why don't you take a nap. From what you've told me, Kewri and Senara can handle things while you get some rest."

I didn't take much persuading. My back felt like every bone was lined with brambles, my neck crunched each time I moved my head, and I could barely think straight. Ren ushered me to his bed and pulled the furs up to my chin. It was blissful to have someone care about my health and wellbeing for a change. Ren stacked logs on the fire and filled his pipe with dried weed. I'd not felt this safe for a long time. Within moments of closing my eyes, I was asleep.

When I awoke, much of the day had passed me by. Ren was standing by his door, holding the skins to one side and peering out. I used the piss pot, stretched my back, and made my way over to see what had grabbed his attention. Posies of meadow flowers were stacked up against the carved icons outside Endelyn's hut. There were pots of grain, a couple of hares, a fine new tunic, and a few other bits and pieces lined up near the doorway.

I looked at Ren. "Strange offerings to the gods."

He shook his head. "Not offerings, gifts for the priestess. Virtually every family in the compound, and a few from beyond our walls, have been paying tribute to her all day."

"Do they not know she's in my hut?" I walked outside to get a clearer view.

Ren followed. "She's not anymore. Senara helped her to move back into her own place while you were asleep. Thought she'd feel better with her own stuff around her."

"Blydh?" I asked tentatively.

"No sign of him. Kewri's lurking about and Senara is still with the priestess, but all is eerily quiet about camp."

This was a shame that would linger in the memories of all our people. I thanked Ren for his kindness and made my way over to the carved icons. Their magnificence was already beginning to fade. The damp and cold conditions had stained the wood and the northern faces were tinged green. They lacked the vibrancy and vigour they once had, when our men first erected them at her door.

I called out and rapped my knuckle against the wooden panel. "Ho there. May I enter, priestess?"

Senara removed the creaking panel and welcomed me inside. There were more gifts within, some of food, others of carved trinkets, but the most stunning of them was a bouncing pup of just a couple of moons in age. It tumbled and rolled about until it landed at my feet, then proceeded to chew my toes through the gap in my pattens. I bent low and picked it up. It was a young bitch, filled with love and high spirits. "Where did this little terror come from?" She even managed to bring a smile to Endelyn's face, particularly as the pup bit down on everything and anything in its path, including my fingers.

"Ren brought her over earlier." Senara said, grinning at the playful antics as I returned it to the rushes.

I had no idea that he'd left the hut while I slept, let alone traded for a dog. "That was thoughtful of him. She'll guard you well when she's grown." I muttered to the priestess with a weak smile.

Senara puffed out her chest. "Until then, I shall make sure Endelyn's safe. You can rely on me, Fur Benyn."

I touched her shoulder on my way past. "I know I can, my dear." Sitting on the edge of the bed next to the priestess, she tried to shuffle over to give me more room. Even that seemed to cause her pain. She was far from over the worst. "I've sent Tallack out to get poppy resin. I'm sure he won't be long. Until then, have you enough willow bark to keep you going?"

Endelyn nodded.

"And, um… would you like me to make you a tonic to hasten the bleed? Just in case…"

Endelyn shook her head. I have to admit, that really surprised me.

She looked at me with those huge doleful eyes, the water pooling in her lower lids. "If this is what the gods have chosen for me, I shall bear my fate."

How could she entertain the notion of keeping the result of such an ordeal, if indeed she was with child? "Are you sure about this, Priestess?"

Endelyn nodded again. "I have been tested by the gods. My faith is strong, Fur Benyn. I will endure."

"Well, if you change your mind, you know where to find me." I stood up to leave, sensing that my skills were no longer required.

Endelyn reached out and squeezed my hand. "Thank you, for…" She glanced over to Senara and then back at me. "For everything."

As I approached the doorway, I glanced back over my shoulder. "I'll send Kewri over with the resin as soon as it arrives." The puppy pounced on the bunk and licked Endelyn's face. Senara chuckled and joined them. If it weren't for the harrowing circumstances that brought these two together, I'd say they looked to be blissfully happy. For a brief moment, I saw something between them, something greater than friendship, something more than a sisterly connection. Maybe I was mistaken.

With my duty of care concluded, my focus shifted to the impossible terms set out by the Duro elders to secure a lasting peace between our people. I had to find my nephew, Tallack and give him the uncomfortable news.

CHAPTER TWENTY-TWO

Tallack was not in the Long Hut, but Blydh was. I could hear him boasting to his men about his conquests from outside. He'd already taken more ale than was appropriate under the circumstances and his men did little to discourage his excesses.

From their muted responses to my nephew's bragging, I guessed that they feared him. It wasn't a case of them being unable to fight against him in single combat, but more like the laws of our tribe forbade such disobedience. None dared to test his right to have them flayed or burnt alive for making a stand. Only Tallack could safely gainsay Blydh, and as the events from the night before illustrated, even he had little sway over his actions.

I returned to my hut to clear up the mess and prepare my supper, keeping a weather eye on the main paths through the compound in case Tallack had returned. Tribe's folk kept delivering gifts and tributes to Endelyn right up until darkness fell, each of them showing their support for the priestess in her troubles.

Kewri came in clutching the back legs of a rabbit. "Endelyn sent this for you by way of thanks." He muttered, lifting the limp carcass under my nose.

"That's kind of her, but not necessary. We have plenty."

"I said that too, but Senara insisted that I take it. Something about there being more than they could cope with." He sighed and slumped down on a stool by the fire.

"You've patched things up with her then?"

He pulled a face worthy of a sullen child. "No. She won't have me back."

It was hard to feel sympathy for the giant. He'd strung two women along at the same time. He was lucky that Senara didn't take offence and slice off a sensitive part of his body in revenge.

When the moon was high over the palisade walls, Ren appeared at the door. "Meliora, you'd better come."

"What is it? Has something happened to the priestess?" I grabbed my cloak and scuttled after him.

"She's fine. It's Blydh. He's out of control." Ren's great strides were hard to match. He was practically at the Long Hut door before I'd left my house.

"Where's Tallack? Isn't he back yet?"

Ren shook his head. "No." He stopped and waited for me to catch up.

"What about their mother?" I puffed, sending clouds of steam into the night air from my lungs.

"That's why I fetched you. He's screaming at Cryda now."

A vision flitted through my mind of the willowy Cryda, the babe Delen in her arms, fending off the dark spirit inside her son. What if Blydh mistook his mother for the priestess and decided to punish her all over again? In a blind panic, I hurried into the Long Hut, frightened by what I'd find.

Cryda sat in her usual seat at the top table, with Blydh lounging in his brother's carved tall chair. She was without her child, which was a blessing, although I thought her presence might snap my nephew out of his delusions. Cryda looked petrified. Her slender hands gripped the arm of the tall chair while she pleaded with Blydh to be reasonable. At their feet lay a slave girl; her head turned unnaturally over her shoulder, her tongue lolling from her open mouth. A short distance from her body was the upturned mess of what looked like stew, strewn across the floor.

I could guess what had happened. As much as it saddened me that a slave girl's life was so expendable, the priority was to secure Cryda's safety. In Tallack's absence, there was no one else who could approach Blydh with any kind of status in the tribe. Knowing that my interference was likely to inflame matters, I had to deflect his ire away from his mother.

"Ho there, Chief." I moved with caution closer to the top table. He could definitely see my approach with his good eye; his lip curled as I drew near. Undeterred, I tried to keep my tone of voice light so as not to provoke him further. "Can I tempt you with some roasted rabbit or a little duck perhaps?"

He twisted his head around to face me and snarled. "I want nothing from you. You're just as likely to poison me as that kyjyan bitch, Brea did my father."

"Now, nephew, that's not fair. I loved your father as well you know. What happened to Aebba was a tragedy. She will pay for what she did." I stopped walking, making sure I was out of the reach of his arm and sword.

Blydh scoffed. "That's a joke. You and Brea were great friends, just like my kyjyan half-brother, who you let escape." He grabbed his cup and drained the contents.

I wanted to correct him, but figured that it would do no good to implicate poor Kewri further. He'd suffered enough for his mistake in accidentally setting Paega free.

"We were all deceived by Brea, Chief, and we all feel Aebba's loss keenly. Not least your poor mother."

Cryda took my cue and piped up. "I still haven't laid his bones to rest."

"And nor shall you until Brea is made to pay for what she's done, along with all her collaborators." Blydh growled, turning his glare back to me. I'd succeeded in drawing his wrath away from Cryda, only to have him snap at me instead. As I backed away, he kept his scowl fixed in my direction. Cryda used the distraction to make her excuses and move to a seat with the elders' wives further away. She was safe for now, but Blydh was likely to turn on anyone.

Edging out of the rear door, I called out to the nearest slave. It was a grim task for them to bury one of their own, but someone had to dispose of the girl. There would be no grave goods nor blessing, just a hole next to the midden pile big enough for her crouched body. I waited near the roasting pits for them to retrieve her.

She had dark skin. It reminded me of my Jago and the lurid way in which he was killed. Why were the lives of this girl and my slave worth nothing, when those born unto our tribe were deemed valuable? Were they not children of grieving parents? Were they not skilled in their own ways? Were their contributions to tribal life less important than our weavers, butchers or the smith? I shook my head in frustration.

When the slaves had finished clearing up the mess in the Long Hut and refilled the ale jugs, I slipped back inside and sat as far away from the top table as I could, mingling with the elders and listening to their gripes. All the talk of Brea and the Duros had stirred up their emotions. How was I ever going to persuade them that a peace between our tribes was in all our interests? Most of them were too young to remember my brother, Cador the Cruel. Both he and his son, Aebba attempted treaties between our tribes and all for nought. The Duros continued to attack our borderlands and we theirs.

Kewri and Ren joined me on the benches closest to the door. They poured themselves ale, but there was nothing to celebrate. We were down a significant amount of metal and ruled by a dark entity that was too powerful to be ousted by Endelyn's ritual at the sacred springs. What foul deeds would this beast lead the men into in the name of protecting our people?

Ren lowered his voice so that only we three could hear. "I must say, Meliora, there's a certain justice in using the same plot that Brea cooked up with the Novantae against her."

"You're assuming that it'll work. We discovered the Novantae treachery before they could carry out their plans and look how that turned out for them." I couldn't stop my cynicism from leaking out of me. The sleep I'd had in Ren's hut barely touched the surface of my exhaustion. Every moment of waiting for Tallack's return, heighten my anxiety levels, keeping me jittery all evening. I peered about the Long Hut, noting the spaces on the warrior's benches and that many of the elders had already returned home with their wives for the night. The entire place was abnormally quiet.

Ren guessed what I was thinking. "The elders may not be able to stop Blydh's disgraceful actions, but they can choose not to encourage him."

It hadn't occurred to me until it was pointed out. There was no singing, no pipers blowing out a merry tune, no laughter nor tales of yore. A few of Blydh's senior warriors remained, but I got the impression it was more to keep watch than to drink and carouse.

"He's lost their respect." I muttered, thinking aloud.

Ren and Kewri both nodded their agreement. Old Aebba the Wild would be mortified if he knew the depths to which his son had sunk. Both he and Cryda always assumed that Blydh would be the greatest leader of our tribe in generations. His solid, dependable form of brutality was tempered with reason and restraint. He only ever sliced heads off our enemies and only in retaliation for their crimes against our people and lands. This imitation of him was hard to swallow.

I thought about the Duros' demands in return for peace and quailed. "What are we to do?" I said out loud before realising.

"The men told me that word was sent to the mines at Bentewyn before we set off for the sacred springs. The order was to bring more tin from their stores. If Kenver can ship more to us soon, it might be alright. There is a chance that the Duros' will accept less." Ren offered.

I blew out my cheeks. "I wasn't thinking about the demand for metal. That can always be found or beaten down to something reasonable."

Ren understood the sticking point better than most. "You've got me there. It's insurmountable." We all watched as Blydh tried to goad his warriors into a wrestling match in front of the top table. They gave him awkward smiles in return, unsure how to refuse his request. Our warriors were not entertainers. To suggest that they should fight one another for sport was an insult. It pained me to witness my kin sink so low.

When at last I spotted Tallack hovering in the doorway, I was greatly relieved. Struggling to my feet, I ambled over and took the small pot of resin from his hand. "Oh, thank Cernonnus. That will ease Endelyn's pain and keep me stocked for a long time. Wherever did you find it?"

"Don't ask, Aunt Mel. I had to trade the weapons we took from the Belgae for that. I'm just glad I wasn't carrying my special sword, or they would have taken that too." I was humbled by his sacrifice. He'd clearly travelled the entire day and long past darkness to provide what I needed. He was shaping up to be a fine Chieftain, one we could all be proud to call our leader. "How is the priestess?" He wiped his cuff across his sweaty face, smearing the mud and filth from his journey.

"Faring better than your brother." I cocked my head in Blydh's direction and sighed. Blydh was out of the tall chair and roaming around the empty benches, spilling ale wherever he went. I couldn't put it off any longer. "Senara's back from the crossing on the River Sid."

"Oh, what news did she bring?"

Steadying myself, I knew that what I had to tell him would not be received well. "The Duro elders are amenable to a peace treaty, but their terms of agreement are harsh."

He narrowed his eyes at me. "Go on."

"Huge quantities of tin, an ongoing trade agreement that is frankly ridiculous… something along the lines of equal tin to copper exchange."

Tallack hissed. "They can shove that up their kyjyan arses for a start."

"Yeah, I think they are starting high but expecting to come down to something respectable later. That's not the issue."

"Then what is?"

"They have a plan to overthrow Brea with little bloodshed and they've made it clear to us that we're not needed to bring this about. According to the scout, they're happy to just kill her and be done with it."

"I see."

"The only way they will hand her over alive, is if we give them someone in return." I couldn't look him in the eye. My nerve failed me. I bit my lip until it hurt, hoping that he would comprehend the rest and save me from actually voicing the words.

"And who had they in mind?"

"They wish to punish the leader of our Head Hunter Clan; the man who has taken the lives of many of their people from the borderlands." My eyes welled up. I sniffed back the drippings accumulating at the tip of my nose.

Tallack drew a sharp breath. "You mean to say they want to swap Brea for Blydh? That is out of the question." His voice rose beyond a whisper until he was rasping at me. I'd anticipated his response, but was not able to think of anything to offer in solution.

"Well, I guess that's the end of that idea. We can't possibly forge a peace with the Duros under those conditions."

"Under what conditions?" Blydh said. I hadn't noticed him looming up behind me and neither did Tallack. "Why would we want peace with the Duros?" He trained his good eye down on me. "What's all this about, brother?" I wasn't sure who was in charge of my nephew's body. His voice was tempered; he sounded like the Blydh of old.

"It's nothing to bother about." Tallack said, reaching out to Blydh's shoulder and guiding him back into the centre of the Long Hut.

Blydh shrugged him off. "No, tell me now. I have just as much right as you over tribal matters. What's this about striking some deal?"

Tallack took a long breath. "It was just something Aunt Mel and I were considering, but it didn't work out. No harm done."

"You and Aunt Mel? Not me." He slipped past Tallack and rounded on me near to the door. "The Duros are our sworn enemy. Just exactly what was this Duro spy suggesting?"

"Brother, please."

"No! I want to hear it from her." He shoved a finger into my chest, pushing me backwards towards the wall. "Tell me, Aunt Mel…" The way he sneered when he said my name made me shudder. "What precisely has that kyjyan bitch Brea asked you to do this time? Eh? Snake in the camp. What was it?"

My head banged against the wall, knocking out some of the dried daub. His finger bruised my breastbone. "I am not Brea's spy. I'm loyal to you and Tallack. Please, Blydh, we are kin." I could see my pitiful reflection in the shine from his helmet. How could he think that I would betray our tribe?

"You're no kin of mine. You're a snake. What was the plan, another fatal poisoning, maybe a leather strap fastened about my neck while I slept, or a blade across my throat?"

"I promise you, none of those things. I would never harm you." I shrieked as his finger became an insistent knuckle pressed to my chest, pinning me against the crumbling walls.

"Ha!" He gestured to his glassy right eye. "What do you call this?" And when I said nothing, he tapped the rim of the helmet. "And this?"

"You know full well, I did my best to treat you. Not even the blessing of Airmed at the springs could restore your sight."

He scoffed again. "Yeah right. *The Blessing*." He sneered. "I wouldn't mind betting the priestess is working for Brea too. You kyjyan women are all in it together. A whole camp of vipers."

Tallack tried to pull Blydh off me but he elbowed his brother in the face.

"Stay out of this. I know how to deal with Duro spies."

Before I could escape, Blydh grabbed me around the throat with both hands and squeezed. His fingertips pressed into my windpipe, choking off the air. I scratched and clawed at him to make him release me but he was too strong. As his grasp tightened, cutting off the tubes in my neck, my eyes bulged. I could feel my feet lifting from the floor, the pressure on my spine increasing. Almost on tiptoes, I tried to plead for my life, but all that came out were guttural splutters.

With lungs burning, I closed my eyes and waited for it all to be over. The light flickering inside extinguished, excepting that my time had come. I had earned my journey into the Underworld and hoped that some kind soul would pay Cernonnus for my admittance.

CHAPTER TWENTY-THREE

My world went quiet. With arms limp and lifeless at my side, I felt my life draining away. I had no strength left in me to fight. Before the last moment with my tribe ebbed away, I saw Kewri; his expression passive, considered. He lifted the helm from Blydh's head with one of his massive hands, and with the other balled up tightly, smashed his fist down on the golden disc inside Blydh's skull.

His scalp split open, the golden plate crumpled and pressed into his soft brain. Those angry fingers loosened from around my neck. His left eye twitched, his mouth fell open, and my nephew crashed to the ground. I took an enormous gasp of air, coughing until my spirit reconnected with my body. Blydh bumped and jerked a couple of times on the rushes and then lay still. No one moved. Tallack, Kewri and I stood over the corpse, expecting the warrior to jump to his feet. This was a man who'd survived against all odds. None of us believed he could die.

Tallack was the first to realise the full enormity of what had occurred. He stooped down and rested his palm against Blydh's face. "Sleep well, brother. Save a space for me.

That was when Cryda knew that her first born was gone forever. She howled louder than any wolf and rushed to his side. The more she wailed, the more hysterical she became, pounding Blydh's solid chest in the hope that she could rouse him. Kewri let the helmet fall to the floor and bowed his head.

"Seize him!" Cryda shrieked. "Men, protect your Chief."

Still no one moved, not even Tallack. All could see that Blydh had lost his battle against the evil inside him. Only his mother blamed Kewri for his swift actions.

Between sobs, Cryda wailed the same thing over and over; "This is all Brea's fault."

It felt wrong to leave her sprawled across the body of her son, but no amount of coaxing would persuade her to leave the Long Hut. Kewri sat back down next to Ren waiting for Tallack to proclaim his sentence. I was too stunned to move from the doorway.

One by one, Blydh's remaining warriors and the elders left through the rear door, leaving just us few. None dared to speak. We simply waited for Cryda to accept all that had happened. I looked down at my dead nephew. His eyes were each facing a different direction, but the fury in his brow had gone, taking the hatred and paranoia with it, and for the first time since that terrible night at the Duro camp, he looked serene and at peace. Whether he would walk with his forefathers in the Summerlands or take the journey into the Underworld, I could not say, but he was at last beyond the reach of his enemies.

Cryda lay the blame on Brea. She was the root of all ails in our tribe since the day she poisoned the twin's father. Now Cryda had two cherished family members to bury, while Brea still walked free. When the Long Hut fire burnt low and the torches sputtered and fizzed, Tallack dismissed us. He stayed by his mother and brother on the rushes as we left. I pushed the giant outside and chivvied him back to my hut. The poor lump was dazed and numb. He'd carried out the Chief's orders to the bitter end, protecting me from any attacker. Neither of us knew what his fate would be for saving my life yet again. I tried to thank him but my words came out jumbled. He understood my meaning even if my speech went astray.

I slept poorly that night. My throat pained me and I was too anxious to settle, so that by dawn, I was already up and about my business. Kewri slept not a wink at all. I heard him pacing about the rushes and banking up the fire until the moon was ready to dip below the horizon. He kept himself busy, doing all my chores outside and chopping more wood to stack under the eaves.

As I was returning from checking on the priestess, Tallack caught up with me on the boardwalk. He couldn't stop staring at the marks on my neck. They still hurt and my voice was reduced to a rasp, but I had nothing to complain about. I'd survived yet another brush with death, while a younger family member perished in my place. My emotions were so close to the surface I feared that I'd never stop crying if I set them free.

"How's Endelyn?" Tallack's eyes were raw. He'd obviously grieved in his own time, in his own way. I was glad of that. Nothing good ever came from holding feelings inside, as I could well attest; my belly roiled with a fury that would not be quelled.

"On the mend, I think."

He nodded and then held my gaze. "Mother doesn't want a pyre."

"Oh?"

"She wants full funeral rites for both Blydh and father at the cromlech beyond Hunter's Tor. She's sent messengers out to call the clan leaders to attend."

"And by leaders you mean Kenver from Bentewyn?" Blydh led the Head Hunters and Tallack the Sea Warriors. The only other clan apart from Kenver's Alchemists were scattered when Paega soiled our water supplies. The Priest Sect was no more, replaced by a single priestess from the moors.

He narrowed his lips and nodded again.

"And when he discovers that both Kerensa and Hellyer are dead, what then?"

He shrugged. "I guess we'll find out in time. First things first, Aebba the Wild cannot be interred while he is unavenged."

I closed my eyes. My body sagged with exhaustion. "Brea." It was hardly the time to be thinking of deals and treaties between tribes, but what choice did we have? "Do you think that the Duro elders would be prepared to exchange Brea for Blydh's body?" I braced myself for the biting rebuke, but none followed.

"Mother wouldn't stand for that. She's insistent on the rites. It was the only way I could convince her to forgive Kewri."

A strong fluttering paralysed my chest. "You forgave him? He won't be punished?"

"I thought you'd be pleased. He was only doing as I commanded."

I flung my arms about him and let the tears fall. "Thank you. That's more than either of us deserve. I knew you'd be a fair and wise ruler."

Tallack's face flushed with embarrassment. "My brother died the day that the giant carried him into your hut to operate on his skull. We've been fooling ourselves that he was still around when all the time that dark spirit swapped places with him in the Underworld."

Retracting my arms from his back, I reached up and cupped his face in my palms. "You're a good man."

He did his best to smile, but I could tell he was hurting inside. The bond with his twin was finally broken. Tallack would feel the loss for the rest of his life. Nothing can replace that kind of closeness. I started off towards my hut but stopped just a short distance away.

Turning back to face him, I said, "You know, we have nothing to lose by asking the Duros. What if I can convince them to accept Blydh's death as honouring their terms?"

Tallack frowned. "Wouldn't they just kill Brea to spite us?"

"Then our aims are achieved however it plays out. Not quite vengeance for Aebba, but we would have forged new allies out of the tragedy." I watched him ruminate on my words. Nothing would bring his brother back to life, but if Blydh's death could deliver a swift end to the misery of borderland raiding, then it was worth pursuing.

"Fine. Send Senara to their scout. The sooner we act the better. I doubt the Duros will wait to overthrow that kyjyan from the mountains."

Hurrying back to my hut, I thought about Tallack's order and how settled Endelyn was in the company of Senara, and wondered if it would halt the priestess's recovery to be without her. The Duro scout, Perren, knew both me and Kewri. It was a chance to get the giant out of camp for a day or so until Cryda's wrath had subsided.

When I told him that Tallack bore no grudge over the death of his brother, Kewri almost collapsed from relief. His spine buckled as he sat on his bunk and a lazy grin spread across his face. After the news had sunk in, I explained my plan and told him to make ready. I had a greater task ahead of me; to convince the former Ruvane to give up the body of her child.

Walking the longer route across camp, I found myself dawdling outside Cryda's hut. I knew that her grief would be so raw as to make her oppose any suggestion I placed before her. The trouble was, the longer we tarried, the greater the likelihood of the Duros backing out of the peace treaty.

"Cryda?" My gullet throbbed with pain. "It's me. Can I come in?"

The door coverings flapped to one side as she poked her head out with a pinched expression and clenched teeth. "You've got a nerve coming here. I've a good mind to call to the men and have you whipped."

"I'm sorry for what happened, truly, but you know in your heart that this was not my fault." I held up my palms in supplication.

Her scowl lessened just a fraction. She edged backwards allowing me to enter. "If you hadn't provoked him, that clumsy oaf wouldn't have needed to protect you." Her voice trailed off when she caught sight of my bruised neck. "Well, it was still avoidable." She sniffed, blinking fast. I moved closer, sensing that she needed my support. She lowered her head to my shoulder. I embraced the poor mite, stroking her back and rocking her gently from side to side.

"There, there. That's right, let it all out, you'll feel much better." I said when the sobbing began. Although I felt her suffering as acutely as my own, I also felt a fraud. There I was, soothing her in her time of grief to make it easier for me to bend her to my will.

I told myself it was for the good of the tribe, but in truth, I wanted to prove that I was right. Senara may have come up with the idea to pursue peace with the Duros, but I was the one who'd pushed for the treaty to put an end to tribal war. More than anything, I was determined to bring peace to both our lands.

Blydh's body lay on a table to our right. She'd already begun to strip and wash him. The golden sun disc poked out from his scalp, bloodied and slick with brain matter. If only I had asked the smith to prepare a thin plate of silver, his life would be spared. I kept my musing to myself. That poor decision of mine brought about Blydh's death and left his baby sister at risk. Delen had lost her half-sister Derwa, banished to the mountain people, and now Blydh, who had assured the sun at her naming ceremony. What will become of her now that she only has her mother and Tallack to protect her?

I waited until Cryda had taken her fill of solace and then sat by her fireside. She joined me and we quickly fell into a comfortable chatter. We didn't share the same blood, but we'd grown close over the winter. Just as I was plucking up the courage to ask her, she threw out a request of her own.

"Will you help me to prepare him for the ritual, Meliora? Not like with Aebba. I don't want it taken over by priests or strangers or anyone. I want his passing to be honoured, not spoiled." It was more than I'd expected and a task I felt ill equipped to perform. Not only were my own emotions in tatters, but my knives were gone, taken by the Belgae. Our tribe had never experienced such a dearth of resources in all my summers. Even if I could borrow a blade sharp enough to deflesh the body, the thought of carving up one so close and so young as Blydh would finish me. I chose not to answer her.

"Cryda, I have something important to discuss with you. Please know that what I ask is a terrible imposition, and under any other circumstances, would not be entertained, but you must hear me out."

I went on to explain the situation between the Duro elders and their plan to overthrow Brea. Her frown turned into a scowl at the mention of her name. "The thing is, they are willing to trade Brea with us in a peace accord." I pressed on, hoping that she'd see what it would mean to our people. When I got to the part where our enemies had demanded her son in return, I hesitated. Blydh was beyond harm. His reputation among our people sullied forever by his recent inexplicable actions. This one trade off, could go a long way to restore his once good name. Despite this, I was sure that she would refuse. Her narrowed eyes made it hard for me to concentrate on how to proceed.

"The Duros are happy to hand over Brea to us, alive, if…um…"

"What… if what? What do they want from us in return?" She snapped.

I swallowed and took a long breath. "They want the leader of the Head Hunter Clan, to appease those who had suffered from Blydh's vicious raids in their borderlands."

Her nostrils flared, but she remained in control.

I continued with caution. "I think I can convince them to accept his death as proof that we've honoured their terms."

She pursed her lips, tilting her head to one side. "They can't have him. They'll defile his body and parade him around like some grotesque trophy. I won't have it, no. That's my final word."

"I agree, but what if I can persuade them to an alliance by only allowing them sight of him as proof that he is gone? We'd have new allies, a trade route through their lands and our people would be safe from attack. I promise I won't let them take him."

Even Cryda could see that it was a good deal by any standards. The question was, could I deliver on my promise? It took a little more cajoling for her to come around, but eventually she saw the sense in my plan. She even offered to accompany me to the crossing on the River Sid for the negotiations, but I reminded her that it was no place for the baby Delen, especially since it could take a number of days for the Duros to stage their revolution against the tyrant, Brea.

I left her a short time later to make the preparations. Kewri loaded all that we needed, plus Blydh's wrapped body, on to Aebba's old wagon and hitched up the ponies. Tallack insisted that we took along three of his trusted warriors, in addition to Renowden and Massen. We were a sombre crew, treading the same familiar path back to the borderlands and our meeting with the Duro scout.

Kewri appeared to be the most disturbed of us all, riding his huge cart horse alongside the wagon carrying the remains of the man he killed. I sat alone on the driving bench of the wagon, steering the ponies. It suited me to be at one with my own reflections. Ren and Massen led our party, with the three warriors from Tallack's clan behind.

The closer we got to the River Sid, the more I felt the chill in my bones. It was never a happy place for me; too many past tragedies and heartbreaks on which to dwell. Sometimes I wished that my memory was impaired, if only to make the sad times easier to bear.

There were no delays on our half day's ride to the meeting place. Perren's fire smoke was visible for some distance, allowing Ren to ride ahead and check that the scout was alone. He may have been Senara's friend but he was still a Duro and there was a chance that we'd been duped. We waited a short way down the track for Ren's signal that it was safe for us to approach before riding up to the hidden campsite. I made sure that Blydh's body was well covered, but he was already beginning to attract flies.

Perren stood with an arrow nocked in his bow. He had it directed at the ground as we dismounted. When he saw Kewri and me, his nervous stance relaxed a little. "Where's Senara?"

"I made her stay behind. She has other duties to attend to." I straightened up and offered him my arm in greeting. "You remember me?"

He scanned us all in one sweep, deciding whether we were to be trusted. As his gaze fell once more on me, he eased the bowstring and took my forearm. "I do. You are the one they call, Fur Benyn."

I sniffed. "Meliora will do, lad. We have ale if you're willing to share your fire with us." I beckoned him to sit on a log at my side. It was important that he took our message without twisting its meaning. The last thing we needed was for him to enrage the elders further with news that Blydh was already dead. I was also aware that it could be a few days before their plan was put into action, and by then Blydh's corpse could well be unrecognisable.

Over the course of a cup or two of ale, and a little of the rabbit meat he'd roasted over the fire, I prised scant information from the man. Every attempt to steer the conversation around to that of the Duro elders, he deflected with unusual mastery. He was no dim wit. With the night creeping fast on the horizon, I dispensed with subtlety and got straight to the point.

"Perren, I need you to go this very night and take a message to the one who will lead when Brea has fallen. Tell them that we agree to their terms and wish to meet them as a matter of urgency." Ren and Massen gave each other furtive looks. They understood the risk I was taking in gambling with half-truths.

"Begging your pardon, Fur Benyn, but I know for a fact that he won't parley with anyone but the Chieftain of the Dumnonii. Unless Tallack himself comes here to assure the terms of the treaty, and the sacrifice of his brother, the elders won't trust its validity."

CHAPTER TWENTY-FOUR

"What game is this? Do you take us for fools?" Ren stood and towered over the slender young scout. "First you demand the head of one of our Chiefs and now you expect us to deliver the other." It surprised me how quick he was to flare. Ren was generally the easy going one.

"I can assure you that this is no game, nor trap. They will take the power away from Brea whether you agree to terms or not. Part of the promises given to our people in return for their support is that the Dumnos are made to pay for the lives taken in our borderlands." Perren cowered away from the reach of Ren and Massen. I have to say, the boy had more courage than I anticipated.

"The same could be said about our land and people. The Duros have raided our homesteaders for generations." I said, trying to find the middle ground.

"That's also true, and it's why our elders are prepared to sit down with Chief Tallack and forge an alliance which benefits all, but only if he agrees to the conditions sent with Senara to your camp."

Ren was losing his temper. "And I suppose it has nothing to do with your elders needing our tin?"

"Another good point, which they are willing to discuss."

All the men looked at me to break the deadlock. In mulling over the problem, I inadvertently glanced at the back of the wagon, before quickly averting my eyes. The last thing we needed was for Perren see the body at this stage in the deception. "Bring your new leaders here with Brea alive, and we will make sure that Chief Tallack is here to greet them." I gave Ren a tiny shake of my head, signalling for him not to make a fuss. "But go this moment, young Perren. This offer will spoil quicker than day old cream." I pushed him towards his horse and flicked my wrists to hasten his journey every time he glanced over his shoulder at me.

When the Duro scout was out of sight and hearing, I turned to Massen. "Ride faster than the wind and explain to Tallack what's happened. Tell him that I suggest he comes with a show of force." He knew my meaning, and without delay, mounted his horse and sped away like Cernonnus was chasing him. Ren and the others looked askance. Perhaps I had overstepped my bounds, but this was a chance in a lifetime opportunity and I was not about to squander that.

"I'd better find a safer meeting place. This one is too enclosed." Ren said, starting to walk away.

"No need." I called after him. "The meeting will take place on the bridge." I'm no great shakes at battle strategy, but I know how to spot a kill zone. The river was the border between our two lands, the midway point of the bridge, to be precise. It was a safe bet that the new Duro leader would come with an immense number of warriors, so it was only fair that we did too.

"You know what's at stake?" Ren lowered his voice to a whisper and leaned into my neck.

I stepped aside. "I do, but this is worth the risk" Of all people, I'd hoped that Ren would be on my side, see the benefits to be had by forging this alliance. At best, the Duros would accept the sighting of Blydh's body and negotiate a settlement over tin trades. At worst, they could take great offence and launch an attack from across the river. Either way, we'd be prepared for them.

We had time to eat, forage and extend the shelter for the night ahead of us. Ren took first watch at the river side of the forest, while I plucked and gutted a couple of ducks for the pot. We moved the wagon under the dense canopy of the trees to shade it from the heat of the sun. I sent the men among the oaks to collect as much moss as they could carry while I carefully unwrapped Blydh's corpse in the rear of the cart.

When I revealed the crater in his skull and the damage to his forehead, a sudden recollection from my youth made me queasy. Then, as with now, the Duros were heavily involved but it was my close kin who had broken my heart that day. I pushed the memory down and got back to work, packing the cool moss around every part of my dead nephew and wrapping him tightly. It was an old trick, but it kept some of the maggots and flies from taking their fill of flesh. Short of removing his guts and smoking him like a fish, there was little more I could do to preserve him.

The men took turns in keeping watch throughout the night, insisting that I slept in the warmest part of the shelter. Not that I could drop off with all my worries and fears swirling in my head. It was not long after dawn when I first heard the rumble of hooves on the dry earth. Ren met our warriors on the track. He suggested suitable lookout spots for the guards, before guiding Tallack to the camp. Ren's mood seemed noticeably brighter with so many fighting men at our backs. The plan was tenuous at best, but having Tallack's support made it feel like a possibility.

My nephew was less pleased to see me. "I told you to send Senara, not go yourself. Are you out of your mind?

We have no idea whether the scout, let alone the Duro elders can be trusted. He might have had warriors waiting to slaughter you all." He slid from his horse's back before it had come to a full stop. Grasping my shoulders, he was about to shake me until he peered down at my face and softened. "What am I to do with you?" The shake became a hug that made it hard for me to breathe. When he finally let go, we sat together with Ren and talked through all the ways in which the Duros could try to deceive us.

By midday, our warriors had built their shelters and were well stocked with provisions. Tallack made them camp in the open, close to the crossing so that any Duro scouts keeping watch would see our numbers and preparedness. Ren built fires around the wagon to keep scavengers at bay and then joined us to eat. To my surprise, he brought with him a young shield maiden.

"Look who I found building a shelter with the men." Ren said, almost in a chuckle.

"Senara!" My mouth hung open. "You haven't left the priestess alone, surely?"

Tallack snorted. "She's with my mother."

It was hard not to laugh. I wanted to say, *hasn't the poor woman been through enough?* But I didn't think Tallack would see the humour in my remark. Despite everything, we were quite at home in the woodlands next to the river. Senara and I caught up with news from the compound while Tallack checked on the men. Kewri slept the afternoon away. He was rostered alongside the men after dark for guard duty.

At dusk, Ren appeared. He was holding the reins of his horse with his hand extended toward me. "Come for a ride, Meliora. I want to show you something."

Curious, I grasped his arm and let him push me up on to his pony. When we were both mounted, he kicked the horse's flanks and directed the pony towards the river bank further north. We didn't need to go far, just to where a wide meander had dug a steep gouge in the highest slope of the valley. As the sun set behind us, we could see right across the vast expanse of Durotriges' land bordering the Sid.

I squinted until my old eyes adjusted to the light and the distance. Where just a moon or two ago we saw Duro warriors felling and moving tree trunks, building palisades and trenches, we now saw smoke - more black billowing smoke than I ever saw before. Women and children ran in all directions, their homes and shelters dancing in flame. The whole camp was in chaos.

"That's the Duro elders rebelling. Burn Brea's badly placed compound and in the confusion, take over leadership."

It was a smart move. Her paid guards would all be too busy putting out fires and saving livestock to protect her. Once the new leader was proclaimed, and in control of all tribal wealth, her warriors would fall into line with their kin. There was one ambitious girl from the mountains who'd be lucky to live out the night.

We watched for a little longer, before the black smoke obscured our view. The Duro elders did not delay in carrying out their plan. We had yet to see whether they would keep their word over delivering Brea to us in one piece.

Tallack did not appear pleased to hear the news when we got back. He nodded briefly acknowledging his understanding and then retired to the shelter to sleep. Senara caught a duck and gave its life in offering to the gods. I heard her blessing and request as she muttered it quietly at the fireside.

"Keep Endelyn safe until I return, Cernonnus, and if the Great Mother, Cerridwen will bless her I promise to make another offering tomorrow."

I pretended not to hear, moving swiftly away to give her some privacy. How quickly those two women had become solid friends was astonishing. It must have been quite a wrench for her to leave the priestess in her time of need. I could only imagine how she was getting along with Cryda, of all people.

All our most senior warriors were at the river side with us. Only Treeve was missing from Tallack's trusted crowd of people. Perhaps Senara should have asked Cernonnus to protect our own compound with Treeve left in charge.

Still, there was enough to keep my mind busy going on all around me. Before I turned in for the night, I took a stroll in the woods to relieve myself and found Tallack sitting in the back of the wagon at his dead brother's side. As I crept closer, I could see his lips moving by torchlight. I knew that he would find it hard to let go. As much as I wanted to hear what he was saying, my intrusion would've jeopardised my relationship with him. It was strained enough as it was.

When I got back to the shelter, Ren had shaken out my bedding furs and padded the ground with fresh cut rushes. "What have I done to deserve such treatment?" I grinned, shucking off my shoes and cloak and settling down for the night.

Ren said nothing. The smile on his face said it all. He wanted to spoil me. I've no idea why. There was just enough light thrown from the fire outside to see my way to the corner of the shelter. A quick fidget and a roll and I was both comfortable and warm. It was almost better than being at home, as much as I love my goats and my bunk. When Ren snuggled down beside me, resting his head against mine, I knew without doubt it was better than home. I didn't dare move in case he realised what might be implied by such an action.

We stayed in the same position for what seemed like half the night, waiting to see what the other might do next. When Kewri returned from his watch at the crossing, Ren turned over with his back to mine and fell asleep. The long moment was over and with it my fleeting glimpse of happiness.

Tallack didn't return to the shelter the whole night. I suspect he spent it in the back of the cart, mulling over his troubles with Blydh's corpse. There was nothing I could do to ease his suffering. Not even poppy resin was strong enough to dull the pain of grief.

By mid-afternoon, Perren returned. Our men escorted him across the river and along to Senara's hidden campsite as though he alone could fight and kill all our tribe. Tallack refused to speak with him, pursing his lips and turning his back to the messenger. I could see what had made him so angry. Our great Chief was summoned and made to wait on the whim of a new leader.

I sensed that the whole endeavour could crumble about me if I didn't act fast. "Perren. Good lad. What message have you brought?"

"Fur Benyn. I see that you heeded my words. You are wise indeed. Our new Chieftain is a fierce man and must prove himself worthy to all the other elders who were vying for his place. He must show his strength."

"Humiliating our Chief is not the way to do that, Perren. Surely you understand?"

He nodded. Sweat poured from his brow and down his neck. I couldn't tell if that was from nerves or the exertion of riding so fast.

"What do they call this man?"

"His name is Fane. He has three grown sons who are all formidable warriors and will lead the clans."

"Is he changeable or good as his word?" I watched Perren for signs of hesitation. There were none.

"He keeps his word, always. That's why few could oppose him when the rebellion was first put forward."

I offered the scout ale, mainly to give myself the chance to think. With men such as Fane and his sons in charge of the horse warrior clans, they would become a mighty force. If Fane chose to make us his next target, it would mark the end of our family line, maybe the whole Dumnonii Tribe too.

Power does odd things to people. Some get giddy with wealth, others abuse their control, but some rule with a wise head. We had yet to discover what sort of a ruler Fane would be.

"What were you tasked to tell us?" I prompted, when Perren failed to divulge the information.

"Right, yes. Firstly, he wanted me to be sure that Chief Tallack himself was present for the parley."

I pointed at my nephew across the camp. "And as you see, he is. What else?"

"I was to make sure that Chief Blydh was present too."

I snorted, giving him a shrivelling glare. "Did you expect us to toss our Chief into a cage for delivery? The nerve. Would you have me throw in the Chiefs' mother and baby sister for good measure too?" I blustered, hoping my display of outrage would force him to back track. "Enough of your demands. Tell Fane to meet us on the bridge at first light or not at all. We will be friends or enemies from the morrow there on." Perren picked himself up and scurried back under armed guard to the Duros.

Tallack waited until he was gone and burst out laughing. "Do you think he wet his leggings?"

I forced myself to titter, but I was in no mood for jollity. "They are stronger now than they've ever been. We could be walking right into a battle in the morning." I rubbed my eyes and clicked the bones in my neck.

"Maybe." He sounded so indifferent. Didn't he understand what my meddling had done?

"They outnumber us by a significant number."

"You said that about the Belgae and we still wriggled free." He took his shiny mystical sword from its scabbard and cleaned it with the edge of his tunic. "The gods are on our side."

After the losses we'd endured since they sacrificed my white hart, I was disinclined to agree with him. We'd lost good men, good women and our best fighting Chief. If anything, I'd say that the gods were delighting in punishing us. The chatter among the warriors close to the river quietened at nightfall. Tallack doubled the number of guards on watch and spent the night walking and talking among them.

Kewri bunked down in our shelter, leaving just enough room for Ren and me to sleep either side of him. As warm as the giant was, it wasn't the same as sharing my furs with Ren. I fell asleep late into the night in the firm belief that I would never experience another moment as intimate with Ren again, and that come dawn, we could all be run through with swords and spears.

At sunrise, I was too anxious to eat. I drank a little water and pulled on my cloak and shoes and walked out to find my nephew. The men were packing away their belongings and readying the horses. Whatever decision was made in the middle of the River Sid, they were not likely to be spending another night in camp. I carried on along the river until I could see the clearing on the Duros side of the bank. There were more warriors lining up in rows than I've ever seen before. Each of them held shields and spears, and many were on horseback.

At their centre was a man wearing an impressive bronze breast plate, sitting astride a black stallion. On either side of him, were three warriors, all of whom were stocky and grim. They had to be Fane and his sons. This was not a tribe in chaos anymore. They were frighteningly calm and ordered.

CHAPTER TWENTY-FIVE

Every one of the Duro warriors stood tall and proud as Fane trotted in front of them bellowing a rallying speech. My gut plummeted inside from the sheer panic of what lay ahead. Had I led our men into a trap? Trembling from head to toe, I managed to scamper down the slope towards the bridge. Tallack stood leaning against his horse.

"Are you not concerned, Nephew?"

He shrugged and stuck a long stem of grass in his mouth, sucking at the sweet sap.

"There are so many of them." I didn't mean to say it out loud, but then I was gradually losing control over my composure.

"Uhuh. They have a lot of men." Tallack turned around and put his arm in the air. From out of the trees came not just the rest of our men, the Head Hunters, the Sea Warriors and any other boys who could raise a spear in defence, but our young women appeared too. Tallack had brought our sharp aimed archers, their quivers bulging with new arrows, their wrists guarded with leather and wood.

One by one, our people lined up in front of the crossing, almost equalling that of the Duros in number. I knew that those women could bring down a horse at a gallop before it was a dozen boat lengths away. The span of the river was no distance at all.

The new Duro leader may have a point to make with his people, but our show of strength would give him fewer reasons to provoke a war. Only a fool would lead an attack on our land through a tiny crossing point as the bridge. Our archers could leisurely pick off one warrior at a time. They needed our tin, we needed them to stop raiding our borders and give us Brea. We had to hope that the demand for Blydh's head was just to appease his people and would not render the whole deal void.

Fane turned his horse about in front of his line of men and faced us. He scanned our women nocking arrows and taking aim from a safe distance, our Head Hunters lining up in front of them on horseback, our Sea Warriors forming a wall of shields and spears. Tallack mounted his horse and secured his shining sword in its scabbard.

"Be ready on the cart for my signal, Aunt Mel. Bring Kewri with you, just in case." He didn't wait for my answer. He rode to the crossing and stopped his horse on our side of the bridge. His Sea Warriors shuffled forwards to surround his back, the archers pulled on their bow strings and took aim. Fane kicked his heel into the stallion's flank and trotted to the opposite side.

The two men sized one another up, gauging their strategies and intent. The large Duro with the grey whiskers made the first move, urging his steed on to the bridge. Tallack responded likewise, until the Chiefs were close enough to have sailed in the same boat.

I climbed up on to the wagon and waited for my cue. The view above the men was clearer from my vantage point, but it was impossible to hear what was being said. Keeping close watch of their expressions and gestures, I guessed that things began with formal greetings and cordial talk. Tallack's face was hidden from me, but I could see Fane's calm indifference and hoped that it was a good sign.

At length, Tallack twisted in his saddle and waved. I reached around and heaved a pole carrying the white banners upright on the wagon, securing it with leather straps. The breeze caught the fabric, sending small ripples along its edge. The men and archers parted, allowing me clear passage to drive the cart directly onto the crossing. Kewri sat at my side with his hand tightening around the shaft of a spear, his other clutching a shield at his knees.

"I don't understand. A white banner for surrender or of peace?" Fane said, tilting his head to see around my nephew and into the rear of the wagon. "You bring me a swaddled body? Where is your brother? You have brought me here under false pretences."

Standing up on the cart, I released the reins and held my hands up. "Chief Tallack, may I speak?"

My nephew looked surprised at my actions, but nodded his consent. I rather thought he was glad of me interrupting. Fane was an imposing figure and not to be goaded with idle promises.

"Forgive this intrusion into what's generally men's business, but I am wholly to blame for this entire situation."

"And who are you to speak so bold, old woman?" Fane growled loud enough for his tribe's men to hear.

"I am Meliora, daughter of Henwin, sister to Cador, aunt of Aebba the Wild and of Chiefs Tallack and Blydh, all of whom are descendants of Kamber." I held my head high and gave him a moment to process our lineage. We'd held the Dumnonii lands for many generations, unlike some of the other tribal regions further north. Stories of old passed down through songs claimed that we shared the blood of a great leader who ruled over all the land, but tales get twisted and altered with time. While no one questioned its validity, I could use those connections for all they were worth.

"Speak, Meliora of noble blood. Your wisdom has value here." Fane bowed his head in respect to me.

I glanced across at all his warriors. Every one of them clung to my words. My innards clenched and my mouth dried, but I was able to appear composed nonetheless. "This thirst for vengeance must stop. We have no quarrel with you, nor your family. In the past, Duro men shared ale and bread with my kin in the hope of trade deals and alliances. It is Brea alone who has stirred the pot of bile, a mountain girl who had no right to lead your tribe. Chief Fane, your people and ours have suffered enough. This tribal feud serves no one. It's so old, it no longer has teeth with which to bite us. Will you not forge a lasting friendship between our families and become known as the Chief who ended all wars?"

Fane stroked his beard and a wry smile bloomed on his face. "You speak well, Meliora, descendant of the great Kamber, but you fail to account for the many heads taken by your nephew in the frequent raids of our borderlands. If this feud was as toothless as you claim, why then would he go on killing and taking his fill of plunder?"

I could see Tallack biting his bottom lip. The Duro warriors were equally as fond of killing and raiding, but to point that out to this untested leader would be folly.

"Agreed, neither side is blameless, but we can begin a new era of peace, work together to bring about better conditions for all our people." I watched him glower at my nephew, taking his time to ponder.

His stare settled on the back of the cart and the body-shaped linen behind me. "Am I to believe that the bundle in your wagon is that of Blydh, and more to the point, you expect me to hand over Brea in return?"

"You're welcome to examine the body, Chief Fane, but I wouldn't get too close to him. My nephew was stricken by a dark demon from the Underworld. His infection was accidental and deeply distressing. I killed him to prevent the spirit getting loose in our compound."

I figured that it would make more impact if I claimed responsibility for the death. Fane covered his face with the back of his arm as if being on the same bridge as the evil spirit was enough for it to jump into his mouth. He gave us a slow nod of understanding. I elbowed Kewri in the shoulder, prompting him to clamber into the back and unwind the bindings from Blydh's face.

With some hesitation, Kewri lifted the upper part of the corpse to allow the Duros to see. Moss and bits of skull sloughed from the top of Blydh's head and landed on Kewri's arm. The poor giant jumped as though he'd been scalded.

"I've seen enough. If this evil spirit is as dangerous as you say, then you must send him back to the Underworld in all haste." Fane grumbled. I could tell that he was disappointed; no doubt he'd planned all sorts of depraved acts in the ritual sacrifice of my kin to prove his strength to his tribe. As Kewri plucked the cloth back over the rotting body, Fane took a deep breath.

"If you want Brea alive, you are going to have to pay handsomely for her."

I could barely contain my relief; I'd been right all along. The Duros main reason for agreeing to meet was based purely on our tin supplies. Brea and Blydh were little more than chattel. Now that Blydh was worthless to them, Brea was reduced to that of goods fit for trade.

Sitting down on the wagon seat, I gathered up the reins and fought with the horses. Kewri hopped down and urged them backwards, pushing the cart from the bridge. Massen and Ren kept the archers on alert while Tallack and Chief Fane thrashed out the terms of the deal.

By the time we were safely on our side of the bank, I turned to see Tallack holding out his hand in offer of friendship. Fane wavered for a moment, and then leant from his horse to grasp my nephew's forearm. Despite the show of alliance between our tribes, it was too soon for the men to trust one another.

I craned my neck in search of the Lady Brea on the opposite bank. All I could see were the neat rows of Duro warriors and their own line of shields defending them. Tallack was still atop his horse in the middle of the bridge. Any one of Fane's men could have shot him through with a half dozen arrows before he could make it back on dry land, but by the same token, we too could have slain their new leader.

Brea was heard before she was visible. Her shrieks and squeals unsettled the horses as the Duro men dragged her from behind their lines. Her arms were bound, her clothing was filthy and torn, and she had severe bruising to her face. The more she fought against her captors the more they gripped her upper arms tightly.

"You kyjyan low-life scum." She spat at Fane on her way past him. "Watch him men, he'll sell your soul to Cernonnus for less than a mangy fox pelt."

The warriors escorting her over the crossing pulled a gag up from her neck and fastened the knot behind her head. They stopped halfway, still clinging on to her arms. Kewri and I swapped glances. What price had Tallack agreed in exchange for the mountain girl?

My nephew pulled the reins of his horse to the left until it turned about in the confined space and began trotting towards us.

Addressing the whole host of our people, Tallack said, "The Duros will only give us Brea if we pay a substantial amount of tin and agree to favourable trades in the future. We don't have enough tin with us to complete the deal. Chief Fane does not trust us to keep our word that we will deliver the metal as soon as it arrives from the mines at Bentewyn."

All at once I saw the slippery Duro's mind. He expected a life for a life; an assurance that we would keep our word. Panic welled inside me, wondering who the old man had selected as his captive.

Tallack swallowed hard and continued the address to his men. "Fane has given me his arm in friendship, along with his guarantee that our people will be treated with dignity and respect."

Massen's shoulder's slumped. He stepped forward from the line of our warriors and grit his teeth. "I will stand as assurance, Chief." Such courage, such sacrifice. He was willing to put his life in the hands of our enemies to bring about peace, without knowing what the Duros would do to him once they had him imprisoned in their camp.

"You are brave and courageous, Massen, and I thank you, but Fane's demand is for two of my best warriors."

The contents of my stomach erupted in my gullet. We all knew to whom he was referring; Renowden had to give himself up to the Duros too. He did not need asking, my best friend in the whole world stepped forward before Tallack could get the words out.

"I'll go, Chief." He said, looking straight ahead at the line of warriors on the opposite bank.

I felt my heart splintering in my chest. My ribs contracted until I could hardly breathe. "No!" I whimpered, but it was too late. Both Ren and Massen were on the crossing before I could object. As our brave men reached the centre of the bridge, the Duros gave Brea a shove and produced leather straps with which to bind their hands.

I climbed from the cart and hurried over to Tallack. "What have you done?"

My nephew leaned closer to me and spoke softly. "I had no other choice, Fane wanted you."

I was reeling. My breath refused to steady, my heart thumped inside my chest and the grief of the last few days exploded in noisy sobs. Memories of my youth flooded my brain, ruining my judgement. It was as if I was taken back in time, only this Duro Chief wanted my life, not my body. Even still, why should two experienced warriors take all the risk in my place?

"Nephew, they can take me. I surrender freely. I'm old and of no use to anyone. Let the men be spared." I pawed at his legs to gain his attention, but it was all for nought. Ren and Massen were bound for the Duro camp, each tied to a long rope and running behind the warrior's horses.

Tallack dismounted and approached Brea. Her garbled ranting was impossible to understand with the gag in her mouth. He pulled the cloth down and glared at her.

Within moments, her spite and venom vanished. "Chief Tallack. You are fair and honourable, I know that you'll be willing to come to some sort of arrangement, won't you?" Her words were glazed with honey, her smile as poisonous as the berries she slipped into Aebba's meal.

I waited for Tallack to rebuke her, shout, scream or beat her. He did none of those things. With a slow glower of revulsion, he looked down his nose and said; "My mother will decide how you'll die. She's had a long time to think up many slow and painful methods of execution."

There I stood, rooted to the spot among a throng of warriors and archers as they started back for our camp. When almost everyone had left the crossing, that fateful place of death and upset, Kewri put his arm about my shoulders and helped me on to the wagon. Blydh oozed and stank in the back, but I was numb to all sensations.

I don't remember the return journey. The rumbling cart jogged me into a daze. I had achieved a peace accord with no bloodshed, but lost my best friend in the process. Fane had given Tallack two moons to make good on his promise of metal, or our men would be tortured unto death.

When we arrived at the island compound, Paega's cage was made secure so that Brea could await her sentence under the stars, with only a stream sullied by horse kawgh and piss for sustenance. I went straight to my hut and burrowed under my bedding furs. As soon as word spread around camp about Brea, the pipers and drummers started their infernal noise.

They had cause to celebrate I know, but the speed at which they forgot the cost was staggering. There was no way of knowing whether Chief Fane would keep his end of the bargain and treat our men well while they were at his mercy. From the state of Brea, I knew that he was fond of beating prisoners and Cernonnus knows what other ordeals she must have suffered.

As much as I wanted to shut out the world and hide under the covers until the gods came to take me, I was curious as to what Cryda had chosen for Brea's death. She was fond of spectacular shows and elaborate schemes. Her mission in life was to be the focus of all the tribe's attention, something at which she excelled.

Wearing the hood of my cloak up, and having partially covered my face, I sneaked into the rear door of the Long Hut sometime after dark. The men were already deep in their cups, lounging on the benches and goading each other into brawls. It seems that they had prepared themselves for battle and were disappointed in the outcome.

Why they were so keen to join their ancestors instead of compromising will always be a mystery to me, but then I am neither warrior nor shield maiden. Perhaps I will never fully understand. Senara was sitting near the front door of the hut cradling the young pup Ren gave to Endelyn.

Edging closer to the top table, I saw the priestess. Tallack had invited her to sit at his side in the Ruvane chair between that of the Chiefs'. Young Treeve look most annoyed, sitting next to Blydh's empty wolf's head seat with a scowl that would not relent.

CHAPTER TWENTY-SIX

Cryda took the chair next to Tallack, nursing the baby Delen with an air of serenity I have not seen in her for many springs. Her husband would at last be avenged. Aebba could sit with his forefathers in the Summerlands watching over us all, instead of roaming the Between Worlds lost.

I ordered a slave to bring me a stool and a cup and waited patiently for the announcement. By the rear door, I was out of sight to all those seated at the top table. Every elder and warrior before me stuffed themselves with rich meats, fine fish and more ale than they deserved. My appetite for celebration had vanished. It was a victory of sorts, barring the death of Blydh and the unknown fate of Ren and Massen.

When the stars shone brightly in the clear sky, Tallack barked at his men to fetch Brea. It was time for Cryda to declare her decision. She handed Delen to her slave and preened her hair. It flowed down her back in golden ringlets, unclipped and unadorned. All her metal belonged to the Belgae now. I could tell that she was savouring every moment of attention.

As the men dragged Brea into the Long Hut, she punched out and kicked at them, her final acts of defiance. Wives of the elders hissed at her as she passed them. Many had lost sons, and some their daughters too, in the attack Brea led on our camp. She was hated in every corner of Dumnonia.

Two burly warriors held Brea in front of the top table. The room hushed. Cryda stepped down from the platform, stood face to face with our old adversary and slapped Brea hard about the cheek. Brea's skin glowed red, her eyes watered but she did not cry out. This mountain girl knew pain well. As the least favoured of Aebba's wives, she suffered nightly from his brutal treatment. It was an education in endurance and no doubt what forced her to poison him in the first place.

Tallack stood in front of his tall chair; his face stern and lean. This was to be his first formal sentencing as sole Chieftain of our tribe. I could see from his pain-etched face how seriously he took the role. It gave me hope that the Dumnonii were in safe but firm hands for the future.

"Brea of the North Kembran Ordoviches, wedded to Aebba the Wild of the Dumnonii, and interim leader of the Durotriges Tribe; you are charged with killing my father, responsible for countless deaths of our people, and of attempting to murder my aunt of noble blood not once, but twice. Do you wish to say anything before your sentence is announced?"

Brea snorted at us all. "You self-righteous kyjyans stood by and let that monster brutalise me every night for more than six cycles. Did you expect me to go on tending my bruises and broken ribs without fighting back? There is nothing noble about your blood. You are all born of animals." She spat at Cryda's feet but missed by a hair's breadth.

Cryda encircled Brea, looking her up and down and sneering. "If it were in my power, I'd see you die a hundred times for what you've done to my family."

Brea scoffed. "If you had at least tried to treat me as one of the family, protected me from Aebba's cruelty…"

Cryda slapped her again, preventing her from explaining her actions. I could see both sides of the argument, but her manipulations of the twins negated any sympathy I once felt for the girl. Power wielded by the vengeful is a dangerous thing.

The former Ruvane stepped closer to the prisoner. "I have thought long and hard about your death." Cryda was so close to Brea their noses were almost touching. "At first, I wanted to see you choking down the same berries you fed to Aebba; watch your tongue blacken and swell, see you gasp your final breath, but that would be over too soon."

Cryda moved back and took a long look at the crowds in the benches; the expectant faces of our warriors and elders, all waiting to support her decision.

"I have made up my mind. Brea will be ripped asunder and eaten by a pack of wolves."

The proclamation was met with silence and confusion. It was a punishment no one in our tribe had ever tried before. The surprise and vacant looks from those around her, I suspect, stemmed from puzzlement over how it might be achieved. Cryda looked distressed by their lack of encouragement. I started the foot stamping, which roused the warriors into cheers and thumping their fists down on the tables. It was certainly a novel way to kill our sworn enemy, and a messy one at that.

Tallack rose from his tall chair and lifted his palm to silence the crowd. "My mother has spoken; it shall be done. Take the prisoner back to the cage and sluice her down. She stinks." The raucous chatter and hollering lasted just a few moments more, before Tallack returned to his seat and beckoned some of the elders forward.

As far as I could tell, he was asking their advice, but none knew how best to harness the fury of a pack of wolves. I stared down in my cup. There was one man who would know the answer, but he and his fellow Sea Warrior friend were a day's ride away in the Duros' camp, that's if he was still alive.

Around the corner of the top table platform, I could see the older men shrugging their shoulders and shaking their heads. They were not experienced warriors, nor hunters. They were little more than weavers, dyers, cattlemen and leather workers. How would they know the ways of wild things?

It wasn't long before I heard the command I was expecting. "Fetch my aunt. I would have her counsel." Tallack looked on while the elders backed away and turned their gazes in my direction. There was no point in concealment now.

"I'm here, Chief."

Tallack moved to the end of the platform and peered down at me. "Why are you hiding down there? Come and sit by me."

It was a strange request. There were few seats on the top table and even fewer that did not already have one of his favoured people occupying them. I struggled to my feet, weary of tribal life and heartache. Glancing up at Treeve, Endelyn, Tallack and Cryda, who had returned to her son's side, I elected to sit at my old table in front of them, alone. My kin had dwindled in number, my friends and allies further still.

They could not see that I was suffering loss as much as they. Did they truly believe that age and wisdom make you immune to grief? My heart was not yet stone. It beat though it had no right to, when younger lives were snuffed out before mine.

"Tell us, Aunt Mel," Tallack began. "How do you…?"

"Dig a pit the length, width and depth of a mid-sized boat with a thick section of tree trunk leaning from the edge to the bottom." I interrupted, my voice heavy and disinterested. "Tether a goat within, but not one of mine. As soon as the wolves climb in after the bait, heave the trunk out with ropes and horses." I couldn't help but feel despondent. When would the bloodshed end? "Now if you'll give me leave, Chief, I have business to attend." I didn't wait for his permission. With my knees clicking and my back popping as it straightened, I headed for the door.

Before I reached the last row of benches, Tallack called after me. "We will get them back, Aunt Mel. I promise." It was another promise he could not be sure of keeping. Ren and Massen's lives were no longer in his control. Everything rested on Chief Fane's word and the speed at which our Alchemists could deliver enough tin to appease him.

The sun was low in the sky when I left. Slaves sat in the back of the Chieftain's cart, repacking Blydh's wrappings with more moss. I should have stopped to ask them what orders Cryda had given them, but I didn't want the subject of defleshing his bones to resurface. One thing was certain, it would take some time to prepare for Brea's inventive death, and even longer to organise the interment of Aebba and Blydh. My nephew would have fully rotted before then.

I was so used to seeing ducks, rabbits or often fish suspended beneath my eaves, gifts from my friend Renowden that my heart sank upon reaching my door. With no fire, food, nor tin with which to trade, I went to my bed, sank into my furs and cried for a long time. Whether the tears fell for my grief over Blydh, my failure to keep him safe after his head was smashed in, or because I was frightened for my friend Ren, I couldn't say, but they gushed from me unimpeded.

Long after nightfall, Kewri bustled in the hut, moaning to himself about the chilly air. I had a shrewd idea where he'd been, but was in no hurry to confirm my suspicions. The poor giant was suffering too, in his own clumsy way. Senara's affections were no longer his to take for granted. She had moved on to new pastures. I had my suspicions over her new infatuation, but no evidence with which to support my hunch. Time would tell.

The morning brought a frozen water trough in my goat pen and steam on the piss pot. There was enough fresh milk and grain to make a little porridge, but only after Kewri had lit a fire. While he grumbled and walked to another hut for a couple of glowing embers to ignite a handful of kindling, I wandered in the direction of the priestess's hut.

I could hear her and Senara giggling while the pup frolicked and growled. "Can I come in?" I called out with as cheerful a tone as I could muster. Stepping over the newest gifts and offerings at her door, I waited for the reply and pushed through the door flaps. Every space was filled with more lavish goods and foods. I spied a necklace of exotic glass and clay beads, a bronze hair pin and several stylish belts of leather.

The women looked at me as though I was trespassing. It was the first time I'd felt uncomfortable checking on a patient in more moons than could be counted. "I… um, came to see how you were. Do you need any more poppy resin?"

Endelyn got up from the bunk and scooped the pup into her arms. "I'm fine, Fur Benyn. You have no need to worry about me. Senara has been taking care of me." They exchanged a long and intimate look.

"Glad to hear it, Priestess. You know where I am if you change your mind about a hastening tonic." I ducked back outside and heard them giggling together once more.

It's odd, because I was sure that I heard her whisper as I left; "Nothing will stop me bearing this child."

I hope to Cernonnus that I'm wrong, but if she is carrying Blydh's baby, that makes it the heir to our entire land. Tallack's liking for his crewman, Treeve had lasted for much longer than his usual relationships. At some time in the near future, he would have to take at least one wife and continue his line or we'd end up in the exact same tangle as the Duros.

Sighing, I stepped up onto the newest boardwalk to catch a glimpse of our prisoner. The route took me past the smith. I lingered, curious as to why he was removing the sheepskin lining from Blydh's helmet. He bid me good day and turned to throw the metal dome in his melting pot over the hot coals.

"What are you doing?" I shrieked, but it was too late. It had begun to sink into the molten pool with all his other broken spearheads and blades.

"Chief's orders." He yelled above the roar of the flames as his apprentice worked the bellows. I turned my palms upward and shrugged, waiting for an explanation.

"Tallack wants Chief Blydh to take a great battle axe with him to the Summerlands. He said that the helm would remind him of his weaknesses at the end and told me to reuse the metal." The smith gave me a pitying smile and returned to his labours.

I knew why Tallack had insisted on destroying the helmet. It made perfect sense to me. He didn't want the evil spirit trapped as a stowaway inside his brother's head for all time. I could imagine the shame it would bring to our ancestors if that should happen.

The bronze was also about all we had left to pay Cernonnus, God of Death and the Wild Forest. Perhaps his interment would be more fitting of a Chieftain, when the Alchemists arrived with a shipment of tin.

Brea was shivering in her cage. As I arrived, one of the weaver women threw scraps from her table at the prisoner. At least she was getting some sustenance. After the huge mess Kewri and I made over Paega's captivity, I decided to stay well away.

Over the course of a few days, Tallack sent warriors out to dig the wolf pit, more were dispatched to our northern mine to give word to Clemo about the fate of his nephew and his boats, and Cryda taunted Brea in her roofless cage on a daily basis.

Just as I was coming to terms with the routine of camp life, Cryda turned up at my door. She was wearing her pleading face, that infuriating pout that was so effective on Aebba.

"Meliora, you said you'd help me to prepare Blydh's body. He'll turn fast if you don't do something."

I wanted to shout at her, tell her that I made no such promise, but her plight was one of desperation. We'd heard nothing from the men tasked with capturing a pack of wolves, and the tin delivery was nowhere to be seen. The closer we got to the next full moon, the more fretful I became for Ren and Massen's lives. The slaves attended the body morning, noon and night, but they were not able to prevent putrefaction.

There was always the possibility of borrowing a blade from one of our warriors for the defleshing ritual, but I was not confident in wielding an unknown dagger; at least, that's what I told Cryda. The truth was that I couldn't bring myself to cut his bones from his flesh.

"But what are we to do? They'll be nothing left to bury if we leave him in this heat." Cryda was right, of course. It had been a dry spring, with frosty nights and scorching sunny days.

"I spoke to a man at the midsummer gathering one time, who told me about a rare funerary ritual that preserved the whole man like a fish." I muttered, more to myself than to her. The recollection was vague and I wondered if I could remember the precise details of what had to be done.

Cryda had screwed her face up in disgust. "He's not a salmon, Meliora. He must have the same dignified end as his forefathers."

That, I almost laughed at but managed to stop myself. There was nothing dignified in Aebba's ending nor Blydh's. She would have to go back as far as my own father to find an honourable Chieftain's death. At least he was chosen by the Morrighan at the battle between us and the Brigantes of East Iwerdon.

I'd put it off for too long. Blydh could wait no more. Giving Kewri a list of all the things I would need to borrow, I set off with Cryda to wash and preserve her son until his burial. The slaves lifted the body to the riverbank, where we unwrapped the swaddling and moss and washed him clean.

His pale skin had mottled in dark grey patches and parts were open like a wound and seeping pus. The scar where I'd stitched up his scalp had dried and shrunk, like his lips. It gave him an unnatural grin that made my stomach churn. The worst parts were his eyeballs. They could no longer hold their shape, being wrinkled and pitted where the liquid had oozed out.

I closed his eyelids, not wanting him to give me that evil stare I'd grown used to while he lived. Cryda didn't seem to notice the foul stench of maggoty offal or the festering kawgh as I sliced into his belly to remove his guts. She shovelled them into a clay jar and sealed the lid with wax as though she was changing the moss from little Delen's arse. This was a mother's love, unending even beyond death.

We had but two choices to make. Either we placed Blydh in a huge amount of salt, or we dried his flesh over a smoking fire. I knew that Cryda would prefer the salt option, but we had no tin to trade for enough salt to complete the job. I also knew that she would object to the use of fire, since it was too similar to a pyre used for the common warriors and elders when they died.

With those considerations in mind, I chose for her. "There is no other way, Cryda. He must be dried." She squeezed out a tear or two and wailed a bit, but it had little effect on me. I left her by the stinking remains of my nephew and went in search of warriors to lend a hand.

I'd made it all the way to the southern end of the island before I spotted a few of Tallack's Sea Warriors jumping onto the riverbank from a row boat beyond the gates. Treeve was among them.

"Ah, Treeve, just the man. I need your assistance with something important."

He tied off the rope, his wide-eyed stare filled with panic. "Can it wait a while, Fur Benyn? Kenver's ship from Bentewyn is in the estuary. He'll be here before sundown."

CHAPTER TWENTY-SEVEN

Now I understood the wild expression and fear in his eyes. Treeve knew the danger of Kenver coming to our compound more than anyone. Whether it was he or my nephew who killed Kenver's daughter, I doubt I shall ever know, but young Treeve disposed of the body in the marshland and not before he'd rifled through her pockets and taken the wealth hidden inside the quill necklace she wore.

Delaying him would not benefit anyone. "Run along and tell Tallack. I'll sort something else out."

"If you're sure?" He said, but didn't wait for me to change my mind. He ran as though he had an ember caught in his leggings.

My feelings about Kenver's arrival were mixed. There was now a chance that we could secure Ren and Massen's release from the Duros with the tin he'd brought from the mines, but I also knew that he would expect to meet his daughter, Kerensa in camp. There were so many secrets that could tip the balance of power in his favour and turn the Alchemists against us for all time.

The messengers had not yet returned from the meeting point where we'd left Clemo and our horses on the northern shore. He was Kenver's brother and responsible for the mining settlement there. It was only a matter of time before the whole story came out. The Alchemists would need careful handling if we were to avoid a catastrophic breakdown between our clans.

I found some of Blydh's Head Hunters and explained my problem. They were only too happy to help. While they set about building a structure in which to smoke the body, I hurried back to the Long Hut to speak with Tallack. It was critical that we all used the same lie about the fate of Kenver's children.

As soon as my nephew saw me, he widened his eyes and shook his head. "I know, I know. It's all in hand."

I walked closer squinting, hoping that he would elaborate.

He waited until I was almost at the top table. "Both Kerensa and Hellyer were received into the Summerlands, having bravely fought and died for their tribe. Hellyer remains in Belgae lands and Kerensa was honoured on the pyre with our fallen warriors."

"You know that's risky. You told our people she had ridden home." I hissed, trying to keep my voice low.

"No. I told Blydh she'd ridden home whenever he was confused. Everyone else believes that she fell during the attack on our island."

It was his decision, when all was said and done, but our people carried the fallen to the pyre. They knew precisely which warriors were dead, those who were injured and who survived. One slip of the tongue and our tin supplies could be lost to us forever. I returned to Cryda at the stream more anxious than ever.

When most of Blydh's innards and the golden sun disc were removed from his body, we poured salted water into the cavity and let it drain out. Cryda stayed at his side until the men came to carry him to the smoke chamber. I left her with her slave and Delen to watch the row boats come ashore with the cargo from Kenver's ship. The leader of the Alchemist Clan was in the first boat, standing at the bow with a beaming grin. As he stepped onto the riverbank, he held out his arm in greeting but then changed his mind. He grabbed my shoulders and touched his forehead to mine, as though we were close family.

I blushed. "It's good to see you, Kenver. Have you kept well, my friend?"

"I have, yes. And you? You look well, Fur Benyn."

We batted idle chatter between us for a while, walking up to the southern gates and stopping periodically to watch the men unloading the bars of tin and a few green tinged rocks in baskets.

"As soon as Tallack sent word about the copper deposits on Lizard Point, we went in search of them. A couple of us have tried to extract copper, but we're not quite there with purity yet. We brought these rocks to compare with the one your niece's husband found. Is he still here?"

"Ah, no. She and her husband returned to the mountains, where they will both stay." I didn't think it necessary to explain Derwa and Glaw's part in their escape plan for Paega, especially since they were banished when Kewri was forgiven for accidentally setting him loose. That giant must have the gods favour to be spared punishment for two heinous crimes, or perhaps Tallack could see how useful it was to have such a warrior on our side.

"That's a pity. I was hoping to speak with him, maybe share a few smelting tips." He rested his hands on his hips and took in the surroundings. "This is a fine new compound you've built here. Most impressive." With his hands rubbing together he began walking towards the

Long Hut. "Now, I'd like to share a cup of ale with my daughter. Where is she?"

I gulped down my anxiety and tried to smile, overtaking his slow pace to avoid answering him. There were few warriors around Tallack's fire that day. Most were about their business, training new recruits or helping Cryda with the preparation of Blydh's body. That made it a little easier for my nephew to relay the sad news of Kenver's children passing.

The Alchemist took the blow with poise and stillness, although I knew him well enough to see through the mock composure. The poor man was beyond distressed. Tallack emphasised the bravery of Hellyer, praising him lavishly to make up for the scarce information regarding Kerensa's passing.

Kenver lowered himself down on the bench where I normally sat. He was stunned for some time, staring at the flames of the central fire and refusing food and ale from the slaves. I offered to forage for fresh mallow sap to cure his melancholy, but he just shook his head. When at last he looked up at me, he said; "Did you see my son fall?"

"I did. It was a quick death, he didn't suffer."

He held my gaze searching for more, but I had none to give.

"And Kerensa?"

I looked away, unable to face him. "No. I was not nearby for that tragedy." It was all I dared offer him. His stare bored into the side of my face, warming my cheeks. I tapped his back with affection and rose to leave.

"Fur Benyn, thank you."

"For what?" I spun about, baffled.

"Your kindness to my children. Those medicines were all that kept us going through the winter ague. I won't forget that."

The lump in my throat would not ease, my eyes blurred with sorrow. I had to leave before I blurted the whole shameful event out, casting dishonour on his daughter's name for all time. By the time I'd made it through the front door, Tallack caught up with me. I cuffed my humours onto my sleeve, mopping up the tears and sniffing the watery snot.

"There's more than enough tin to trade for Ren and Massen, but we also need weapons and grain. Our stores are empty and the harvest is five moons away."

I frowned at my nephew, unsure as to what he expected me to do. We had already cleaned out all the tin from the northern mines, and Kenver was unlikely to return to the mining camp at Bentewyn anytime soon, having been summoned by the former Ruvane to participate in the rituals for Aebba and Blydh. Even if he did, it would take half a cycle to replenish the tin supplies squandered on the Belgae. Without a solution to offer, I shrugged.

Tallack looked pitiful. "What I'm saying is, that it might take a bit longer than anticipated to get Ren and Massen back."

I gasped at his suggestion. "You can't be serious. Chief Fane gave you two moons to make good on your word. Where do you suppose that we can find more tin before then?"

"So, you would have our people starve instead?"

My lips pursed; my jaw set. "You made a promise to both me and the Duros. We can ration the grain, send the warriors out hunting and have fewer ridiculously wasteful feasts. You must get Ren released. He and Massen will suffer a horrific fate if you fail them." My nephew had no concept of starvation. Those beyond our walls knew how to eke out their provisions. One small piece of meat in a stew would feed a family for two days. Tallack felt deprived if he only had the choice of goose or duck.

He failed to give me an answer. Instead, he screwed up his nose and marched off towards the priestess's hut. I watched him for a few moments, as he stopped next to the carved poles and bowed his head in communion with the gods. Perhaps they would somehow talk some sense into him.

Blydh's body took days of smoking to dry out. When the warriors lifted him out of the cabin, his knees tucked to his chin, his arms crossed over his chest, the skin had taken on a leathery brown appearance. Cryda burst into tears and ran back to her hut the moment she caught sight of him.

Directing the men to the shelter Kewri built for my patients, I took clean fabric and set about wrapping his body. It shocked me how light Blydh was now that all the moisture had gone from his flesh. If it wasn't for the broken skull and shrunken stitches, I'd never have known it was my nephew's body.

With a continuous guard at the door, Blydh stayed in the shelter away from the camp dogs and stray foxes for more than a quarter moon. I kept myself busy with my goats and spring gathering of new shoots and herbs to blend into balms and tonics. Tallack spent an unhealthy amount of time in his hut with Treeve, while Kenver sought counsel and made offerings at Endelyn's house almost daily.

My warning about over indulgence and preserving our food supplies seemed to have had an effect on Tallack. There were no feasts nor wanton ale binges about the island at all. He ordered the wooden panels fixed across the doors of the Long Hut and conducted private discussions with the elders and his mother in his own round house. It irked me that Treeve was present for all such talks, where I was not invited, but at least I was able to grieve in my own way without bumping into Kenver too often.

Several times during that quarter moon, I caught Tallack on his way to his mother's or Endelyn's hut and asked him when he would send word to the Duros about the tin exchange for Ren and Massen. Every time, he avoided a direct answer. It was either, *soon*, or *not long now*, or *after we have buried my brother*, but never *today*. I was starting to think that he would not keep his promise.

On the seventh day after Kenver's arrival, I went back to my hut after a day of foraging to find Kewri bundling his bedding furs up with his knife and pipe.

"Moving out?" I said with more than a hint of glibness.

"One of the warriors came back from the forest near the River Teign. They have four wolves trapped in a pit. The rest of the pack were too wary to climb in after them and fled." His manner surprised me. Kewri was not one to glorify violence or revel in blood spilled. Perhaps his loyalty to the tribe was stronger than I thought. He was almost eager to see the end of Brea, although her actions had not affected him personally.

"You're heading out there then?" I had no idea where he and I stood. He was neither my slave, nor a clan member. His actions were borne out of a combination of Tallack's orders and my requests. I could no more forbid him from leaving than any other elder in the tribe.

He stopped packing and peered down at me. "I thought we were all going. Wasn't that Cryda's decision, to watch that kyjyan, Brea die and then walk on to the cromlech to bury the Chieftains?" He was right of course, but I hadn't envisioned the whole tribe turning out for the occasion. Our family were so few in number we needed the support of the warriors, elders and their families to ensure a decent funerary send off for Aebba and Blydh. I nodded at him, disappointed that the trip to the wolf pit would take precedence over releasing Ren and Massen. Nothing I could say to my nephew or Cryda would put their safety above the rites of two fallen Chiefs.

After my nightly fretting about the captives, I fell asleep on the opposite side of my round house to the giant. The entire compound was hushed but for the odd howl from Endelyn's pup. Kewri woke early and prepared our horses, eager to be on the track at dawn. I hurried along the boardwalks to see Brea. She was shivering from the nip in the air and covered in filth. Initially, she pretended not to see me, turning her head away from where I stood and scratching at the lice in her knotted hair.

Although I could hear the men tramping down the boardwalk to collect her, I didn't move. Eventually, she turned to face me.

"What do you want from me, Meliora?" Her spite made my spine prickle.

"You know, it might make a difference if you apologised to Tallack. He has the authority to spare your life."

She almost exploded with laughter; her own brand of desperation. "That spineless rat would never defy his mother. Besides, I'm not sorry for killing that animal; he got exactly what he deserved. You're wasting your time, Fur Benyn. Leave me to my misery." She practically spat my name; such was her anger.

As the men led her away, I thought that she was going to get exactly what she deserved too. I can't condone how Aebba treated her, but to bed his son before the body was cold and go on to lay blame at another's door, was beyond calculated. At least I tried to reason with her, give her a chance to show remorse. Whatever her fate would be, my conscience was clear.

By mid-morning, many had gathered for the long procession to the pit. Kewri was itching to ride ahead, but Tallack was insistent that we all travelled together as one long unit. Cryda and Endelyn both sat on the Chieftain wagon. Baby Delen and her slave travelled in the back with Blydh's preserved body and the pot of Aebba's bones. Both sets of remains were packed with fragrant meadow flowers and surrounded by their possessions and gifts to the gods to pay their passage into the Summerlands.

Brea was bound at the wrists, with the remaining length of rope attached to the back of the wagon. Every few moments she was tugged forwards, forcing her to run or be dragged along the track on her face. She had a prime view of the bodies, and plenty of time to reflect on her mistakes, but I doubt she used the time wisely. She will meet Cernonnus in the Underworld, where she will pay for her actions. There will be no offerings for this mountain girl and no grave. What the wolves can't eat, the worms will.

I rode behind the wagon and Brea, next to Kewri on his massive cart horse. The Sea Warriors trotted up front with Tallack and Treeve, leading the way, while the Head Hunters and Kenver followed the elders and their families at the rear. Some had horses, others walked, making our journey tedious and slow.

Senara was sat astride the same pony I had taken from Tallack before sending her out on her first scouting trip. It seemed forever ago, and yet he'd not noticed the horse missing once. She trotted alongside the Chieftain wagon, staying close to the priestess. Thank Cernonnus they had left that unruly pup behind with a few Sea Warriors and the slaves. I could imagine the boisterous creature taking a bite out of Blydh before we could lay him to rest.

It was not far to the forest along the River Teign from the island on the Exe. Even with our least nimble elders on foot, it was less than a quarter day's walk. The warrior who had delivered the news of the wolf pack led us straight to the pit.

I could see that they had followed my instructions precisely. They'd used their common sense to dig a sheer-sided hole into the soft clay of the river bank, avoiding the troublesome roots and stones of the forest just a short distance away. The sodden earth was piled high in a great ridge next to the river.

Their ropes and tools were packed up at their campsite, their ponies readied for the next leg of the journey. I slid down from my horse and handed the reins to Kewri so that I could lean over and peer into the hole. A short pole stuck up in the centre with a chewed tether and the remains of the sacrificial goat.

As soon as the wolves heard us, they sniffed the air and growled. One was much larger than the others. I assumed it was their pack leader. When more people crowded around the edges of the pit, they bared their teeth and snarled, backing away into the furthest corner from us. Endelyn and Cryda parted the crowd and stood in a prominent position.

Cryda jogged the babe in her arms, too close to the edge for my comfort. "Yes, this will do well. I am pleased. They should be good and hungry by now." And to Endelyn she said. "Will you speak to the gods on our behalf? I should like them to take this vile wretch as an offering. They will be receiving my husband and son into their embrace shortly after."

The priestess nodded. What was happening? A few days sharing a hut and now they were best friends? Had Endelyn tamed the former Ruvane into compliance while we negotiated with the Duros, or was pity Cryda's main motive for befriending this wild thing from the Nine Maidens stone circle?

Tallack moved the masses back to a respectable distance and gestured for the men to lead Brea closer. Her wrists were raw and chaffed, her arms and legs burned by the sun. Her ripped tunic was soiled with her own piss and kawgh. She was hardly recognisable as the same person.

She chose this very moment to appeal to Tallack, using their once close relationship as a needle to stab at his good nature.

CHAPTER TWENTY-EIGHT

"Can't you see that I was just defending myself?" Brea began. "All I ever wanted was to be accepted by your family, not treated like a slave from the Ordoviches' mountains."

One of the warriors offered to cut her ties, but Tallack shook his head, turning the pathetic woman around to face the hole in the ground. The wolves snarled louder. My nephew pushed her harder, until Brea was balancing bare foot on the edge.

"Please, Tallack, I beg of you. It's not too late for me to make amends. We had fun once, you and I, didn't we? We can do that again." Her pleading was more insistent the nearer to death she stepped. Tallack stopped pushing and looked away. He was finding it difficult to carry out the sentence on someone for whom he once had feelings. His soft heart would not win favours with the Head Hunter Clan. He needed to be decisive and strong to gain their respect.

Cryda lost patience with him. She shoved Endelyn out of her way and stood next to Tallack and Brea. "Say your words, Priestess. Let's not waste any more time listening to the lies of this deceitful bitch." Before Tallack could step away and let the women take over, Cryda reached to his belt and took his blade.

I thought that she would cut the ropes binding Brea's wrist to give her a fighting chance against the wolves.

Instead, she slashed the knife across Brea's upper arm and then across the other. Both were shallow flesh wounds but they trickled blood down her torn tunic. Brea flinched. The wolves sniffed the air again, huffing to each other that their supper was being served.

Endelyn tipped back her head and raised her palms to the air, her eyes rolling in their sockets. "Cernonnus, God of Death and All Things Wild, we commend to thee an offering of the highest order. Take her temper, take her spirit, take her blackened heart and do as you will with her. Temptress, betrayer, murderer, and liar, we cast her into the pit so that you may carry her into the Underworld. There to submit to a fiery torment for all time." Endelyn nodded to Cryda.

The former Ruvane glowered, smiling. Relishing every moment of Brea's distress, she extended two fingers and pushed her in the chest. Brea toppled on the edge, her cinched wrists jerking about trying to balance, her eyes wide with fear. She landed flat on her back, knocking the air out of her. The cracking noise told me that one or two bones were broken. Gasping, she struggled to her knees, coming face to face with the drooling maws of the four wolves. Their growls grew louder, more urgent. The largest one snapping its jaws close to her neck.

Brea screamed, waving her arms about in an attempt to scare them away, but they had smelt her blood and were starving. For a few moments, Brea clung to the belief that she could fight them, until the wolf on her left took a bite out of her side. She screeched in agony, the ragged strips of skin and rib jutting from her middle. There was nowhere for her to run, nowhere to hide. As she glanced up and caught my eye, I saw her defiance turn into resignation.

The pack leader lunged, securing its fangs over her nose and chin before ripping it from her bones. A second wolf went for the belly, tearing the soft flesh and spilling her entrails over her lap. When they finally chewed at her throat, I knew that her end had come. Her only movements were from creatures as they tugged at her bones.

Endelyn continued her babbling and god's speech while the tribe looked on. I'd seen more than enough and turned away, but I could still hear the yelps and bickering as the wolves fought over the tastiest parts. Cryda's expression remained the same throughout. If anything, her smile broadened a little more to see the animals ingesting her foe.

I stood by the horses, waiting for Tallack to call an end to the show. It wasn't long before Kenver joined me. He was already numbed by death. Neither of us spoke, for what was there left to say? The ponies were deeply unsettled by the noise from the pit. I had to call for Kewri's help to stop the cart horses from bolting, taking the bodies of my kin with them. Endelyn's chanting stopped, the elders and warriors stepped back from the edge, and Cryda's smile faded.

Tallack returned the dagger to his belt. "My father is avenged; we can now lay him to rest in peace." He gave orders for the warriors who had dug the pit to stay behind. They were to replace the planking in the hole when everyone had left, allowing the wolves to climb out. When all that remained were bones, Tallack asked the men to fill the pit, preventing further dark spirits escaping from the underworld. I thought that a most sensible precaution.

Before setting off for the burial site, most ate the provisions they'd brought along. I gave mine to Kewri.

After witnessing such carnage, my appetite had completely gone. While I ruminated over the tragic loss of lives, Cryda skipped around with such a lightness of step and happy countenance, it was hard to believe that she was about to bury her husband and child. Her focus was entirely on seeking revenge, she'd forgotten to grieve. Perhaps that would come in the fullness of time.

The sun was already past the midpoint in the sky when we set off along the Teign Valley, following the course of the river heading west. As the crow flies, it was no distance at all, but our path was heavily wooded and the trail overgrown. Without the savvy guidance and navigation skills of Ren to help us, Tallack chose to stick closely to the winding river. It was slow going with the wagon, and some of the more elderly in our group struggled with tiredness.

Senara was the first to give up her horse to another, helping the old man up on to the pony's back and walking alongside with the reins. Others saw her gracious act and copied her, lifting the ailing or injured on to warriors' steeds and leading them in turn. Kewri offered up his massive cart horse, but its sheer size and strength put them off accepting. Little did they know that the creature was as gentle and placid as his rider.

We fell back into roughly the same order as before, with Tallack and Treeve up front and the Head Hunters trailing behind. Kenver caught up and trotted next to me. Our conversation was stilted for a long time, which was to be expected given all he had discovered over the past few days. I began to get used to his silence, almost reassured by the absence of idle chatter. The trail seemed to have its own sort of bumpy rhythm, lulling me into a trance.

"Who prepared my daughter's body for the pyre?"

The question shocked me from my musings. I stammered, unsure what to say. "Um, I don't know. I'm sure that she was treated with respect." The memory of seeing Treeve lugging her lifeless body under the gully at the eastern side of our palisade walls and across the marshlands crowded out all other thoughts.

"Could you at least tell me what killed her? Was it an arrow, a spear, was she fighting another warrior, what?"

My throat tightened; I couldn't swallow. He watched as my face flushed hot. I shook my head. "I'm sorry, Kenver. I know little of how it happened." Which was the truth. I could not with confidence lay the blame at anyone's feet. All I knew for sure was that Tallack ordered Treeve to dispose of the body. That much he'd confessed.

"Then can you tell me who would know? I should like to speak with them. Her mother will need the details before she is likely to accept her death."

I squirmed, trying not to let my discomfort show. "There were many lives lost that day. Brea planned the raid, the leader of the Duros led the attack and lost his fight in the process. Too many of our young folk were sent to sit with the gods. Each and every one of them, were washed and placed with care on the pyre. Tallack insisted on offering sacrifices for them all." My words were truthful and honest, despite leaving out the part where Kerensa was not actually laid on the funeral fire.

He opened his mouth to speak again, but I interrupted. "If you'll pardon me, I have urgent need to speak with my nephew." What else could I do, but kick my horse into a canter and overtake the cart until I could squeeze between Treeve and Tallack on the trail. I knew it made me look suspicious, but I was never adept at lying. Any more time spent with the grieving Alchemist and I would have cracked.

Treeve always made it difficult to speak with Tallack alone. That excuse for a warrior pushed his way into our family business all the while. If my nephew hadn't invited him into his bed, the lad would still be manning the fishing boats. I did all I could to warn him that Kenver was asking awkward questions but he had more pressing concerns on his mind.

"Not now, Aunt Mel." He flicked his head towards the tor cresting the valley on our right. "See up there."

I looked for a good long while, leaving my horse to steer while I was distracted. The ridge at the top of the steep incline was bare of trees. There was a rocky outcrop near to the highest point that looked like a giant bigger than Kewri had spent many summers stacking the stones. "What am I looking for?" I muttered, glancing in long sweeps to the north. A shadow flickered between two jagged scree slopes, but I paid it no heed.

"Look again." Tallack grumbled. Training my sight on the spot where the dark area moved, I thought I could make out the shape of a man. The more I stared, the more convinced I was that we had a scout on our tail. Before long, it moved into view; a scuttling rake of a man, all bone and sinew, dashing between the bumps in the ridge. My mouth fell open.

"Paega." Tallack said, letting out a noisy breath. "Slimy kyjyan has kept pace with us since the wolf pit."

My mind reeled. I thought I'd seen the last of my nephew after he gave Kewri the slip that fateful day. Why would he stick around on the borders of the moors? He could have run to any region in the land and started afresh where he was unknown. There was nothing left for him in our tribe. Was he, perhaps trying to find his scattered

Priest Sect to reassert his power over our family? I dismissed the notion immediately. Even if he could gather them all together, they were no match for the Sea Warriors and Head Hunters combined.

"Do you think he wants to earn your pardon?"

Tallack blew out his lips. "Not him. He doesn't know the meaning of the word."

I let the matter rest for some time, until the pressure to speak got the better of me. "As soon as we are finished here, can we take the tin to the Duros and get Ren released?"

My nephew peered at me from the corner of his eye and grinned. "Yes, Aunt Mel. I gave you my word. Ren will come home to you."

What did he mean by that? Of course, we needed our best warriors back, but they'd be coming home to us all, not me specifically.

We walked on for the rest of the day until the trees blotted out the last rays of the sun, but my thoughts wouldn't settle. One moment I sweated over Ren and Massen, the next I fretted about Kenver. As soon as I had a handle on those problems, the memory of the skinny waif following our path slipped into my head. I was too old to cope with such worry. What I needed more than anything was rest, but I was unlikely to get that for some time.

Stopping where the Teign diverges, we watered the horses and discussed our options. We were in a clearing of pasture, with the wooded vale at our backs and the gentle slope up to the Drewsteign burial chamber. Cryda and Tallack wanted to push on past dusk, but the elders and their families were exhausted. They were not accustomed to travelling and groaned about the lack of comforts they were used to in the compound.

I was concerned that we were in an exposed position. What if Paega was scouting for a larger crowd of Priest Warriors, waiting for an opportune moment to attack us while we were most vulnerable? I said as much to my nephew, meaning to keep my voice low, but one of the elders heard me. Before long, the whole long line of us was buzzing with the news. That put paid to any thoughts about making camp in the clearing.

On we went, tramping up the hill to the flattened pasture at the top. The long and narrow mound of turf was just visible as we crested, more so when the moon rose and cast its shadow across the valley. The excitement and elation of Brea's death still bubbled among the young. Those of us who were longer in the tooth, remembered what lay beneath the mound. There would be a great deal of hard work come the dawn.

Every able body among us would be required to dig out the earth from the stone structure inside. At the heart of the mound, were three upright tall stones, capped with another huge rock of monumental proportions. If we were lucky, we would find the gap between the entrance stones and form a tunnel into the burial chamber inside. There lay the bones of our Chieftains of old, from long before my grandfather's time.

Trust Cryda to ask for a funerary ritual that was long since passed remembering. My brother, Cador the Cruel, and our father before him, earned their places in the barrows at Stonehenge. It was where we left Aebba's skull, allowing him to enter the portal to the Summerlands as soon as Brea died. Having his long bones on our hallowed ground, gave him the ability to roam far and wide. Aebba could watch over his people, or commune with the gods and other Chieftains at the henge.

I was unsure of the destination of Blydh's journey. None of us spoke about it, but I dare say others were thinking the same thing as me. He did not die in battle, nor was it an honourable death. By rights, he should be on his way to the Underworld, but Tallack was sure that we lost Blydh the moment the golden sun disc was slotted under his scalp. We can but hope that he will be accepted alongside his father, but then Aebba was in a similar position. A once great warrior felled by his own wife's hand. Despite this, his acceptance into the Summerlands was assured by the highest priest at the midsummer gathering.

The fires were small, the meals tiny and unsatisfying, but enough to stop our bellies groaning. On the exposed hill top, we all huddled for warmth with those whom we knew the best. I slept next to Endelyn on one side of me and Cryda and Delen on the other. I noticed that when most people were drifting off to sleep, Senara burrowed under Endelyn's furs. I'm making no judgement, but I've a feeling that the priestess might be the reason why Kewri will go on being spurned by Senara. At least both she and Endelyn are safe and relatively happy.

Barring the night watchmen, the only person who did not bunk down around the fires was Kenver. I could see him in the cold light of the moon, staring up at the sky. His breath billowed into mist with every sigh.

Come dawn, we all rose and shared a watery porridge, warmed through over the dying embers. Tallack organised teams of warriors, some to dig, others to hunt, more to collect wood for the fires, and to build a temporary shelter for his mother and sister. I wandered back down the slope, picking, gathering and snacking on what edible offerings the landscape had to give. Kewri kept me company, although he'd lost his jubilant attitude at seeing Brea ripped asunder. The return to being the quiet and plodding giant was heartening. It was almost like being back at home among the wild flowers and willow bark shavings, if it wasn't for the dangers involved in opening a burial chamber.

The men worked hard throughout the day, scraping, digging and moving the soil until the base of the stones were exposed. After a short break, the toil continued until one man could squeeze into the central space under the capstone and still have room to manoeuvre. I watched as the men eased a sharpened pole beneath the floor stone of the chamber and prized it up from the compacted mud.

Endelyn tapped Tallack on the shoulder and gave him a bracelet she'd made. It was a fine plait of horsehair, with beads woven at intervals. "Wear this for protection, Chief. I had it blessed by the holiest in all the lands one summer." My nephew took it from her and wound it around his wrist.

Cryda looked up from her nursing babe and touched the priestess's hand as she passed. "Thank you, my dear." She whispered. It seemed to me that Endelyn had just about charmed everyone in our whole tribe. The warriors heaved and pushed until the floor stone worked loose and could be removed to reveal the cavity for the older bones.

Tallack was nervous. I could tell by the way he fiddled with the charmed bracelet and hesitated at the mound's edge. Cryda carried the jar containing Aebba's long bones, while two from the Head Hunter Clan lifted the dried body of their leader from the cart. The afternoon sun beat down with such ferocity, some of the men removed their sweat soaked tunics and let the breeze dry their skin.

When the route to the chamber was cleared, Cryda crouched low and stepped inside. Tallack lit a torch and held it close to the capstone roof for her to see. There, she finally laid her husband's bones to rest. His offerings were modest, since his famed bronze shield and swords sat beside his skull and other finery at Stonehenge. I did not see what personal items of his she placed with him, but from the lazy grin on her face, I thought it might be something that evoked the memory of a secret only they had shared.

Tallack reached his hand out to steady his mother as she struggled from the chamber. It was his turn next. She took the torch from him so that he could receive the crouched corpse of his twin brother. Ducking low, he cradled the wrapped figure and entered the tunnel. From the hideous crunching sound, I guessed that the space was too small to accommodate the body. Tallack had to snap the joints to make it fit. On his return, Tallack's face was drawn and grey.

Treeve dashed forward to offer assistance, but my nephew pushed him away. I can only imagine how that must have felt, knowing that Blydh would be unable to walk to the Summerlands with broken leg bones. Cryda plucked a polished battle axe from the rear of the wagon, all shiny and new, forged from the metal of Blydh's helm. It took moments for her to shimmy back inside and leave it with the body.

All the elders looked to Kenver next. He held a bronze spearhead in his palm, a token from the Alchemist's Clan to protect Blydh in his afterlife. I had a similar one from my bundle, but it was only fair that Kenver went first, he was a clan leader after all. His deposit was swift and uneventful, leaving me to play my part in the ritual.

It wasn't so easy for me to crawl inside. My joints were less supple, my muscles weaker and sore. As soon as I was under the capstone, the sickly smell of death made me gag. It was infused with the strong odour of woodsmoke that no meadow flower could conceal. Suppressing a cough, I held my breath and groped about in the darkness for the location of the bones in the chamber by my feet. In my clumsy exploration, my fingers tore through something soft and squelchy. Blydh was not fully preserved. I didn't know whether to throw up or wipe the offensive humours on my tunic. That was about all I could stand. I launched the spear head in the hole and hurried outside.

Cryda was rummaging in the back of the cart, her frown teetering on the edge of tears. "I was sure that he had it when I was washing him in my hut." Her nose wrinkled, her features pinched holding in the emotions.

"What have you lost?" I asked, wiping my hand on the grass.

Tallack answered for her. "The golden sun disc."

"Oh, I have that. I cleaned it so that Delen could have it back." I said, heading for the bundle strapped to my horse.

"Are you addled, Meliora? Do you want my daughter to suffer the same fate as my son?" Cryda screeched. "Give it to me."

"But it was part of Delen's naming ceremony, when Blydh assured her the sun." I was puzzled by her reaction.

Endelyn stepped between us to calm the storm. "Sweet, Fur Benyn. The sun disc must be buried along with Blydh so that the dark spirit can return to the Underworld and cause no more harm to our people."

Such a ridiculous notion, since Blydh and the spirit were now under ground, but it was not the time to argue. I was overheated, tired, and hungry, and the priestess still hadn't begun her babbling and chanting to the gods. Collecting the disc from my pack, I gave it to Tallack. He completed the offerings, climbing back inside the chamber for the last time.

We formed a half-circle and joined hands, with Kenver on my left, and Tallack on my right next to Treeve. Just as Endelyn was winding herself up for the ritual blessing, Treeve said;

"Wait just a moment. I will burst with heat if I don't take off my tunic." He let go of Tallack's hand and we all watched as he grabbed the hem and pulled it high over his head. My eyes fell to the prominent ribs of the skinny little boy at my nephew's side.

Kenver's sight alighted on something else. "Why are you wearing my daughter's quill necklace?"

All eyes fell to Treeve and then to Tallack as Kenver began to draw his own conclusions. This did not bode well.

***

If you enjoyed this novel, and have a moment spare to express your opinion, **a review would be greatly appreciated**.

For more information on the rest of the series, please go to: www.carantocpublishing.com/sam-taw

The next book in the series is entitled **Pagan Siege**

JOIN MY READERS' GROUP AND RECEIVE THE EXCLUSIVE EBOOK NOVELLA,

PAGAN FURY

Three unsuitable lovers.
Two valuable metals.
One critical mission.

The Dumnonii have no copper for their forges. Without a new supply, there will be no more bronze weapons for the inevitable battle ahead.

Joint Chieftain, Tallack, must cross the western ocean to negotiate an alliance with the obstinate Dathi of the Ivernii and complete an impossible task to gain his trust.

Can he succeed where once his father failed?

Join the young warrior and his crew in a lust fuelled, intense quest on the shores of Iwerdon and find out for yourself.

This story takes place between book one, Pagan Death, and book two, Pagan Curse. Please be aware that there will be spoilers that might ruin the enjoyment if they are read out of order.
Sign up here:

www.carantocpublishing.com/sam-taw

About the Author
Sam Taw is the pen name for fiction author Sam Nash. Sam is committed to delivering novels in two distinct genres, historical thrillers and a unique blend of science fiction and international espionage stories.

She lives in a small market town in the south of Leicestershire, in the UK but dreams of one day owning a woodland on the Cornish coast.

For information regarding the work of Sam Taw, please visit:

www.carantocpublishing.com/sam-taw

For information regarding the work of Sam Nash, please visit:

https://www.samnash.org

Printed in Great Britain
by Amazon

70222176R00174